STRAWBERRY SUMMER

T0125720

Praise for Melissa Brayden

First Position

"Brayden aptly develops the growing relationship between Ana and Natalie, making the emotional payoff that much sweeter. This ably plotted, moving offering will earn its place deep in readers' hearts."
—*Publishers Weekly*

"*First Position* is romance at its finest with an opposites attract theme that kept me engaged the whole way through."—*The Lesbian Review*

"You go about your days reading books, thinking oh, yes this one is good, that one over there is so good, and then a Melissa Brayden comes along making everything else seem...well just less than."
—*The Romantic Reader*

Waiting in the Wings

"This was an engaging book with believable characters and story development. It's always a pleasure to read a book set in a world like theater/film that gets it right...a thoroughly enjoyable read."
—*Lez Books*

"This is Brayden's first novel, but we wouldn't notice if she hadn't told us. The book is well put together and more complex than most authors' second or third books. The characters have chemistry; you want them to get together in the end. The book is light, frothy, and fun to read. And the sex is hot without being too explicit—not an easy trick to pull off."—*Liberty Press*

"Sexy, funny and all around enjoyable."—*Afterellen.com*

Heart Block

"The story is enchanting with conflicts and issues to be overcome that will keep the reader turning the pages. The relationship between Sarah and Emory is achingly beautiful and skillfully portrayed. This second offering by Melissa Brayden is a perfect package of love—and life to be lived to the fullest. So grab a beverage and snuggle up with a comfy throw to read this classic story of overcoming obstacles and finding enduring love."—*Lambda Literary Review*

"Although this book doesn't beat you over the head with wit, the interactions are almost always humorous, making both characters really quite loveable. Overall a very enjoyable read."—*C-Spot Reviews*

How Sweet It Is

"'Sweet' is definitely the keyword for this well-written, character-driven lesbian romance novel. It is ultimately a love letter to small town America, and the lesson to remain open to whatever opportunities and happiness comes into your life."—Bob Lind, *Echo Magazine*

"Oh boy! The events were perfectly plausible, but the collection and the threading of all the stories, main and sub plots, were just fantastic. I completely and wholeheartedly recommend this book. So touching, so heartwarming and all-out beautiful."—*Rainbow Book Reviews*

Kiss the Girl

"There are romances and there are romances...Melissa Brayden can be relied on to write consistently very sweet, pure romances and delivers again with her newest book *Kiss the Girl*...There are scenes suffused with the sweetest love, some with great sadness or even anger—a whole gamut of emotions that take readers on a gentle roller coaster with a consistent upbeat tone. And at the heart of this book is a hymn to true friendship and human decency." —*C-Spot Reviews*

Just Three Words

"A beautiful and downright hilarious tale about two very relatable women looking for love."—*Sharing Is Caring Book Reviews*

The Soho Loft Series

"The trilogy was enjoyable and definitely worth a read if you're looking for solid romance or interconnected stories about a group of friends." —*The Lesbrary*

By the Author

Waiting in the Wings

Heart Block

How Sweet It Is

First Position

Strawberry Summer

Soho Loft Romances:

Kiss the Girl

Just Three Words

Ready or Not

Visit us at www.boldstrokesbooks.com

STRAWBERRY SUMMER

by

Melissa Brayden

2017

STRAWBERRY SUMMER

ISBN 13: 978-1-62639-867-2

This Trade Paperback Original Is Published By
Bold Strokes Books, Inc.
P.O. Box 249
Valley Falls, NY 12185

First Edition: April 2017

Credits
Editors: Lynda Sandoval and Stacia Seaman
Production Design: Stacia Seaman
Cover Design by Sheri (graphicartist2020@hotmail.com)

Acknowledgments

I've always been fascinated by how important our formative years truly are. Humans are living longer these days, and reaching age 100 is no longer as shocking as it once was. Yet the years between age fourteen and twenty continue to be our most memorable and influential. This is the time when we decide who we are or who it is we want to become. We learn a variety of life's lessons, take risks, and have our hearts broken, much to our own gut-wrenching surprise. These experiences stand out in our memories like no other—raw, wonderful, and vivid. I very much wanted to explore those formative years when I set out to write *Strawberry Summer*, and oh, what a nostalgic journey it turned out to be!

Thank you: Bold Strokes Books for giving my voice a home and being a great place to cultivate creativity; my fantastic, patient, and wise editor, Lynda Sandoval, for continuing to push me in the best way; my copy editor, Stacia Seaman, for making me look good and being so seamless to work with; my friends: Rachel, Nikki, and Georgia, for being you; Carsen Taite and Barbara Ann Wright for sitting in a tiny cabin with me and being great cheerleaders as I hammered out the middle section of this book; to my family for making me feel like I'm awesome (whether I am or not); my dogs (Apple and Ryder) for snuggling up to me while I write; and Alan for being my rock and keeping the world at bay when I need it to be.

For my first love.

Now

Courtney Carrington was the last person on Earth I wanted to see.

Yet, there she stood. Big blue eyes, sun-streaked blond hair, and even more gorgeous than the last time I'd laid eyes on her—five years and three months ago, to be exact. Not that I'd kept track. God, what was she doing back in town anyway? I hadn't planned on this, on the Courtney effect, but here it was. My palms felt clammy and I wasn't sure which words to choose, stripped of that ability. Damn her for that.

Courtney seemed almost as uncomfortable as I did, which was something. As my eyes landed on hers, it felt as if the world around us paused. The everyday sounds dulled and everything went intricately still. Uncomfortably still, in response to the history we shared. If it weren't for the acute pain that slashed in my chest at merely the sight of her, I would have thought this moment a dream.

"Maggie," Courtney said. The statement hadn't come with any additional words. Instead, Courtney eased a strand of hair behind her ear. It's what she did when she was nervous. I hated that I knew that. I hated how much I used to love it.

Somehow, I'm still not sure how, I found my voice. "What are you doing here?" I managed to say. "You weren't at the funeral, so I didn't expect—"

"No. I'm sure you didn't." She shifted uncomfortably at the reference to her father's service and adjusted the leather attaché that matched perfectly with the designer suit and jacket combo. I hadn't glanced down, but I was fairly confident there were designer shoes to complete the ensemble. Courtney always had been too sophisticated for this town, and looking at her now, it was clear that the divide had only increased with time.

"Hey, Maggie, you okay?" my cousin Berta whispered from her spot at my elbow.

"Hi, Berta," Courtney said and offered a small smile. "It's really good to see you."

"Courtney." Berta nodded back, then softened because Berta had a huge heart. "I'm sorry about your father."

"Thank you."

I discreetly reached to the side and gave Berta's hand an "I'm fine" squeeze, grateful she was there for this absolutely fantastic moment in my life. Sigh. She and I had met for lunch at Drew's Deli that afternoon, one of those quick drive-by lunches people have in the middle of the week before racing off to work again. In our cases, Berta to her salon and me to the McAllister property. I was scheduled to show the home three times that afternoon and had no intention of being late for the first appointment. Unfortunately, Drew's had been down a counter guy and lunch had run long, which was why Berta and I were scurrying across the square at the precise moment Courtney approached from the opposite direction. Sometimes the universe was a cruel, cruel place.

"The store is in disarray," Courtney explained. "Someone needed to take the reins and put things back in order. So here I am."

"And out of everyone at Carrington's, they chose to send one of their vice presidents?" It wasn't likely and we both knew it.

"Of course not." Courtney glanced at the ground, then met my eyes again, the connection making my stomach tighten. How could she still do that after all this time? Damn it. "I volunteered to come back to Tanner Peak. Carrington's is an important fixture in this town, and I wanted to make sure that doesn't change. As you know, this particular store is very important to my family."

"Very noble of you," I said.

She closed her eyes briefly. "Please don't. I wanted to come back."

"I'm sure the town appreciates your concern, but I'm late for a showing and better run."

Courtney backed up as I moved forward. "I don't want to keep you, but I thought maybe we could find a time to talk. Over coffee, perhaps?"

"Uh, yeah, I don't think so." My own uniquely developed code for *hell no.* "I'm not sure talking is necessary."

"Isn't it? Maggie, I have a lot—"

"Margaret. My name is Margaret."

Courtney closed her eyes briefly at the insinuated formality. "Fair enough. *Margaret,* I'm only asking for a few minutes." She passed a quick gaze to Berta and back to me, dropping her tone. "There are things I want to say, if you'll just give me that chance."

"Yeah, except I'm swamped this week unfortunately. I'm booked with showings and we're at the peak of—"

"Summer harvest," Courtney finished. "I remember. I also ran into your father this morning. He invited me to help pick the leftovers. Said it was a really good year for the strawberries."

"It was," I conceded. "We were lucky. Fewer freezes. But I think we're good on help, actually, so don't go out of your way."

"Too late," Courtney said. "I already told him I'd be there Saturday."

Fantastic news. The afternoon couldn't get any better. Truly. "Awesome," I said flatly.

Courtney attempted a smile in the midst of all the awkwardness. "I'll let you two get back to what you were doing. Think about that coffee, Margaret. If this week is bad, then maybe next. I'm here for a while."

And just like that she was gone.

I stood there in disbelief, my heart beating out of my chest in traitorous thumps. Courtney Carrington was back. Right here in Tanner Peak. Really? This was happening?

CHAPTER ONE

The first summer

When you're approaching the end of your junior year of high school, Fridays become the beacon of light you crawl toward on your hands and knees throughout the rest of the school week. I lived for Fridays, dreamt of them, wanted to have their children and not care about who judged us for our love.

However, today was not a Friday I was looking forward to, which said a lot about its potential for suckage. I was a less-than-popular kid at Tanner Peak High School who was about to get up in front of her entire U.S. history class and give a much-dreaded presentation. When it was over, I could cling to the promise of a weekend of reading, swimming, and working outside under the big blue sky.

I repeat, when it was *over*.

First, however, my worst fear would be realized in living color.

The topic of my presentation, the tactics of persuasion Abraham Lincoln employed on his cabinet members in an effort to abolish slavery, was one I was actually interested in. I didn't mind the research or the speech writing or even the rehearsal period. However, getting up in front of my classmates, who already found me boring and uninteresting, sounded about as enjoyable as a root canal on my birthday. Tanner Peak was a small town, and once you were deemed a "farm kid," your social calendar remained relatively open. Wide open. I'd always done my best to be friendly but stayed out of the line of teenage fire. So far, so good. I didn't have a lot of friends, but I didn't have any enemies either, and that was key.

"Margaret, you're scheduled to start us off today," Mr. Blankenship said from behind his overly ornate oak desk. I still wasn't sure how he'd gotten it through the door of the classroom to begin with. I thought on it often. That desk was ridiculously large. "Margaret?"

Right. It was now or never.

"Yeah. I'm ready." I stood and took a deep breath, reminding myself that in six short minutes this whole thing would be over, and in a couple of hours I'd have the weekend stretched out long and luxuriously in front of me. Maybe I'd take a dip in the creek later. The temperatures had been climbing.

I walked to the front of the room, already self-conscious but doing my best to mask it. I'd spent the better part of my week selecting what would hopefully be a non-offensive outfit for this very occasion with the goal of simplicity. As hard as I tried, I was no fashionista, and my style seemed to fall about a year too late to be trendy. However, it's difficult to screw up jeans, a slim-fitting maroon T-shirt, and Chuck Taylors. So that's what I went with. I'd pulled my hair into a clip so it wouldn't do something stupid like fall into my eyes.

I surveyed the room made up of twenty-four teenage faces. Mark Osgood was laughing at something Alexis Windell had just whispered to him. The cluster of cheerleaders already wearing their uniforms blinked back at me with mild tolerance. I could hear my heartbeat in my ears and wanted desperately to sit back down again, but that wasn't really an option. Just as I opened my mouth to speak, the door to the classroom swung open and Vice Principal Hendricks entered and held up a hand.

"Sorry to interrupt, Mr. Blankenship, but I've brought you a new student." On cue, twenty-four heads swiveled in unison as a striking blonde entered the room. We didn't get a lot of new students. This was a big deal. "This is Courtney Carrington, who is joining us from Chicago."

"Wonderful. Courtney, you can take that desk there," Mr. Blankenship said, indicating a desk near the front of the room. The girl smiled confidently as she passed my classmates en route to her new desk. The desk next to mine.

Perfect. Another ultra-popular girl who thought the world existed to make her feel superior. Just what I needed.

With a wave, Mr. Hendricks departed the classroom and all eyes were back to me. The new girl, Courtney, looked up at me expectantly. I was, after all, standing in front of the classroom as if I had the floor. Except I was rattled now and trying to remember what it was that my presentation was about exactly. What I did notice was that the new girl's skirt fell slightly above the knee and was made up of navy and maroon plaid. Instead of heels or sandals, she wore lace-up gray boots. I'd never seen lace-up boots look like that before. A skirt and boot combo would have never occurred to me in a million years.

"She ever goin' to say anything?" Travis Oakham asked loudly. He was the wide receiver on the football team and thereby everyone's favorite human. That was beyond unfortunate for a myriad of reasons.

"Allow me to begin," I said quickly in response, vamping as my pulse accelerated to a pace I didn't stop to analyze. *Allow me to begin? Did I actually say that in front of my classmates? Kill me now. Notify my family it wasn't pretty.*

Travis made a sweeping gesture with his arm and then accepted a note passed his way from the gaggle of cheerleaders at the back of the class. The cheerleaders lived to pass Travis notes. He smirked at its contents and I attempted to focus.

Time to get my A in spite of it all. I came here with a goal, and I'd achieve it if it killed me.

"Abraham Lincoln was more charismatic than Travis Oakham," I said with confidence. All eyes shifted to Travis and then back to me. It wasn't the opening I'd planned on, but I went with it. "And we all know Travis is charismatic. Like Travis, Lincoln knew how to hold court. People listened to him." The confused look on Travis's face let me know that I had his attention, and for the remaining five and half minutes of my presentation, I held on to it, along with the rest of the room. I wasn't a rock star up there by any means, and the applause when I finished was tepid at best, but I felt steady on my feet when I returned to my desk. I hadn't crashed and burned, which was everything. I'd remembered my material and Mr. Blankenship seemed pleased as he jotted away on his legal pad. The jury was still out on how my opening comments about Travis had been received, but I'd worry about that later. One lily pad at a time, I reminded myself.

"That was really good," the new girl whispered as I sat down. "Truly. I'm not just saying that."

"Thanks," I said, briefly meeting her eyes. She was unfortunately even prettier than I'd thought and apparently polite. I didn't trust it but was brought up with manners. "Welcome to Tanner Peak."

Her smile widened. "Thanks. This is my fourth school in five years," she whispered with a weary smile and then crossed one leg over the other, lace-up boots and all, as she focused on the next presenter. She would do well here. Travis and his flock would scoop her up and place her square in the world of the elite and sought after. It was only a matter of time.

Flying high on my not-a-failure of a morning, I floated into the cafeteria following fourth-period geometry and dropped my brown bag lunch on my standard table. My cousin Berta, also a junior, smiled at me. "And? What was the verdict?"

"I didn't choke. I almost choked. Then didn't choke. It was a record save."

"Proud of you," she said. "You earn a strawberry tart made from your family's very own awesome fruit." Berta tossed a Saran-wrapped tart in the air and I caught it handily.

"Score. Oh, and we got a new girl," I said. "Yet another —"

"Is anyone sitting here?"

I glanced up, stunned to see Courtney Carrington holding a lunch tray and smiling nervously down at us. I passed a glance to Berta, who smiled back at Courtney. "Uh, no," I said. What the hell was happening?

"Great." Courtney took the seat next to me, and I marveled at this turn of events because why wouldn't Courtney sit with Melanie Newcastle or Travis Oakham or all the other Kens and Barbies? Didn't matter. They'd recruit her soon enough. "I'm Courtney," she said to Berta and extended her hand across the table. Interesting. You didn't see a lot of teenagers shake hands. She carried herself with a certain maturity I wasn't used to.

"Roberta Wicks, but everyone calls me Berta. You must be new."

"It's my first day," Courtney said and hooked her thumb at me. "We have history together. It's Margaret, right?" I cringed a little. I hated my name. Always had and probably always would.

"Yeah."

"What's your last name?" Courtney asked.

"Beringer," I supplied.

"Oh, like that strawberry farm on the way into town. There's a cute hanging sign in the shape of a strawberry."

"Yeah, that's my family's place."

"Seriously?" she asked, sitting up a little straighter. I was reluctant to answer due to my whole farm-kid status. It hadn't been easy. Tanner Peak was a small town in the hills of California made up of roughly twelve thousand people. Within that, the makeup was divided into those who lived in the center of town and those on the berry farms that made up its perimeter. I'd heard the term "dirt under her nails" used as a shorthand one too many times. Nevertheless, I nodded.

"I've lived there all my life. On that farm."

Berta looked my way. "The Beringers are one of the largest producers of strawberries in probably a hundred miles."

"Wow," Courtney said. Again, this girl was making an effort.

I inclined my head. "Berta is my cousin, I should point out, and thereby predisposed to say that."

Courtney nodded. "Cousins, huh? You know, there is a slight resemblance, now that you mention it." And there was. Only the boring brown straight hair on my head was curly and fun on Berta's. What was more, Berta always seemed to know how to tame it into a cute and sassy style, a talent I lacked. Berta's eyes were brown. Mine have always been described as more hazel.

Courtney looked thoughtful. "It's amusing that your family is known for berries and your last name is Beringer."

"Trust me," I said. "The irony is lost on no one."

"So where are you from, Courtney?" Berta asked as we dug into our lunches.

She took a minute to finish her bite of salad. "Originally, Chicago, but my family moves a lot. My father's line of work. It's not the easiest, moving so often, but I've been told that we're settling down for good this time. I guess we'll see about that."

"What does your dad do?" Berta asked.

"He owns a chain of department stores." Courtney took another bite and Berta and I froze. I played back her name in my head. Courtney *Carrington*. Of course. I was an idiot.

Berta set her cream soda down in shared shock. "Are you talking about Carrington's Department Store? You're *that* Carrington?" For the past four months, it was all anyone in town could talk about. We had three stoplights, a handful of restaurants, and finally the town was getting its very own department store. This was *huge*. Monumental. There would be no more forty-minute drive to Westover for school shopping. No half-day commute just to buy a decent birthday present. In only a few short weeks, we could shop for clothes or appliances right here in town. It was still hard to imagine.

"Right," Courtney said. "My father grew up in Tanner Peak, so it was important for him to open a store here at some point. I guess 'at some point' means now."

"I just can't believe it," Berta said, shaking her head in awe. "You realize you're a celebrity. At least to people like us."

Courtney laughed. "Trust me. I'm not."

"It's cool of your dad to bring a store here," I told her, remembering what my parents had said on the topic. "It's going to bring a lot of jobs to Tanner Peak and probably make it more attractive to outsiders looking for a place to land."

Courtney inclined her head in thought. "Well, I'm sure it had to be a favorable investment as well, if I know my father. Plus, my grandmother still lives around the corner from the school, so there's also a personal connection."

Berta pointed at me. "Netta!"

It all came together in my head. "Oh my God. Netta Carrington." The woman gave out whole Snickers bars on Halloween and was practically a grandmother to everyone she met. We just never realized she was the department store Carrington. And why would we? She was Netta to us.

"Yes!" Courtney said. "You guys know her?"

"Everyone knows her," I said. "She's awesome, so I'm guessing your dad must be."

"Oh, let's not get carried away." There was an almost eye-roll that came with the comment, indicating that she didn't think her dad was so great. My intuition steered me past it.

"So what's there to do around here?" Courtney asked. "I've been here ten minutes and haven't really had time to explore."

I opened my mouth and closed it, looking to Berta for help because there wasn't much. "We have a movie theater," she said, offering up our two-screen Cineplex.

I nodded. "And a pretty okay sandwich shop."

"There's a park."

"And a kick-ass Laundromat," I said. "I spend most of my Saturday nights at the Laundromat. Everyone who's anyone is there." Horror slashed across Courtney's face and I held up a hand in reprieve. I may have been a low-ranking high school socialite, but I wasn't a lost cause. "Just a joke. I'm kidding, which I tend to do a lot. Probably a nervous thing. As is announcing to others when I'm nervous. Just a heads-up for you."

Courtney relaxed into a grin. "Helpful tip. Thank you."

"Don't worry," Berta told her. "There's plenty to do, especially when you add in school activities."

"I play tennis," Courtney said, brightening.

Of course she played tennis. I mean, *of course*. Instead of rolling my eyes at the cliché, I decided to be helpful. "We have a team. There's only a few weeks of school left, but you could maybe see about practicing with them."

Berta joined in. "Official tryouts happen in August for next year. You'll want to hit up Coach Barnhart."

Courtney scribbled a note in her spiral. "Barnhart. Got it. This is awesome. Thanks, guys."

"Anytime," I said.

"Hi, there. We haven't met yet," Melanie Newcastle purred as she landed alongside our table. *And here we go. Pretty much right on time.* Courtney stood and offered her hand with a smile.

"We haven't. I'm Courtney." Instead of accepting Courtney's hand, Melanie did what she and her friends always did and pulled Courtney into an embrace, the multitude of bracelets on her wrist cling-clanging along. This time I actually did roll my eyes.

"And I'm Melanie. We're so glad to have you. How about I introduce you around?"

Courtney's smile doubled in wattage. "Oh, I'd love that." With Melanie's hand on Courtney's shoulder, they headed off in the direction of the beautiful and sought after.

"We'll catch up later," Courtney said over her shoulder. She held my gaze and nodded sincerely. I couldn't help but wonder how long it would be until that sincerity was replaced with the sugar-coated niceties germane to the elite.

"Bye, Margaret. Bye, Berta. You two enjoy the rest of your lunch," Melanie said in a friendly/false farewell. Yeah, kinda like that.

I sighed and smiled at Berta as we picked up the remains of our lunch and headed to the trash can. The new friend possibility had been nice while it had lasted.

Onward and upward.

CHAPTER TWO

The afternoon sun beat down gloriously over the farm, making the green seem extra vibrant and the color on the strawberries pop for days. I snagged a ripe one on my way into the farm and bit into it, closing my eyes at the burst of sugar and fruit that filled my mouth. Nothing like it on the planet. The sea fog from the Pacific had rolled off for the day and in its wake had left a mild afternoon, maybe even warm enough for that swim in the creek if I was lucky.

"What's up, Scrapper?" my brother Clayton asked, approaching from the cooling rooms. The nickname he'd given me from childhood had stuck. What could I say? It was better than Margaret, and I wore it as a badge of honor. I'd always been tenacious about proving myself on the farm. Scrappy I could cop to.

"Well, I've survived another week of public education and have returned home at long last."

"You're so dramatic."

"I am not. I'm what you call a realist. My existence is a struggle."

"It is not. Your nose has been in too many damn history books. You're not one of the oppressed. You're a middle-class kid living in Southern California. This is the time in your life when you should be soaking it all up, enjoying yourself," he said, wiping down the windshield of his pickup. "High school is the best."

Well, yeah, it certainly had been for Clay, who had graduated three years ago with titles like quarterback and prom king and favorite student in all of the universe. Girls lusted after him. Guys wanted to be him. Strangely, I hadn't received the same adoration during my time in high school.

"I think we'll have to agree to disagree on the whole high school high-note thing," I said. "But it's fine. What's going on around here? Need any help?"

"Nope. Knockin' off for the day. The guys are laying the last run of plastic to the northern fields. Pop's out there with them now, wrapping up. Berries are looking good this year, kiddo."

"Tasting good too. We were lucky. Not too many storms."

He whistled. "I'll take that luck again next year."

We were easing out of peak season, in which everyone on the farm had to put in immense amounts of overtime. There were still plenty of strawberries on the plants to harvest, but the bulk of the work was behind us. Kinda nice to see my brother breathing a little easier as we moved into the summer months. My father would now shift his focus to some of the administrative tasks it took to keep the farm up and running as Clay focused on replanting the fields for the fall harvest. My brother had taken over a good chunk of the responsibility on the farm in the last year. At least the parts my father was willing to relinquish to him. Beringer's had belonged to my grandfather first, passed down to my father, and one day would belong to my brother and me. Something Clay took very seriously.

He tossed the hand towel into the truck bed. "You just missed your buddy on the refrigeration truck."

"Oh yeah? How's Jimbo?" I was sad to have missed him. Jimbo happened to be my favorite of the drivers. Quick witted. Smart.

"He left a book for you. Something about Hemingway's life. I put it on the kitchen table in the big house." The big house, where I lived with my parents, stood on the southern end of the farm, closest to town. Clay occupied the smaller cottage a few fields over to the east. It gave him space for…extracurricular activities.

"He knows I've been on a Hemingway kick."

Clay laughed in disbelief. "Whatever bookworm gene came your way by birth certainly skipped my hard head."

"Whatever. You just prefer the outdoors, and I can't say I blame you." I rolled my shoulders and stared skyward. It sure was a nice afternoon.

Clay walked to the driver's side of his truck and called to me over his shoulder. "Headed to town for beer and Oreos. Coming or not?"

"Coming." I'd been following Clay around religiously since

childhood. He pretended to tolerate me, but I knew he enjoyed the company. I ran inside, dropped my backpack on the kitchen table, and scurried back out to the truck.

"Margaret Eileen Beringer, get back in here!" I froze at the sound of my mother's voice, held up a finger to Clay, and headed calmly back inside.

My mother stood in the entryway with a hand on her hip. Her hair was a shade lighter than mine, closer to Clay's blond locks, and cut to her shoulders. I'd always found my mom pretty. "Yes, ma'am?" I asked, already aware of the infraction.

"I know my only daughter did not just race in this house and then out again without a word about how her history report went when I've been waiting to hear all day, checking the clock."

I grinned. "I'm very sorry. I'm a thoughtless daughter ready to make it right."

"And? How'd it go? Were you nervous? Did you forget anything?" My mom had always been my biggest cheerleader.

"Petrified as always, but it went really well. Best part of all? It's over and I don't have to agonize over it ever again."

"That's great, sweetheart. I'm so proud of you. I knew you'd ace it. Now, where are you running off to like a crazy child?"

"Klein's Grocery with Clay. He's craving beer and cookies. He might be pregnant."

"Well, he should lay off the beer in that case. Wait a second." She walked to her purse and found a ten. "Please pick up some white vinegar. The coffee machine's been going nuts and I can't work if I can't caffeinate."

"Will do. Back soon." My mother, believe it or not, was a romance writer. As in, the torrid kind of sexy romance you see in the checkout lines at the grocery store. The ones with the shirtless man with rippling muscles on the cover that make you feel embarrassed to be alive. She chose to write under the pen name Bella Charmed but would happily talk about her work to most anyone who asked, and those who didn't, for that matter. While I found it slightly embarrassing where my classmates were concerned, I was also really proud of her and all she'd accomplished.

I kissed my mom on the cheek, tore out of the house, and jumped in the truck just in time for Clay to pull away. "Turn it up," I said, and he blasted the Beach Boys, as we were nothing if not throwbacks. With the windows down, "Fun, Fun, Fun" on the radio, and the entire weekend laid out ahead, I didn't think the afternoon could get much better.

The parking lot at Klein's was overflowing when we arrived, typical for a Friday afternoon when the weather was nice. Various barbecues, picnics, and get-togethers would certainly be taking shape. But it was the blonde sitting in the rocking chair in front of the store that snagged my focus. Courtney Carrington, still wearing the plaid skirt and the boots, sat there writing something in a notepad. No, wait, drawing something. She'd glance up briefly and then go back to her page, biting her bottom lip in concentration. Her long hair was now pulled into a side braid that rested on her shoulder. She looked infinitely more relaxed than the last time I'd seen her, as if in her element. I stopped to watch her draw for a moment, captivated by the serenity of it all.

"You coming in?" Clay asked way too loud. "Or are you gonna stay out here and weirdly stare at strangers some more?"

Damn it. I wanted the ground to swallow me up then and there. Overhearing the comment, Courtney's gaze snapped to mine and I felt the warm blush hit my cheeks without delay. I turned red at the slightest embarrassment. Probably the lamest thing about me.

Courtney, however, smiled, which eased the mortification. "Well, hey there, Margaret Beringer."

"Hey." I made my way up the three wooden stairs to the store's porch. "What are you doing out here?"

She gestured to the gas pump out front with her chin. "There's this little bird just below the pump having the best time with the gravel. Picking it up and tossing it around. I just had to capture him." It wasn't something I would have noticed on my own, and the fact that Courtney had didn't fit with my initial characterization of her. Wasn't she destined to be superficial and shallow? The guilt kicked me swiftly in the gut.

"You didn't mention you were an artist." I peered at her drawing. It was really good.

"We didn't get to talk for that long," she said. "Unfortunately."

"That's right. You were whisked away to the land of…" I abandoned the sentence, hearing how it would sound out loud and a little tired of my own rush to judgment.

"The land of?"

"Never mind. I should find my brother."

"That or stare weirdly at more strangers."

I laughed at the zing. Courtney was different than the average teenage fare around here. She was harder to predict. That had my attention. I held up my hands. "For the record, I didn't mean to stare."

"For the record, I'm not at all offended."

My laughter was of the nervous variety. "Good."

Courtney straightened. "What are you up to tonight? I'm bored and seem to have very few prospects."

"Oh." I paused, not really sure where to go from there. "I figured Melanie and her gaggle of girls would have you circling the square with them. It's kind of what they do."

"She did mention it." The fact that Courtney hadn't jumped all over that opportunity scored her additional points in my book. And she already had a handful.

"And you're not joining them?"

"I considered it," she said and flashed a smile. "But now that you're here, I thought I'd see what you have going on."

"Weighing your options."

She tilted her head from side to side. "Something like that. So what does Margaret Beringer, heir to the strawberry throne, have in store for herself tonight?"

"Okay, um…" God, I wished I had something more exciting to offer. "I was gonna play it pretty low key, one could say. Maybe go for a swim later."

Courtney seemed to perk up. "Oh yeah? So you have a pool?"

I suppressed a laugh. "No, but, um, there's a creek down the hill a bit from the park."

"A creek, huh?" Courtney seemed to mull over the concept.

"Yeah. If you follow the path just next to the pavilion, it leads down to the water."

Courtney began to pack up her sketchpad and pencils. "Great. What time will I find you there?"

Wait. This was happening? This was a bad idea. "Oh. Probably a little after eight." Damn it all! I was a betrayer of self.

"Perfect. I'll see you at your hidden creek later," Courtney said.

"I'm up for moonlight swimming. We can hang, get to know each other."

What had I done? I felt the dreaded blush again. "Yeah. Okay. I'll see you later, then." So we'd go swimming together. Me and Courtney Carrington. Who was very pretty. And who I probably had nothing in common with. Why not? So much for my relaxing Friday night. I was an idiot.

Searching for white vinegar and my wayward brother, I headed into the store. I found him near the bakery's glass display case. Darlene, the doe-eyed baker, was chatting him up. She batted her eyes and swatted his bicep with a girly giggle. *Subtle, Darlene.* As I waited for the super stud to tear himself away, I reflected on the fact that I had actual plans of my own later. Not a big deal. Except it felt like a big deal. I had all this extra energy and my palms were itchy as I strolled the aisles of Klein's in an attempt to shake it off. Only now, my stomach muscles tightened as I recalled the image of Courtney biting her lip thoughtfully while she sketched. What was that about anyway? Just a girl drawing. Nothing to ruminate on.

Only she was a beautiful girl.

Deep sigh to the gods above.

I considered calling Berta to join Courtney and me, take the pressure off the conversation responsibility, but remembered she was headed to Santa Barbara to visit the grandparents on her father's side. No-go there. It would be fine, I decided, moving myself past it. We might even have fun together.

"You're extra quiet for such a chatty kid," Clay said on the drive home.

"I am? Just thinking, I guess."

"You know that girl out front of Klein's? I've never seen her before."

"As of today, she sits next to me in history. Just moved here from Chicago. She's a Carrington, as in the department store variety."

Clay whistled low. "So, loaded?"

"I guess."

"The prodigal son returns home after all. I'd heard the family might move back when the store opening was announced a few months ago."

"What does that mean?" I asked. "The prodigal son."

"Think about it. You ever hear Netta Carrington mention her son?" I shook my head. "Because he's a moneygrubbing asshole who practically abandoned her. Hasn't visited once in the last ten years is what people say."

"How do you know all this?" I asked.

"People talk to me, Scrap." Right. There was that. "Plus, he and Dad went to school together. Never got along. Rumor has it Dad decked him in front of the school."

"No way," I said, shaking my head. "Dad wouldn't hit anyone."

Clay passed me a dubious look and my jaw fell.

"Seriously? Why have I never heard about any of this?"

"Probably because you've never struck up a friendship with the Carrington kid before."

"Huh. Good point."

We eased into the circular drive in front of the big house and I jumped out and carried my share of the groceries inside. My parents were both in the kitchen, a very common occurrence an hour before dinner. They tended to prepare the meal together and catch each other up on their respective days. It was sweet in a way. My father sliced a tomato and my mother read to him from her laptop. "Wordlessly, Jeffrey kissed her, and not softly. He owned her, every inch of her. He eased his leathery hands—"

"Whoa, whoa, whoa," I said, holding up a hand. "Child in the room. Child in the *room*."

"Don't worry. It's a short scene," my mother said, waving me off.

I gaped in outrage at her dismissal. "I thought we had a 'no reading sex scenes out loud before dinner' clause. If not, we need one. I so move."

My father raised his gaze from the tomato, his eyes thoughtful. "Wasn't Jeffrey the crooked farmhand in the last book? I thought he stole a bunch of money and everyone hated him."

"Yes," my mother said, nodding. "That's him. But Chastity has had a major influence on his view of the world and makes him want to be a better man. In more ways than one." My parents locked eyes and tiny little parent sparks shot into the air all around them. Oh, man. Cute as they were, I just couldn't.

"There's also a 'no flirting in front of your daughter' clause."

"There most certainly is not," my father said sternly, but there was a twinkle in his eye. "Oh, Jimbo left a book for you."

I grinned. "I heard. Hemingway!"

"What's another word for thrust?" my mother asked.

I put fingers in my ears. "La-la-la-la-la. Please yell upstairs when you're ready for me to set the table. Until then, I'll be in my room saving up for therapy." My mother grabbed me as I passed and placed a loud smacking kiss on my cheek. I couldn't help but smile in the midst of my mock outrage. My parents, while annoying, were pretty great in the scheme of possible parents I could have been paired with. I was lucky that way.

Snagging the book off the table, I took the stairs two at a time and spent the next ten minutes thumbing through the description of Hemingway's childhood, intrigued to read that his mother was said to have dressed young Ernie as a girl until he was four. He could join me in therapy. As hard as I tried, however, I couldn't seem to lose myself in the book—a rare happening, as I was a voracious reader. Too keyed up, I decided. Maybe from the brief encounter with Courtney, a potential new friend. Maybe because I was nervous about us hanging out. Or maybe it was because I knew the actual underlying cause of my anxiety.

I was into girls.

This wasn't a brand-new revelation. I'd known for a while, but this was the first time that a girl had made such a startling impression on me, and I'd only known her for a few hours. But Courtney was also a seemingly friendly and intriguing person. I didn't know a ton of those. God, I didn't want to do anything to make it weird. So for the next ten minutes, I did things like pace the length of my room, look over my swimsuits to make sure I didn't choose a stupid one, and run my fingers through my hair just because. In other words, I behaved like a crazy person.

"Where are you off to?" my father asked an hour later as I stood from the dinner table with my plate in my hand.

"I didn't say I was going anywhere."

"Don't have to." He exchanged a look with my mother. "You got that look. Clay said you made a new friend. Is that where you're headed?"

I took in the expectant expression on my father's face and the amused one on my mother's and then passed Clay a stare of my own that said, "Traitor, I will pay you back for this if it takes me until my dying breath." He grinned happily and shoved a forkful of green beans into his highly offensive big mouth. Underneath the broad shoulders and sandy blond hair, he was just a big kid. I shook it off and aimed for nonchalance when answering my father. "I'm going to the creek. It's finally warm enough to swim. I won't be late, though."

"Curfew is ten," my father reminded me. "And make sure there's no swimming by yourself after dark."

"Yes, sir."

My mother inclined her head in curiosity. "Who's the new friend?"

"Oh. Her name is Courtney. She just moved here."

"Well, then bring her by," she said. "We'd like to say hello."

"I'll see if she's available."

"You forgot to mention her last name," Clay said. He dodged my death glare by way of intense concentration on his obnoxious mound of mashed potatoes.

"Don't you have some sort of hot but less-than-intelligent date to pick up?" I asked with a raise of my eyebrow.

"It's seven thirty on a Friday," he pointed out with a twinkle in his eye. "The night is young."

"What's her last name, then?" my father asked, his interest now piqued. Damn my brother.

I met his gaze. "Carrington."

"Mitch Carrington's girl?" my father asked, setting down the plate of spinach he'd just picked up.

"I believe so, sir." I held my breath, hoping this information wouldn't get in the way of my plans tonight.

My mother placed a calming hand on my father's wrist. "Has to be. Bring her by after you swim. We went to school with her dad. Your father could put together one of his famous strawberry shortcakes for dessert."

My father didn't say anything.

"I'll see if she's free."

My mother sat back, pleased. "Wonderful. We'll hope she is."

I thought about the exchange on the ten-minute walk to the creek's edge, curious about my parents and their relationship to Mr. Carrington. What did my dad have against the guy, anyway? I passed through Town Square, waving politely to those I recognized, which, let's be honest, was just about everyone in a town the size of ours. Some bluesy music spilled out from Lonesome's Bar and the sweet smell of hamburgers frying permeated the air near the Berry Good Café.

And oh, good. There was Travis and Melanie and their dutiful followers, all gathered around Travis's new car. He'd recently turned seventeen and had thrown one of the biggest blowouts the teenage Tanner Peak had seen in years. Berta and I had dropped in but were long gone by the time the cops arrived to bust it up for noise complaints and underage drinking.

"Beringer," Travis said indifferently as I approached. He wore his letterman jacket, which in May seemed oppressive, but hey, it was a choice. It wasn't as if we'd forget who he was or his laundry list of athletic accomplishments. As if anyone would ever allow that.

"Hey, Travis," I said politely.

The group broke a little and I saw Courtney standing in their midst, laughing at something Melanie had said. Gone was the plaid skirt and in its place jean shorts and flip-flops. She appeared infinitely more casual and relaxed.

"Margaret, hey," she said, catching sight of me and smiling. She gestured generically at the group. "These guys are talking about roasting marshmallows at Melanie's house." Cue Melanie looking instantly uncomfortable at the insinuated invitation. I had never really been a part of their set.

"You can come if you want," Melanie said reluctantly with a shrug, averting her eyes.

"Oh, no. But thank you. For the invitation." My gaze skated from Melanie to Courtney, then back to Melanie again. "I'm good, though."

Melanie showed off the plastic smile, her claim to fame. "Have fun, then."

"You guys, too." I nodded and waved and headed off on my own path. It wasn't so much that I didn't want to hang out and roast marshmallows in the land of social people. It was more the stress of holding my own with those kids that had me heading the other direction. I didn't say the right things, or know the right clothes to wear, or listen to the most popular music, and surely there would be a giant sign over my head that notified them. So I chose to remain on my own, and that would be just fine. I could convince myself of that anyway, if I said it often enough.

The last little bit of daylight clung to life as I arrived at the peaceful creek. The sky held glimmers of pink from the sun's descent, and I took a moment to really appreciate its brilliance. The water lapped leisurely against the bank in serene accompaniment. This was my spot. I let out a relaxed breath at how at home this place made me feel.

Safe. Comfortable. Calm.

I stripped off the shirt and shorts I'd worn over my one-piece suit and slipped easily into the water, hissing as the cool liquid pressed to my skin. I pushed back from the edge with my foot and floated on my back, acclimating to the temperature. God, I loved the rush I got in those first few seconds. A surge of adrenaline that shouted, "This is too cold to live," making it a moment I fully embraced. I liked living dangerously. Well, in small, controllable scenarios quite close to my own backyard.

"You weren't lying. There's a creek out here after all." I righted myself abruptly and whirled around at the sound of the voice, surprised to find Courtney standing at the water's edge. "Hey," she said and offered a little wave.

"Oh, hi. I thought you were gonna—"

"Marshmallows don't really excite me. Plus, I haven't been swimming in I don't know how long."

"You came to the right place for that." It was the stupidest sentence ever uttered, and I winced internally, willing it back. The turtles on the bank were cooler than I was.

Courtney seemed amused. "I appreciate the tip. So is there any kind of science to this?" She started to unbutton her shirt and at the same time stepped out of her flip-flops. A strand of hair fell haphazardly across her eye. "City girl and all."

I played back the sentence because my brain had been otherwise occupied by the bright blue of her eyes. They sparkled when she smiled. "Oh. I think you just get in the water," I said with a smile, focusing on the simplicity of the question. "At least that's what I've heard."

She shook her head and shrugged out of her shirt, revealing a light blue bikini top with a sidecar dip of noticeable cleavage. I swallowed. "Good thing I have you."

"I do what I can for the city folk of the world," I said, and swam a short distance away, giving Courtney some space. This also offered me a moment to deal with the butterflies that apparently had taken up residence in my stomach—you know, introduce myself and work out some sort of rental agreement.

I heard a splash behind me and turned. "Holy shit, that's cold," Courtney said, her eyes wide. She treaded water a few yards away.

"Give it a minute. Your body will get used to it."

"Shit, shit, shit. Okay." But she was laughing. "Let's see what we can do to speed up that process." Before I knew it, she dove headfirst beneath the water's surface and I was left alone, listening to the quiet sounds of nature at dusk—and waiting for her to surface. I heard a splash behind me and turned.

"You okay?" I asked.

Courtney took a deep gulp of air and tossed her hair behind her. "This really gets your blood going! Wow."

"It does. That's the best part."

"I could get used to this." She was under again. This girl was an adventurous type. For the next few minutes, she explored the area, taking short little swims and dips beneath the surface like an audacious otter. I used the time to pep talk myself into relaxing a little. Courtney was just a girl from school. A very nice girl from school who was nothing like the other girls in town. A very nice, *beautiful* girl from school who chose to hang out with me on a Friday night rather than the infinitely more sought-after kids. There were those butterflies again.

"So, why Abraham Lincoln?" she asked.

"What?"

"Your presentation today," Courtney said, swimming my way. "What made you choose Lincoln?"

"Well, he's arguably one of the greatest speakers in the history of the country."

"He is. You're a pretty impressive speaker yourself. You realize that?"

"I've never really thought so, no. I was nervous and I screwed up the opening." I looked away.

"You're not astute at taking a compliment, are you?"

I considered the statement. "I guess I'm not."

"Trust me when I say that the speech was really good." I opened my mouth to argue, but she beat me there. "Don't say another thing to discredit yourself. A thank-you is all that a compliment requires."

"In that case, thank you." And then I felt the blush hit my cheeks.

Courtney's eyes met mine and she smiled. "You're very welcome." She held my gaze for a moment longer and then swam away again. I decided to take control of the conversation as she flipped onto her back.

"So what do you think of Tanner Peak so far?"

She seemed to ruminate on the question. "It's definitely small."

"Well, yeah."

"And homey, though. Everyone seems to like it here."

"Mostly true."

"But despite the size, there also seems to be a lot to discover. Like this little creek, for instance. First one I've encountered outside of a *Little House on the Prairie* episode."

"Oh, come on," I said, laughing, and feeling a little defensive of my hometown. "I think we're a little farther along than *Little House*."

"I can agree with that. But things do move a little slower here."

"That part is true."

"But in a nice way."

"I think it's the most beautiful place on the planet," I said before hearing myself and wincing. I pretended to study the sky then, embarrassed to have confessed what probably sounded like a really naïve declaration to someone who'd seen more of the world than I probably ever would. Courtney didn't say anything, and when I stole another glance, I caught her watching me.

"What?" I asked, wondering if I had an errant strand of grass on my face, because that would be typical.

"Nothing," Courtney said, and looked away.

"No, seriously. You can say it. I know I must sound small-town stupid to you."

"What?" She had the decency to look outraged. "No. I definitely wasn't thinking that."

"Okay. Then what were you thinking?"

"That you light up when you talk about this place, and you're really pretty when you light up."

"Oh." The comment landed hard, and I felt a little glowy. She thought I was pretty? Now, don't get me wrong, I knew I wasn't a hideous person, but outside of that, I'd always categorized myself as kind of average in the looks department. "Thank you."

"You're welcome."

We swam some more as daylight slid away. The luminous moon

took its place, providing plenty of light and reflecting off the water in intricate little rays. Crickets chirped nearby in a soothing chorus. The night couldn't have been more serene.

"So when does it open?" I asked. "Carrington's. Soon, right?"

"Ten days and eleven hours," she said, doing the math quickly in her head.

"That's specific."

"I'm more than a little excited. The opening of a new store gets my blood going."

I laughed. "Now who's all lit up?"

She shrugged, giving in. "True. I'm pretty much obsessed with the department store world. I wish I could put my finger on what it is I love so much."

"You could give it a shot." I swam in her direction so I was close enough to really appreciate this explanation.

She grinned and looked away. "You'll think I'm boring."

"Trust me when I say I won't." Nothing about this girl struck me as boring.

She studied me, perhaps sizing up the truth of that statement, and bit her lower lip. "Okay. I'm not sure where to start. You sure you want to hear this? You're the articulate one, presenting effortlessly in front of the class as if you were born to do it."

"There was nothing effortless about what happened today. But honestly, I'm interested."

Courtney nodded. "There's something about the hustle and bustle of the customers as they move through the perfectly decorated space in search of something new and untouched to take home with them. Then there's the fact that the temperature is always a cool sixty-eight degrees, the mannequins are forever perfectly dressed, and quiet music plays to offer a little pick-me-up. It feels like an escape from the real world, which can at times be ugly, to somewhere unmarred and beautiful."

I watched her face, captivated by the wonder I saw there. "I don't think I will ever look at a department store the same way again."

Courtney laughed. "Good. Then my work here is done."

"So is that what you want to do with your life? I mean, after school. Work for the family business?"

She didn't hesitate. "Absolutely. Only one problem."

"And what is that?"

"I have to convince my father."

"What? He doesn't want to pass on the store to—"

"To his daughter? No. He has definite ideas about women in business."

"Ouch."

"Exactly."

It made me want to double-check the calendar and what year we were living in. Last I looked, we also had the right to vote. "So what's your plan?"

"Astonish him with my superior abilities once the store opens and convince him to give me an actual job on the floor. Even just a cash register at first. Something small until I can learn more and move to a new position."

"And eventually plant your flag as CEO and take down all department store rivals?"

"Well, yeah." She was dead serious. "Isn't that what you want? To eventually take over the berry business?"

I laughed, then realized she meant it sincerely. "I do love it, but I'm not sure I want to spend my life harvesting fields on a tractor. I guess that's me checking the undecided box as far as my future employment goes."

"Totally okay. In fact—whoa." She slipped, probably on the smooth rocks on the creek bed. But I was quick enough to catch her arm and steady her.

"You're okay," I said, holding on until she righted herself.

She met my eyes and I gently released her, noting how close we stood. "I just lost my footing, I guess. Thanks, Margaret." She must have caught me cringe at the name I'd always hated. "Something I said?"

"Nope. I'm cool."

"Tell me what that was. Your face completely fell."

I sighed in surrender and laid it out there for her. "I hate my name."

Courtney laughed. "You hate your *name*? Margaret?"

"Yes, Margaret. And it's not funny. It's awful and I'll never crawl out from underneath it."

"What don't you like about it?" She was trying to contain her smile and failing miserably.

"Well, in the land of Kendalls, Mackenzies, and Emersons,

Margaret is about as fashionable as a bolo tie. The Wicked Witch of the West was named Margaret in real life, which means I'm cursed! I'll probably just wind up stealing shoes and—"

"Okay, okay." Courtney caught my wildly gesturing hands in hers. "I think I get your passion for the topic," she said, laughing once again. "So how about a nickname?"

I blinked back at her, preoccupied by the fact that she still held my hands. "A nickname?"

"Yeah. What about Maggie?"

I rolled it around in my head. "It's not bad. It's certainly better."

"Done. Maggie. All better. See?"

"If you say so."

"And I do. Hey, *Maggie*, I think I'm ready to dry off. Join me?"

"Sure." I looked on as Courtney pushed herself onto dry land, offering me my first full glimpse of her in her bathing suit. I blinked hard at the image, at how gracefully she moved, at how smooth her skin looked, at the lines that flared into curves that... *Stop it. What is wrong with me?*

We toweled off and sat on the edge of the creek. While it was darker out now, I could still make out her features easily enough and was hyperaware of her proximity.

"So tell me about this Travis guy," Courtney said. Aha. Travis. Probably a crush in the making. I wouldn't have expected anything different.

"Travis is...Travis. Probably one of the more popular guys in the junior class. Athletic. Confident."

"In a good way or bad?"

"Depends on who you ask."

She tilted her head to the side and then bumped my shoulder. "I'm asking you, crazy."

I swallowed and tried to approach the topic as delicately as I could. Sure, I had opinions about the guy, but I wasn't going to color Courtney's perception of him blatantly. "I've had both up and down moments with him. He's okay, I guess. Just has some maturing to do."

"Such is a teenage boy, I'm afraid."

"Yeah, I guess that's it. I'm sure he means well."

"So Travis means well. Got it. Who do you date?"

"Me? No one. Not at the moment." Not at *any* moment, but who was counting? "Just pretty much doing my own thing. I concentrate on school and the farm, mainly."

"The *strawberries*."

"Well, there are a lot of them." Why did I say dumb things? *Why?*

"I'd like to see your place sometime. Try one of those berries for myself."

"My mom wanted me to bring you by tonight for dessert, but because I'm a nice person I will convince her you had to race home."

"But I don't."

"You don't?"

"Have to race home. We should go and have dessert. That would be awesome."

"Are you sure? You definitely don't have to—"

"Come on." She squeezed my hand. "I want to meet your parents. And if there are fresh strawberries in this dessert, I'm a goner." And she was up and moving before I could answer. Courtney, I was finding, was the type of girl who leapt at life and went after what she wanted.

❖

"So when did you all arrive in town?" my mother asked, and set a jar of strawberry topping between us on the table. Normally at this time of night, my mom would be in her nightgown on the couch, sometimes watching *Golden Girls* reruns, sometimes reading a book. But she was still dressed, which only spoke to how much she wanted to meet Courtney. I couldn't decide if that made me pathetic or fortunate to have a mom so invested.

"Three days ago," Courtney told her. "My dad's still in Chicago, though, tying up some loose ends with some of the Midwest stores. He'll join us next week."

I watched as my father sat back in his chair. The subtle movement was enough to tell me he was uncomfortable at the mere mention of Mr. Carrington.

My mom topped her own strawberry shortcake and joined us at the table. "And your mother? Is she settling in okay?"

Courtney nodded. "Seems to be. She doesn't know anyone other than my grandmother, though. I'm hoping she makes a friend or two."

"I should invite her to book club this week."

"I'm sure she'd love that. That would be so nice of you."

My mom nodded and seemed excited by the concept. "Consider it done. We meet on Tuesdays at the café on the square. We're currently reading my new release, but generally we stick with general fiction."

Courtney's eyes widened and she set down her spoon. It was clear she was impressed. "You're a writer?"

"She writes romance," I told her, feeling rather proud. "She has twenty-four books published."

"Oh my God. I have to read one," Courtney said emphatically.

My mother smiled. "Someday maybe. You're a little younger than my target audience."

"I've never met an author before."

"She's a good one, too," my dad said. "More shortcake?" Courtney had blown through the dessert on her plate and I couldn't blame her, as it was every-which-way awesome.

"Sure!" she answered cheerfully. My mother followed him into the kitchen and Courtney turned to me.

"Your parents are like something out of a Norman Rockwell painting." Her hair had all but dried and the blond had returned. It framed her face as if she'd never gone swimming. How was that possible? I'm sure mine was a tumbled mess.

"What? No. My parents, they're just normal parents."

"Inviting your friends over, homemade dessert, hanging out with us? That wouldn't happen at my house. Ever. Just for the record."

"What would happen?"

She thought on the question. "Everyone quiet and invested in their own thing. It's rare we do anything together. We definitely don't hang out."

"Dinner?"

"Usually on our own. Someone will put some food on the stove. Everyone grabs a plate and disperses."

I was leveled with sadness, imagining Courtney eating by herself, no one asking her about her day or worrying about the presentation she had to give in history class. "Wow. So you're pretty independent, then."

She must have noticed the look on my face and instantly toughened. "Don't feel bad for me. I'm fine. It's just nice to see…this." She looked around the room. "It's warm here. Friendly."

"Yeah. I guess it is."

After another half hour around the table in which my dad explained the riveting process of protecting the strawberries from bug invasions and my mother let Courtney read the back of one of her books, I borrowed my mom's Honda to drive Courtney home. It was, after all, past ten, and though Tanner Peak felt like the safest place on Earth, it still didn't seem right to send Courtney out on her own so late. Besides, I was really having a good time. And maybe I'm crazy, but she seemed to be having fun, too.

"Tonight was exactly what I needed," she said halfway into the drive to her house. She'd rolled the window down and stuck her face out to the air rushing past. "I had a good time with you, Maggie Beringer. Swimming in the creek." She laughed. "God, I can't believe I just said that sentence."

"Well, get used to it," I said, stealing a glance at her. "You're not living in a concrete jungle anymore, and summer's on the way."

"Right? Adjustment period in progress." She paused. "How long until summer break?"

"Three weeks and four days."

"It's not like you're keeping track or anything."

I chuckled. "Not at all."

I drove to the house she directed me to on Legends Lane, a three-story mammoth with neatly trimmed bushes and a pale blue door.

"And here you are," I said, pulling into the drive.

"You rock for driving me. Thank you."

"Anytime." I glanced up at the house, noticing for the first time that it was dark, as in completely. Not a porch light, nor a glimmer of light from inside. I gestured to the home, a little nervous for her now. "So, is anyone home in there?"

Courtney shifted. "My mom, but she sleeps a lot."

I nodded. "I guess she trusts you to make curfew."

"Not exactly. When my dad's out of town, I don't really have one. Polar opposite parenting styles."

"I bet that keeps you on your toes."

She shifted uncomfortably. "You have no idea. See you at school?"

I shrugged resolutely. "I'm mandated to be there."

She laughed. "Thanks for hanging out with me tonight. You're a cool girl." She winked at me and closed the door, leaving me no choice but to watch in awe as she walked to her house with a gentle sway of her hips. Once she was inside, I closed my eyes at the prickles that danced across my skin. I touched my cheeks, feeling the blush, but my spirits were much too high to care.

On the drive back to my house, I blared the radio and smiled at this new development in my once boring and uneventful life. Courtney Carrington had come to town.

CHAPTER THREE

Snow cones, hot dogs, dunking tanks, and strawberries galore. These were all the things that made the Peak of Berries Festival one of my favorite days of the year. Practically everyone in town showed up on the set-aside Saturday. Live music played from multiple bandstands, and the strawberry itself was full on celebrated in every way possible. Strawberry cakes, pies, tarts, cookies, slaw, barbecue sauce, milk, marmalade, salsa, salads, biscuits, donuts, ice cream, chilled soup, and more. If you could shove a strawberry into it, it was there and available to sample at the festival for just a few tickets. Hell, you could even get a fried strawberry.

Beringer's, as always, had one of the biggest and busiest booths there. We served a mean strawberry and brie crostini in the midst of a sampling of delicious strawberry-influenced ice cream treats.

"What is this wonderful madness?" Courtney asked over the three people in front of her. She wore white shorts and a blue and white striped shirt and had her hair pulled back in a French braid.

I leaned down from the elevated booth. "Welcome to the Peak of Berries Festival! We do it every year. It's my favorite event!" The festival just brought with it a sense of community that made me proud to be from Tanner Peak. Everyone was there and everyone was represented. The firemen performed demonstrations and posed with kids, the high school held a pie-throwing competition, and the library even had a nook with beanbag chairs and books galore.

"How about a strawberry float? You won't be the same after."

"Is that a good thing?" she asked nervously.

"You gotta trust me on this one."

"One strawberry float, please," she said, and handed me up three tickets.

I held up my hand in protest. "On the house."

Courtney beamed as I handed her down a strawberry float complete with a cookie straw. "Thank you! You didn't have to do that."

"Well, I feel a sense of responsibility to further introduce you to the wonder that is the strawberry."

"And you're doing an admirable job." She took a sip and nodded as I waited in anticipation. "It's wonderful."

"Isn't it?"

"Is that Margaret Beringer I see up in that booth?" Courtney's grandmother yelled as she came up behind her.

"Netta!" I shouted back. "Wait right there!" I quickly made up a second float and walked it down to her. "A strawberry float for you "

Courtney raised one of her perfect eyebrows. "You're going to go bankrupt if you're not careful there, Maggie. You're giving away all of your merchandise."

"I seem to be walking on the wild side today." I was also in a fabulous mood, which helped.

"You girls already know each other?" Netta asked. She had her gray hair in a twisty bun today and wore a festive red hat.

"We do," Courtney said. "Because of Maggie, I know lots more about Abraham Lincoln."

"Well, that's something, I suppose."

I laughed at her very candid response. Netta was a sweetheart, but she didn't pull any punches.

"I was hoping you would introduce Courtney around, show her all the stuff she needs to know. Look out for her."

Courtney looked instantly embarrassed. "Grams, I don't need anyone to look out for me."

"She does, too," Netta whispered.

"I'll do my best," I whispered back.

"If you guys are done conspiring, Maggie, do you think at some point today I could introduce my mom to yours? She could use a friend." The concern written all over Courtney's face was not lost on me.

Netta nodded along. "I think that would be a very good thing."

"Yeah, of course," I told them. "She's working in the booth now, but our shift ends in an hour."

Courtney seemed relieved. "Maybe on the picnic grounds?"

"Sure. We'll see you then." Netta and Courtney disappeared into the throngs and I went back to work. My mother was, of course, more than agreeable, and we found the Carringtons right where they said they'd be. Mrs. Carrington sat in a chair with an untouched funnel cake in front of her on one of the long rectangular tables arranged in rows. She attempted a smile when we approached, but she seemed weary and nervous. Her eyes were red rimmed with dark circles beneath them. She was, in every way, a contrast to my own mother, who stood alongside me vibrant, outgoing, and friendly.

"Well, hello," my mother said, happily approaching the group. She extended a hand to Courtney's mother, who did not get up from the folding chair in which she sat. "I'm Evie Beringer. It's a pleasure to meet you. Welcome to Tanner Peak."

"Thank you," Courtney's mother said shyly. "I'm Beverly. Courtney speaks very highly of your family."

My mother swatted Courtney's arm good-naturedly. "She's just being sweet. Courtney's welcome at our house anytime."

I stepped forward. "Mrs. Carrington, I'm Maggie. Margaret."

My mother grabbed my shoulders from behind. "This one belongs to me. I should have led with that." She turned to Netta laughing, and Netta joined her.

Beverly Carrington's watery blue eyes met mine. "A pleasure, Maggie. I'm glad Courtney has a friend."

My mother, the natural, took her cue and pulled out the chair across from Beverly and took a seat. "Why don't we have lunch tomorrow. We can meet at the café and I can catch you up on all the town gossip in one fell swoop."

Beverly looked up at Courtney, who stood behind her. Courtney nodded encouragingly, and it seemed to be the confidence booster she needed. "That would be nice. What time should we meet?"

"How about noon?" my mother asked. "We can hit up the place in the midst of the lunch crowd and introduce you to some folks. How does that sound?" It must have sounded awesome to Courtney, who beamed at the turn of events.

"I would like that," Beverly said conservatively. But she did seem pleased. I was proud of my mom in that moment for reaching out to someone who clearly needed it.

My mom leaned across the table. "We also have a book club you might like. Though I should tell you that those ladies drink more red wine than a nun on Sunday." She laughed at her own joke the way she always did. "We do a little reading, too."

"This is fantastic," Courtney whispered to me. "Thank you."

I shrugged off the thanks because this was just what people did in this town. They looked out for one another. "No problem. Are you enjoying the festival?"

"It just got infinitely better."

❖

I was actually excited for school that Monday, which never happened, especially not at this point in the school year. Maybe it was because summer was so close I could almost reach out and grab it. Maybe it was because Berta was back from her weekend away. Who knew?

Well, I did.

And it had nothing to do with either of those two things.

As I closed my locker and headed off down the hallway to my anatomy and physiology class, the skip in my step didn't miss a beat as I passed Michael Kersten making out with Mindy Stevenson against her locker. I nodded in their direction. A few steps away, a clique of senior girls chatted about the fake IDs they'd used to get into a club one town over. I smiled and waved. Down the hall was the huddle of academics planning their final exam study sessions. I mentally high-fived them.

As I walked, Berta appeared next to me. "Alert. Louis is headed this way."

"Well, you are looking extra alluring." That earned me an elbow in the ribs. "And aggressive."

Louis Macheski was a kid we'd grown up with since birth. Sweet. Quirky. Redheaded. Sometimes annoying. Always harmless.

He appeared right on cue.

"Berta. Hello. The AV club is doing a movie night. Not this Thursday, but the next Thursday. And it's not just for club members, which is what I wanted to speak to you about, because in fact, anyone can attend. I was hoping you would." He smiled at Berta, braces and all, before remembering me. "You, too, Margaret. God. You should come, too. I should have said that from the start. Everyone's invited. I just wanted to make sure that Roberta—"

"Cool," I said, stopping him before he continued until Christmas. "Maybe we will."

"Do you know what they're screening?" Berta asked.

He nodded as he absorbed the question. "I do not know, as of this moment. But I will check and get right back to you. To you both," he said, making sure to meet my eyes. His exuberance was sweet and made me smile. But then again, I was excited too.

"Thanks, Louis," Berta said, and patted him good-naturedly on the shoulder. A buddy pat—I hoped he understood that component. Louis fled down a side hallway, probably in search of the president of the AV club and an answer to Berta's question. I turned to her in all seriousness.

"His love for you knows no bounds."

Berta sighed and repositioned her backpack. "He's a nice guy."

"You realize you're probably going to have to let him down easy at some point, though, right?"

She turned to me as we walked. "You sure I can't keep smiling and patting his shoulder?"

"Might be cruel and unusual after a while."

"I don't like hurting people's feelings," she said, wincing.

"Which is one of the sweetest things about you. But maybe it's the kinder way to go."

She nodded and slipped into thought before we split for our respective classes.

When the time came for third-period history, I slid into my desk as always and spent the few moments before the bell going over my homework from the weekend, not at all wondering when Courtney would arrive. Not. At. All.

But then Mr. Blankenship stood from his ridiculous desk and class was under way. No Courtney. I forced myself to pay attention as we discussed the fallout of the Civil War and the economic effects of— giggling. There was definitely giggling coming from the back of the room, followed by the sound of it coming to an abrupt halt. I turned along with the rest of the class as Melanie, Courtney, and Lila Jane, the overzealous soccer goalie, took their spots surreptitiously. Courtney passed Mr. Blankenship an apologetic stare as she took her seat next to me.

"Hey," she whispered, moments later, and sent me a smile. I wasn't exactly someone who talked in the middle of a lecture, so I nodded politely. She wore a pale pink sundress with a thin brown belt. She even made a sundress look sophisticated. I shoved the thought from my mind and focused on the lecture, of which I'd already missed a good chunk.

Forty-six minutes later the bell rang and I gathered my stuff.

"See you later, Maggie," Courtney said, dipping her head to catch my eye as I packed up.

"Yeah, see ya."

Travis waited for Courtney outside the classroom and the two headed off down the hallway together. He leaned in and whispered something and she slugged him playfully. On the bright side, Courtney was fitting in and finding friends easily. I would try and concentrate on that particular detail and sideline the unattractive jealous thing creeping up my spine.

Louis decided to join us for lunch that day and went about setting out each individual Tupperware container his mother had meticulously packed for him. Homemade roast beef in one. Mashed potatoes in another. Gravy. And a berry salad.

"You don't mess around," Berta told him in awe. "I literally slap some peanut butter between some bread and head to school."

I nodded. "I'm lucky if I remember to do that."

Louis seemed disturbed by this concept. "Why don't we share? I don't mind sharing. I have plenty. Here."

"No, no," Berta said, holding up a hand. "I was simply remarking on the array."

"Margaret?" he asked, holding up his now gravy-drenched roast beef. He'd always been such a kindhearted person.

"I'm good."

"Let me know if you change your mind."

"That's quite a spread you have there," Courtney said, setting her tray next to mine. I looked up and met bright blue eyes, surprised to see her. My pulse seemed to beat a little faster and I felt this upshot in energy. I really needed to grab control of this little crush. And yes, I could admit that that was what this was.

Louis shrugged, now looking embarrassed. He shifted to an impressive shade of red to match his hair, and I understood that I wasn't the only one Courtney had an effect on. "My mom is—"

"A saint," Courtney finished, gesturing to the food. "Look at the culinary showmanship. Mine's probably still in bed." I sent her a questioning glance, but she waved it off. "So here's the thing. Are you listening?"

I nodded. "I am."

"I was talking with Melanie and Lila Jane in second period, and there's a group heading to Santa Barbara this weekend for a beach party. Melanie's parents have rented a house and we can stay the night."

"That's awesome," I said blandly, and investigated the contents of the less-than-happy enchilada on my tray.

"And we're going."

My gaze snapped to hers. "We? No, no, no."

"Yes. You and Berta are coming with me."

Louis, having been left out of that invitation, looked up feebly, and my heart squeezed for him. If Berta and I fell on the boring list, then Louis could best be described as living on the untouchable one. I turned to her. "I'm not sure we're up for it, Courtney."

"We're not," Berta said more emphatically.

She nodded. "I was expecting that. You don't like those guys and don't make much secret about it."

I balked. "That's not true." Totally true.

"All I'm asking is that you suspend your judgment and come have fun with us. Keep an open mind, and you might actually find that they're not as bad as you think. Louis should come too," she said, passing him a smile. That scored her big points in my book.

He was instantly red again. "Oh, thank you for the invitation, but my parents are taking me fishing."

"Next time, then," Courtney told him and then turned to me. "Tell me why you don't want to go."

"They don't want us there," I told her. "Trust me."

"I've already informed Melanie that I'm bringing you both, and she was 'no big deal' about it. The house is huge and has plenty of room. Everyone's just going to sleep on the floor. Say yes, so I can stop begging."

I held up a finger. "Let the record reflect that there has been no begging."

She turned to me and showcased her big blue puppy-dog eyes of unfairness, blinking back at me sadly. Like there was any possible scenario where I could resist that kind of setup. I sighed loudly. "Okay. I'll go. Fine. You've twisted my arm via your pathetic facial work. But I won't have a good time."

"I'm sure you'll hate every minute of it," Courtney said and dusted off her hands in victory. She turned to Berta. "Well?"

Berta shook her head. "I think I'm gonna pass. But thanks."

Well, that was that. I smiled at Courtney. "When do we leave?"

She took a moment, studying me before grinning back. "I'll pick you up at the farm after school on Friday. We can be at the beach in forty-five minutes."

Berta raised an eyebrow at me and I shrugged back. It made sense that she'd wonder what the hell I was thinking, as I generally avoided Melanie and her clan at every turn. But Courtney had a point. Maybe I hadn't given Melanie a chance. Maybe she was a decent person after all. And it was possible that Travis was just being a teenage boy. Or maybe I just wanted all of these things to be true for Courtney's sake. One thing was for sure, Courtney had me reaching outside my comfort zone.

And it was terrifying.

"Looking for a ride?" Courtney asked from the driver's seat of a blue Mercedes convertible. Wow. I stood in my circular drive that Friday afternoon, clutching my duffel bag and pillow in awe of the car she'd just pulled up in.

"This is yours?" I asked, circling it in reverence. I was promised a car when I turned eighteen, but even then it would be a used model. This was…an impressive piece of machinery.

Courtney flipped her sunglasses onto her head. "All mine. My parents' strategy of not having to do much in the way of kid maintenance, I suspect." I whistled low, still taking in the car. "Don't just stand there drooling. Hop in."

Before I could, the door to the house opened and my mother raced toward us waving. "Hi, Courtney!"

Courtney beamed back from the car. "Hi, Mrs. Beringer. How's the writing today?"

"Jeffrey is brooding again and racing his motorcycle all over town. Chastity can't take her eyes off him."

"Isn't that always the case? The quiet ones pull you in."

My mother nodded quite seriously. "You're a wise one, young lady."

"Are we all set?" I asked, ready to flee the scene and this awkward conversation as fast as possible. Unfortunately, my mother wasn't quite ready to say good-bye.

"So I've spoken to Melanie's mother, who assured me she will be in attendance at the beach house all night."

I nodded. "I already told you that."

She ignored me. "Courtney, do you have a valid driver's license?"

"Yes, ma'am. Would you like to see it? I could—"

"Mom," I said, trying to intervene. Nothing.

"Any speeding tickets?"

Courtney shook her head. "Not one."

"Good." My mother turned to me and took my face in her hands as if I were still four. Mortifying. "You'll call when you all arrive in Santa Barbara? The minute you arrive?"

"I will."

"Please remember that you're representing your father and me, not to mention the Beringer name."

"Of course. May I go?"

She kissed my cheek and offered me a squeeze. "You girls be careful and—"

"Call you," I finished.

My mother blew a kiss. "*Call me.*"

I climbed into the car. With a final wave to my very nervous-looking parent, we were off.

"She's adorable," Courtney said, and flipped on the music. Loud.

I laughed internally at the characterization. I would have gone with *overbearing*. "The cutest," I said instead over the music.

"Ready for a little fun in the sun?"

Despite my trepidation, I was prepared to give this whole thing a shot. "Why not?"

"Now, that's what I want to hear."

We wound our way to the front of the farm, passing the green plants that still held the odd strawberry not yet harvested. The sun beat down from half-mast in the dazzling blue sky. It really was the perfect day for a drive, and the warmer temperature would hold on for another hour and a half at least. I looked over at Courtney. Her blond hair was down and blowing in the breeze. It carried a subtle curl that I decided was most likely Courtney-made. Black Chanel sunglasses rested on her face, and she sang quietly with the song on the radio. It was an image I could stare at all day.

"Sing with me," she said, as we hit the highway, gaining speed.

"As much as I would like to, I'm afraid I don't know this one."

"What?" She gaped at me. "How is that possible? It's the most overplayed song of the year."

"About that? Yeah, I have a confession to make. It's pretty shocking, so brace yourself."

She glanced over at me, dipping the sunglasses. "Okay. Try me."

"I rarely listen to current music."

"No!" she said in mock horror. "Get out of my car!" Then softening, "Okay, so what do you listen to? And if you name a boy band I might actually drop you at the next rest stop."

"Hopefully, we won't pass any for a while." I pulled my phone out of my back pocket and gestured to her radio. "May I?"

"By all means." I plugged my phone into the stereo system and selected the Beatles' *A Hard Day's Night* album and waited in anticipation as "Can't Buy Me Love" filled the car.

"The Rolling Stones?" Courtney asked innocently after listening for a beat.

I collapsed back in my seat as if leveled by a two-by-four, and it felt a little like I had been. I couldn't handle the misstep. This would change everything.

Courtney laughed and put my fears to rest. "I'm kidding. Please know I'm kidding." Thank God. She reached over and touched my knee, giving it a little squeeze. "Beatles. Got it. You like the Beatles."

That smile was killer, but I focused on the importance of the moment, sat up again, and turned to face her better. "I don't like the Beatles. One doesn't just *like* the Beatles. I have an appreciation for the geniuses that are the lads from Liverpool. Music just doesn't come like this anymore. Do you understand what I'm saying? The Beatles are everything."

She nodded along. "I understand the gravity. You take the Beatles very seriously. Tell me something about them."

I didn't hesitate. "Well, they wrote the title track to this particular album in a day. This was also the first album written entirely by them. No outside assistance."

"What else?"

"The last recording session that included all four happened in 1969. Strawberry Fields refers to a Salvation Army home near where John used to live. The BBC banned 'I Am the Walrus' because the lyrics contain the word 'knickers.' There's a version of 'Love Me Do' out there with a different drummer. I mean, poor Ringo. Oh, and the first time Paul—"

"Okay, okay, that's good," she said, laughing. Her hand was on my knee again. "You've proven yourself a true fan."

I regained my sense of calm. "You can't ask me for Beatles facts unless you're ready for Beatles facts."

"I think I get that now."

She'd yet to move her hand, and the warmth that touch inspired was spreading rapidly. "You," she said, "have a dimple on your cheek that I hadn't noticed until now."

"Yes." I touched my cheek. "I do."

"How had I not noticed that?" She returned her hand to the steering wheel and shook her head. "A dimpled Beatles fanatic. What am I gonna do with you?"

God, I had ideas on the subject. Big-time ideas. I just didn't have any intention of sharing them.

We arrived in Santa Barbara a little later than we'd planned, due to traffic. Melanie's vacation house was apparently on Butterfly Beach, one of the westward-facing beaches that offered a beautiful view of the sunset.

"Look at that," Courtney said reverently, as we walked toward the water that was now haloed with brilliant pinks and oranges. She placed her hands on her hips. "You don't often see something so beautiful."

I liked that she'd noticed. I paused next to her just to watch. For several long moments, that was all we did, take in the radiance of that sunset. Finally, I turned to her.

"You sure you want to abandon something as peaceful as this for the group we're about to join?"

Her smile was sincere and her voice quiet when she answered. "This is a really nice spot. I agree."

I nodded, holding her gaze and memorizing the way the sun slanted across her eyes, making them that much more blue.

She opened her mouth and closed it. "I have to say something."

"Okay. What do you want to say?" And now I was focusing on her mouth, mesmerized by it, because how could one not be?

"In some ways, I feel like we were supposed to meet."

I shifted, curious now. "How so?"

She shook her head. "I'm not sure. Just this feeling I have. That we're *meant* to be friends. Almost like I'm right where I'm supposed to be."

"Maybe we are. Meant to be friends."

Courtney blushed. It was a look I'd never seen on her. "Am I being stupid?" she asked. "You can tell me if I am."

I stared at her for a moment before answering. "Not at all."

"Good." She sighed. "Maybe we should go find the others before I decide I knew you in a past life and really freak you the hell out."

I laughed. "If we must."

"Melanie emailed directions." She inclined her head toward the house looming in the distance. "Follow me."

And I did.

The truth was, in that moment, I'd have followed Courtney anywhere.

CHAPTER FOUR

"Martin Shakerman, if you get my hair wet, you are going to die. Do you hear me? Die!" Melanie shouted from a few yards down the beach as Martin chased her with a water balloon in hand. He was shirtless. She wore a bikini. It was all very *Baywatch*.

We'd been at the beach party for a couple of hours now, and most people had mellowed a bit from the initial rush to play volleyball, score a hamburger off the grill, or some other beachy activity to check off the list before our one night here ended.

The sun was gone and the night now hung around us. Some of the boys had built a fire, and the fifteen or so kids in attendance sat around it. Melanie's parents were nice enough to walk some blankets down from the house, which was good because a chill moved in from the water. Half of the group had coupled off, cuddling under blankets together. I sat next to Courtney and made small talk with Lila Jane, while next to me Travis and Courtney seemed to be hitting it off.

"I've just never seen you at one of these things before," Lila Jane said dubiously as she wrestled with a package of marshmallows.

"Right. I imagine you wouldn't have. I haven't been to many."

"So do you just prefer, like, sticking to yourself?" More bag wrestling.

"I guess that's one way to put it."

"You're actually not so bad," she said.

You know, I wasn't sure how to take that. "Thanks, I think. Do you want me to open that for you?"

"See? That's a really nice offer. That's what I'm talking about."

She passed me the bag. I easily tore into it and handed it back. Lila Jane had definitely not grown up on a farm.

She passed back a flask. "To show my gratitude."

"What's in it?" She tossed me a look that said *really?* "Right." I nodded and stared at the metal container. I wasn't someone who drank. In fact, being the rule follower that I was, I never had. But this kind of felt like the night to give it a try. Maybe it would relax me some. So I tossed back a swallow and winced as what had to be whiskey burned a potent trail down my throat. To my right, Courtney giggled and put her hand on Travis's back. I'd never actually heard her giggle before. I realized now that was the laugh she reserved for boys like Travis. He seemed to eat it up, which meant she knew what she was doing.

"You don't like that one?" Travis asked her, laughing as well.

Courtney covered her eyes. "That has got to be the worst pickup line I've ever heard."

"How about this one?" He leaned back onto his elbow and surveyed her. "Are those diamonds in your eyes, or did the stars fall from the skies?"

She shook her head and pointed at him. "No, absolutely not. That was even worse than the first." But she giggled through the sentence. I grimaced and died a little inside. Exactly how many more hours were left of this night?

Travis sat up with a lazy grin across his face. "Now, hold on. I'm not a photographer, but even I can picture us together."

"Wow," Courtney said in earnest. "You've got an arsenal of all things lame."

He flashed his Travis smile. "I've also got a thing. For you."

She flattened her hand against his knee and used it to push herself up. "On that very flattering note, I'm off to freshen up." She offered my shoulder a squeeze as she passed, her fingertips lingering on my neck a bit. I refused to react, as I realized now that she was simply a tactile person. I stared into the fire as it danced to and fro. The heat from it was starting to warm my face uncomfortably. I felt Travis watching me.

"So, Beringer, what's the word on your friend?" he asked, sliding over to me and taking Courtney's spot.

"Can you expand upon the question?" My eyes never left the fire.

"Courtney. Is she into me?"

"I have no way of knowing that."

"So she hasn't said anything?"

I met his eyes and paused because in the midst of the confident good looks, there was a surprising amount of vulnerability. I caved, because I apparently have a heart. Even for Travis. "She did ask me about you."

"She did?" he asked like a hopeful little puppy.

"She did. I told her you weren't a total idiot, which you're not." New discovery: Whiskey makes one say things. Brave things.

"That's gotta be a good sign, right?" More of the bouncing puppy vibe.

"I would imagine."

Travis glanced around to see who was listening and settled on a decision. "Let's walk."

I glanced to my right and left to see who else he might be addressing, because there was no way it was me. No one else seemed to be paying attention. "Me?"

"Beringer, just do this for me? Please?"

I stole another swig from that flask and braced myself for the heat to slither its way down my throat. I gave my head a firm shake and stood. "All yours."

Once we made it down to the shoreline, he must have deemed the distance adequate. "So, I really like her."

"Courtney, you mean? You have a thing for Courtney." Join the club.

He nodded. "I don't know what it is about her."

I did. I knew exactly what it was. Courtney was not only beautiful, but she was exciting, and different, and actually a really nice person on top of it all. She was all of the things. It wasn't surprising that Travis had noticed that, too. I was sure everyone did.

"I was hoping you could help. With intel."

"As in?"

"I dunno. Tell me what she likes. What is she into?"

I decided to throw him a bone. "She likes to draw. She sketches objects out in the world."

"Great. I can work with that. She's artistic, which is hot. What about guys?"

"We haven't talked much about guys."

"C'mon. You're her friend. You two always eat lunch together, and she brought you here. You probably know her best. What kind of guys does she like?"

"Listen, Travis. That's a really broad question, and I honestly don't know the answer." The alcohol seemed to have loosened me up considerably, but it also made my head a little foggy. Was this what it meant to be a lightweight?

"Just tell me what I should do to, you know, make the best impression on her," he said.

Travis was asking me for dating advice? Me, who'd dated no one. The world was upside down.

"Like should I go for it? Make a move? Or play it cool?"

I scrubbed at my face, wondering how I'd gotten myself to this point. I thought about the campfire. About Courtney's giggling, how close she sat to him. She seemed very much into Travis, and who was I to get in the way? That wasn't what friends did for each other, and if nothing else, I wanted to hang on to this friendship. Courtney was starting to matter to me. "I think you should go for it," I said, letting my hand drop in surrender.

His eyes lit up. "Yeah? I'd have a chance?"

"I think it's definitely possible. It's what I would do if I were you."

He knocked me on the shoulder. "I owe you one." He backed away, barefoot in the sand, and pointed at me. "We should talk more."

I pointed back at him good-naturedly. "I'll put it in my date book."

"That's funny. See? You're a funny girl, Beringer, when you want to be."

I stood alone on the beach and watched as Travis approached Courtney at the campfire and offered her his hand. She smiled up at him and accepted, and they headed off down the beach in the opposite direction. The two of them would have beautiful children together. Tiny, popular people who would take over the world.

All was as it should be. Double sigh of sadness.

I rejoined the group around the fire, anything to ignore the tug I felt on my heart over what had been a stupid crush anyway. I waited patiently for the bag of marshmallows to come my way. If nothing else, I could stuff myself with s'mores and chalk up the evening to a junk food victory. Only Cody Timmons seemed to be examining each and every marshmallow before making a selection. I dipped my head and caught his gaze. "Do you need a few minutes alone with those? You're not proposing, Cody. It's a marshmallow. Chop-chop."

That drew laughter from the group.

"Margaret, you should come out more," one girl said. "Not live your life on that farm."

"Beringer's not so bad," came from across the circle.

Apparently, the small amount of alcohol I'd downed seemed to have brought out a bold sense of sarcasm my classmates appreciated. Who would have guessed? Cody playfully tossed the bag my way and Melanie studied me. "What?" I asked.

"You're different tonight." It was an accusation.

"I am?"

She shrugged and went back to her conversation. Just as I decided that I still didn't enjoy her, I was tapped on the shoulder. I turned around with a mild dose of alcohol-fueled irritation and looked up into Courtney's big blue eyes. To my surprise, they flashed anger. "What's up?" I asked.

"Can I speak to you for a moment?"

I glanced back at the group and then to Courtney, not exactly sure of the situation. "Um, yeah. Of course."

She stalked away toward the house and I was left with little choice but to follow. "Why would you do that?" she asked, whirling on me once we were alone.

"Do what?"

"You told Travis to kiss me. I mean, you *told* him to. Why would you do that?"

I held up a hand. "Whoa. I didn't say those particular words."

"But you made him think I was into it. That I was into *him*."

I shook my head in exasperation. "Aren't you?"

"No. I'm not, actually."

"Okay then, I'm sorry. I shouldn't have encouraged him. But you guys were pretty cozy next to the fire, so—"

She pressed her lips to mine and I froze. All at once a warm rush of amazing came over me and I responded, returning her kiss. Surrendering beneath it. Courtney slid her hands around my waist and pulled me closer as our lips moved in slow tandem. I'd been kissed exactly once in my life, by Edwin Elderman in a game of Spin the Bottle at my church youth camp, but it had been nothing like this. I wasn't even sure it had been the same activity. Because kissing Courtney was warm and satisfying and addictive and exciting and it made my skin shiver in the most wonderful way. The proximity came with that intoxicating scent of vanilla and I was gone, lost in a blurry haze of fabulous. It only lasted for a few seconds, but they were probably the best few seconds of my time on Earth thus far. As Courtney pulled back, ending the kiss, she kept her lips very close to mine. "Get it now?" she said quietly.

I nodded, as I wasn't sure what words to pick.

"Good."

That was the extent of our conversation on the topic, and I didn't press for more.

We rejoined the others for another hour around the bonfire before the curfew Melanie's parents had laid out for us hit. I'd never felt lighter in my life as I sat alongside that flickering fire with my classmates. Jokes were somehow funnier, the beach was sexier, and everyone there was so much more fun. My brain remained fuzzy from alcohol or Courtney—it was hard to say for sure which.

By the end of the night, per Melanie's parents' rules, the boys sacked out on the second floor of the beach house and the girls assembled sleeping bags on the first. I picked a spot near the sliding glass door where I could stare up at the sky as I drifted off. The alcohol clung a bit and I wasn't ready to shut my eyes. Courtney wordlessly set up her sleeping bag next to mine and stretched out on her back. Someone killed the lights, but in typical teenage girl fashion, the chatter continued.

"Tell me he didn't actually say that," one of my classmates said.

"Not only did he say it, he tried it," another answered.

"And what did you do?"

"I leaned into it."

Cue the laughter and subsequent teenage girl question-and-answer session. In the midst of the back and forth, a warm hand slipped around my waist from behind. *Courtney.* I hitched in a breath at the initial contact, her hand against my stomach. I closed my eyes and remained still as she eased her body behind mine. The lights were off and we were forgotten in our corner by the sliding glass door. "Is this okay?" she whispered. "You can tell me if it's not."

I nodded and placed my hand atop hers, holding it in place as my heart thudded away. The voices of the girls faded into the background, and it was only us there as far as I was concerned, Courtney and me, her arm around me as we stared up at the night sky. We lay like that for a while as I counted stars and listened to her breathe, her exhales faintly tickling my shoulder. Eventually, it slowed down and evened out, signaling to me that Courtney had drifted off. I set aside a moment to memorize the warm tingles that danced across my skin at her touch, her proximity, and the fantastic scent of vanilla that I now associated with only her. I'd never experienced anything like it. As exhausting as the day had been, I fought against sleep so I could live in this day for just a little while longer.

Slowly but surely, sleep descended and I joined Courtney in welcome slumber. Who knew what the morning would bring? Maybe we'd never discuss what had happened between us that night. It was possible the alcohol would be blamed and the events of the night would be shelved forever. But I dared to wonder. What if this was the beginning of something highly unexpected in my life?

Something memorable.

Something wonderful.

Boring little Margaret Beringer, who nothing ever happened to, was suddenly in the middle of something meaningful with a girl she genuinely liked?

Was it truly possible?

CHAPTER FIVE

By the time Sunday rolled around, one thing was clear. I was in over my head and could maybe do well to ask for a little guidance. I didn't have a ton of reliable options, but I knew of one who wouldn't let me down.

"I need advice," I said to my brother from the steps in front of the shed. Clay lay flat on his back underneath the old tractor. That thing hadn't worked in two years. I had no idea what made him think he could get it going now.

He stuck his head out and showcased a streak of grease across his chin. "Good thing I'm brilliant. Lay it on me."

"I need *girl* advice." This was a big step for me, and I braced myself against his reaction.

He quirked an eyebrow.

"Can we skip the shocked older brother heart-to-heart?"

"If you want."

"I do."

"Got it. So…you're into a girl. Not a total surprise, by the way."

"I don't know how I feel about that statement, but let's press on."

"What's the question? I'm a pro."

I sighed. This was uncharted territory between Clay and me, but I was keenly aware of the fact that he did really well when it came to women and dating and was likely the perfect person to come to. Plus, his heart was as big as his ego, so he'd definitely be willing.

"There's a girl I like."

"I gathered that." He swung his legs around to face me from his spot in the dirt and swept the blond hair out of his eyes. "Does she know it?"

"I think it's safe to say yes."

"Does she like you back?"

"Again with the affirmative."

"So what's the problem?"

I met his gaze. "I have no moves."

"Well, you do say things like 'affirmative.'"

I tossed a towel at him.

"Just ribbin' ya." He took a moment with what I'd said and then, reaching a conclusion, gave his head a firm shake. "Impossible. You're related to me. You have to have moves."

I couldn't help but laugh at the arrogance. "While I see how that might be troubling for your legacy, it's true."

He hopped to his feet and moved toward me with purpose. "Nah. It's not moves you're missing. It's experience. You're new at this whole romance game."

"Also true."

He rolled his shoulders as if gearing up for battle. "Give me the details. Let me know what I'm working with."

"I don't know that I want to go into all—"

"Stop wussing out. Have you kissed yet?"

I covered my eyes because it was the only way I'd make it through this. "Yes," I said quietly and scrubbed my face before refocusing. "But that was two nights ago, and I haven't seen her since. And we didn't talk about it. At all. And now I have no idea what the next step is, or if I should take it or—"

"So here's what you're going to do."

"Maybe I should get some paper," I said, and glanced around for options.

"No, you little scrapper, just listen to me." He ruffled my hair encouragingly. "You can do this."

"Says the expert who's never home on a Saturday night. Ever."

"There's a reason for that." He paused. "A *girl*, huh?"

"Yes, a *girl*." I rolled my eyes. "Are you going to help or not?"

"No, I am. I definitely am." That seemed to usher him back on track and he refocused. "So the next time you see this girl, the department store one, I'm guessing." I cringed at his accuracy. "You're going to work on little touches. Every chance you get."

"I'm going to need you to be more specific."

He took a seat next to me on the steps and gestured toward himself and out again. "Come up with little ways to initiate contact. Nothing works better than serial contact. When you walk past her, maybe give her shoulder a little squeeze or hang on an extra second or two when you hand her something. Little touches let her know you're into her."

A lightbulb flew on. "Oh, my God. *She* does that! That exact thing!"

"Well, then it seems she has a few moves of her own. You're in luck." He grinned.

"Who has moves?"

I whirled at the sound of my mother's voice. Mayday.

"The girl this scrapper is crushing on."

I didn't even have a second to throttle him, and God, did I want to.

"Ohhh! This is exciting! Which girl does she have a crush on?" my mother asked eagerly and rubbed her hands together in anticipation. Say what?

Clay shrugged. "I'm guessing the department store one, though she's yet to confirm or deny."

"Margaret, you have feelings for Courtney?" my mother asked proudly.

You'd have thought I'd just announced I liked spinach.

"Wait," I said, struggling to keep up. "Did we not just skip a step? A very big step. A monumental one."

"What is everyone doing out here?" my father asked, rounding the shed in his work coveralls.

"Your daughter is finally coming out," my mother told him gleefully.

Was this really happening? It was, wasn't it?

"Well, that's great!" my father said, thumping me on the back. "We wondered when it would be."

Clay held up his hands. "I mean, I thought it was possible, but didn't know one hundred percent."

"Well, how could you?" my mom said. "You're not her mother."

"Or her father," my dad said, looking pleased with himself.

"Yeah, but I'm her brother. I pick up on stuff, too. Like when she stared at that photo of Jennifer Lopez I had on my wall in high school for *way* too long."

"Good point," my mother said.

I stood. "Am I even here right now? Can you guys see me?"

My mother kissed my cheek. "Of course we can. I'm sorry, sweetheart. We're just celebrating a little here. Oh! We should all go out for pizza."

"No. No going out for pizza. And shouldn't I get to be in charge of this conversation?" I said in exaggerated outrage. "Because it's kind of important to my history as, you know, a person."

"Of course you should," my mother said and made a sweeping gesture with her hand. "Take it away."

There was a long silence as I tried to figure out what the hell to say. This was so not what I had planned on.

"So…I like a girl," I said quietly, doing my best not to toe the dirt. "And I realize now that this is not the surprise I thought it was going to be or whatever, but it's the truth all the same." Silence. I nodded once awkwardly. "So there's that." Sensing that I was done, my mother broke into applause, and to my shock and horror, my father and brother joined right in. They were applauding my coming out? Embarrassed and reeling, I stomped into the house.

"You guys are such weirdos!" I yelled over my shoulder. But they were *my* weirdos, and I loved them. The sound of the applause followed me into the house, only adding fuel to the remarkable blush I felt heat my cheeks. I made sure to slam the door for effect, but underneath the bravado, I was smiling.

And I'm pretty positive they knew it.

I was officially out, I thought as I lay on my bed staring up at the glow-in-the-dark stars I'd glued to my ceiling in the third grade. That knowledge brought with it a certain confidence. And maybe it was time to put that confidence to work.

❖

"Whoa," Berta said when I joined her at her locker for what would be the last day of my junior year. "What is happening here?"

"What?" I asked nonchalantly. I knew exactly what.

"You look...amazing," she said, turning so she could give me a full once-over.

I smiled at my cousin and enjoyed that little boost to my ego. "Thank you. I thought I'd put in some effort since it's the last day of school and all."

"So this is a celebratory look?"

"Yes. That is exactly what this is." In all honesty, I hadn't done a ton different. But something about the events of the past week had me wanting to go the extra mile. So I'd worn my hair down, which was a rare occurrence all on its own. But I'd also tamed my hair into subtle waves with the use of a product I'd swiped from my mother's bathroom. Then I'd added some lip gloss, and bam—there was an extra spring in my step. I liked the way I looked. It mirrored the way I'd been feeling lately.

"And this has nothing to do with you spending time with Melanie and her minions at the beach? Because if I'm being honest, it feels that way." She slammed her locker and I passed her a disbelieving look as we headed off to class.

"Melanie? What? No way. You realize that's impossible. You have to trust me on this."

"I will. I just...miss you is all. You're so different lately."

I paused and turned to her, realizing that I had been a little MIA. "I'm sorry about that. I miss you, too. We should do something this week. Want to?"

She nodded. "Yeah, that would be great."

We said good-bye and headed to our respective first periods.

The day went by in a haze of raucous teenagers anxious for summer freedom and teachers doing what they could to keep them contained until the final bell. Amidst it all, there had been no Courtney. Her desk sat noticeably vacant in history class.

"Beringer, where's your friend?"

I glanced at Travis, who waited for me outside history. "I actually don't know."

"She's in the office," Melanie said strolling past us. "Withdrawing."

Instantly, we were both following her. "What, leaving school?" Travis asked.

I shook my head, not understanding. "Why?"

Melanie turned calmly. "Listen, I'm just saying what I saw. Her father is asking for her records. She's out of here."

I didn't wait around for more and took off to the front office. No sign of Courtney or her dad anywhere. I dashed outside just in time to see a black Town Car exit the parking lot. What the hell was going on?

I called Courtney's phone, but it rolled immediately to voice mail. I hung up and fired off a text. *You're leaving?*

But it went unanswered.

The remaining hours of the school day existed to torture me as I watched the seconds tick by with excruciating leisure. The clock hated me and I hated it. There'd been no word from Courtney, no explanation, but the news of her departure sure did spread fast. One kid thought she'd been caught with drugs. Another heard she would be commuting to a private school an hour away. It was Netta who broke the news to me.

"I'm sorry to say that her parents are getting a divorce. Her mother has decided she doesn't want to be married to her father anymore," she told me from her porch that afternoon. She had the same blue eyes as Courtney, and today they held sadness. "Courtney is moving back east with her mother."

"For good?" I asked, my heart heavy like lead.

"I'm afraid so. They stopped in to say good-bye an hour ago before heading to the airport in Santa Barbara."

"She didn't say anything to me. Nothing."

She shook her head. "It all happened very quickly, and Courtney hasn't had the easiest time, as you can imagine. I'm sure you'll hear from her once she catches her breath."

I nodded. "Thanks, Netta."

"Sweetheart, can I get you a soft drink or something to eat? We can commiserate together if you like."

I forced a smile, because she really was one of the nicest people. "No, but thank you." I gave her a hug. "I'm sorry about all this."

"Me, too, Margaret. I was so happy to have her here. We were going to catch up on the time we'd missed."

"Maybe she'll be back one day."

She nodded, her gaze falling to the ground. "That would make me happy."

I gestured behind me. "I better get home, but I'll stop by next week to say hi, if that's okay."

She seemed to perk up at the idea and her smile returned. "I would like that very much."

"See you then. Bye, Netta."

"Good-bye, Margaret. Give my best to your parents."

"Yes, ma'am."

I turned and descended the steps as the summer I'd looked forward to, planned on, faded like the waning sun behind the clouds. But more than that, my heart ached for Courtney, for what she must have been going through. Just when she thought she'd found stability, a place she could settle in, it was yanked out from under her yet again.

This weekend there would be gatherings, barbecues, and sales all over town in celebration of the end of the school year. Tanner Peak had a way of going all out when it came to ushering in new seasons. The day I'd been waiting for all year was here, and yet it didn't matter in the scheme of things anymore. Celebrating was now the furthest thing from my mind. With a heavy heart, I headed home, thinking of the girl who wore plaid skirts and boots. Who was smart and kind and beautiful. Who'd affected me more than I would have thought possible, but seemed a little lost herself.

No, the summer I'd longed for didn't seem to matter as much anymore. The edges seemed duller. Courtney Carrington had sparked my life into color, and now that she was gone, everything else felt bleak and gray.

CHAPTER SIX

The third summer

"We have a year of college behind us," Berta said thoughtfully. "Does that seem possible to you?" She sipped from her hazelnut latte housed in a giant mug. Steam rose grandly from its center.

"We are, in fact, sophomores now," I said in amazement and took a pull from my iced coffee in a boring plastic cup. While I was a little jealous of the glorious mug Berta held with both hands, I was unable to stomach hot beverages in the midst of the warm summer temperatures, something I planned to work on. It was good to have goals in life.

It had been two weeks since Berta had returned to town from UC Santa Barbara and I'd taken my last exam at the community branch just outside of town. We were free of college for the summer, and the future now loomed in front of us, big and bold. The world was ours to explore for the next three months.

Berta sat back in the oversized armchair alongside the window at Bag of Beans, Tanner Peak's newly opened coffeehouse. The competition for business between Beans and the well-established café had been fodder for the town's new Facebook page. The youth of Tanner Peak were all about the converted cottage full of couches and the fancy espresso drinks. However, the older generation stood by the traditional cup of joe found at the Berry Good Café. Lately, I'd started every morning at Bag of Beans and enjoyed how much busier it was now that many of my old classmates had returned to town from school. "How crazy is that?" Berta asked. "We're seriously growing up."

"Is it strange that I already feel it? The impending responsibility that will come with actually graduating in three short years?" Well, two and a half for me. I planned to graduate early.

Berta tucked a strand of hair behind her ear and shook her head. "No, because I'm going out of my mind with all the things I need to accomplish before August. Moving from a dorm to an apartment is going to require a ton more stuff. I need to shop and shop like it's my job."

"Luckily you were born with a prominent retail gene."

She pointed at me. "There is that. You're good at seeing the bright side of things, Maggie. I appreciate that about you. Then there's your uncanny ability to detect cookies in the vicinity."

"That cookie thing took years of work."

She pointed at the sincerity on her face. "Nothing but gratitude."

"I'm just making sure you get it."

"Ladies," Travis said, settling next to us with what looked to be a dessert masquerading as coffee. He didn't ask if he could join us, but that was just Travis.

"Aren't you supposed to be applying for jobs today?" Berta asked him between sips.

He gestured to his coffee imposter. "My precursor to rejection."

I shook my head. "You won't face rejection and you know it. This town loves you. There are parades in your honor."

He perked up and smiled. "They do, don't they? Parade would be nice. Just sayin'."

I shook my head at him and laughed. "I'd start organizing promptly, but I'm sure it's in the works."

The last two years had been a big one in terms of our friendship. Travis and I had found a common ground that summer before our senior year. Courtney Carrington and her brief visit had brought us together in a sense. As annoying as he could be on one level, he was actually kind of a cool human on another. Who knew? Along with that newfound friendship, something interesting had happened. The social hierarchy I'd always known high school to be crumbled, and the senior class spent our last year...being people. Maybe it stemmed from the knowledge that it would be our final year together. Regardless, we chilled the hell out and did crazy things like sitting at different lunch tables in the cafeteria. It was a few unique months of wonderful madness.

And now it was all behind us. We'd scattered to various parts of the country and returned, all with tales to tell of all the growing up we'd done. The levels of life we'd conquered.

Well, all but me and Travis. I'd remained on the farm but commuted to Santa Barbara City College for classes three times a week. Travis, however, had jumped straight into the world of employment, working full-time at Amundson's Hardware. Though he was now ready to move on, quite literally, to greener pastures.

"I'm looking for work where I can use my hands," he explained. "Tired of ringing stuff up at a register. Construction, farming, firefighting. Something with an outdoor component so I could put these magnificent puppies to work." He flexed six different ways and I laughed at the fact that he cherished his muscles so desperately. Travis, in my opinion, was an enjoyable cliché sent to brighten my life and entertain me endlessly. The fact that he was totally on board for the teasing made him the best sport ever. I was keeping him.

"You know, you'd be a fantastic firefighter," Berta told him, latching onto the idea.

"But you would have to go to firefighting school," I told him.

He grimaced.

"Stop making that face. They can't have people who don't know anything about fires running into burning buildings all willy-nilly. Think of the mayhem. You'd have to learn how to hold a hose."

He bounced his eyebrows. "I can hold a hose, baby."

I looked at him hard. "You need God."

He ignored me. "So firefighting requires school? Bummer. I'll put it on the list of possibilities, I guess."

"In the meantime, if you're truly interested in farming, my brother is looking for extra help at our place. I heard him say so yesterday."

"Seriously?" Travis sat forward in his armchair. "Can you talk to him for me? Put in a good word. Work the little sister charm?"

I shrugged. "I can try. I'm headed home after this, and I'll see if I can find him. Stop by this afternoon if you have time."

He seemed newly energized. "I'll be there."

Melanie Newcastle breezed past our chairs on the way to the counter. She said nothing, which wasn't shocking. If the rest of us had grown closer over the past two years, Melanie had done quite the opposite. She was meaner and more spiteful than ever. Sadly, she didn't even mask it behind the pretend niceties anymore and had pulled away from most of her friends. She worked in town part-time at Curl Up and Dye, the town's go-to salon, as a shampoo girl. From what I heard, she was pursuing her beautician's license at night.

I avoided her whenever possible.

"Nice of you to say hi, Mel!" Travis yelled at her across the shop. "Great to see you!"

Her answer was to wiggle four fingers at us (and I mean barely wiggle) and turn back to the menu. She was an unhappy human being, I decided. Misery personified over there.

"Well, I'm out," Travis said, and downed the last of his chocolate fudge sundae of a coffee. "Catch up with you guys later. Stay groovy. Dream about me and whatnot." Travis set upon his sojourn of a job search and I turned to Berta.

"What's on tap for you today?"

Her expression was dialed to dread. "Brushing up on my computer science for my summer course. It starts next week and I don't want to show up already behind."

"Such a brainiac over there."

Berta had plans to conquer the gaming industry for womankind, and I was thrilled to cheer her on. She was a science egghead and would go far. My plans were a little less specific. I'd start with the basics and see where the road led me. The farm would always be important to me, family history and all, so whatever I did decide to do with my life would have to go hand and hand with a part-time commitment to Beringer's.

But I did long for a career of my own. Something I could really sink my teeth into and run with. I was still percolating on what that might be.

"What about you?" Berta asked.

"Gonna help with the summer harvest. The largest berries have all been cooled and sent out on trucks for distribution, but the smaller ones are starting to ripen and redden. Clay has the pickers out in full force and can surely use an extra pair of hands at the Pick-Your-Own. Then I'll see where the day takes me. If Clay decides to put me on the machinery and turn me loose in the northern fields, you may never see me again."

"You know he won't do that. He thinks it's dangerous and doesn't want to worry about you."

"It is dangerous, which is why it drives me crazy that he won't. It's sexist."

"Oh, it is not. He's being a big brother."

"An annoying one."

I didn't see Clay when I arrived back at the farm. It was likely he was working in the northern fields and getting them prepped for the larger harvest in the fall. We were luckier than the other farms across the country in that the climate in the valley and our elevation allowed for strawberry production virtually year-round. We snuck in a few pumpkins for Halloween, because who doesn't love a good pumpkin patch photo with their kids in autumn? The pumpkins brought in a ton of foot traffic.

What I did find on the property was handfuls of families picking strawberries by the bucketful. My mother and a couple of part-time workers headed up our Pick-Your-Own program in which customers could pick berries to take home, paying by the pound.

"Hey, Lindsey!" I said to the bright-eyed four-year-old feasting on a giant red strawberry. "You got a good-looking one there. Perfect choice. Ready for harvest."

Her mother smiled at me. "You guys really have the best berries in California."

"Can we quote you on that?" my mother asked, as she weighed a bucket for a couple I didn't recognize—most likely out-of-towners. Lots of folks made the drive to the strawberry farms in the summer months.

"You seen Clay around?" I asked my mother.

"Six pounds and eight ounces," she announced to the couple happily. "I think he's taking lunch around the side of the big house. You'll probably find him sitting on the tailgate of his truck."

"Perfect. Thank you." I walked to the residential portion of the farm and around to the side of the big house where Clay generally parked his truck. It fell under a patch of shade this time of day, which provided a nice getaway from the summer sun. But as I rounded the corner, Clay was nowhere to be found. Instead of the pickup I'd expected to find, I stood in front of a very distinctive blue Mercedes convertible.

"I wondered if you were home."

I turned at the sound of her voice and found myself face-to-face with Courtney Carrington. Her hair seemed blonder, maybe a little longer than the last time I'd seen her. She'd pulled it back on the sides with a clip, and it fell in subtle waves down her back. She wore a white sundress that showcased an admirable tan and beige heels. It had spaghetti straps and small buttons down the side and came to her mid-thigh. Standing there, she was the most beautiful thing I'd ever seen.

"Courtney." I shook my head, my grin growing. "I didn't know you were in town."

"Hey there, Maggie." She lifted a shoulder and smiled. God, that smile. I'd forgotten how it affected me. "How could you have known?"

The point was valid. We'd exchanged a couple of emails after her sudden departure from town two years ago. I could tell then that the divorce had hit her hard, but she hadn't gone into much detail and I hadn't pushed. Gradually, our emails were spaced further and further apart. I figured she'd been absorbed back into Chicago life.

Yet here she stood.

"You look fantastic," she said, gesturing to me. "I mean, *really* fantastic."

"Thank you." I felt fantastic, too. The time since I'd seen her last had been keenly important in the scheme of who I was, or at least who I was trying to become. I'd done a lot of growing up. I'd begun finding my confidence, my self-worth, and Courtney had been there to help set it all in motion. I owed her big-time for that.

"I can't believe you're here. It's so great to see you." I pulled her into a hug, realizing that this was not something I would have necessarily done easily the last time I'd seen her, and—bam. There it was. Vanilla, like a freshly baked cookie. I closed my eyes briefly as the scent transported me to the shelved memories of two summers past. The days that had made my heart flutter and my senses overload in the most terrifying, wonderful, confusing way.

Somehow it was less confusing this time. Still a little nerve inducing.

But every bit as captivating.

"How long are you staying?" I asked, as I released her.

She lifted both hands. "I'm here for the summer."

"Oh, wow." Wow, indeed. Double wow.

"My dad, though often an asshole, has come through this time.

I'll be working at the Tanner Peak Carrington's in an apprenticeship, newly designed. Basically, learning everything I can in a three-month rotation, all on his watch."

"And then?" I pushed myself onto the short retaining wall that lined the drive. Courtney followed suit and joined me there, crossing her legs and turning to face me. I would never be that put together, no matter what I did.

"I'm off to Northwestern."

"You got in to *Northwestern*?" The words tumbled from my mouth before I thought them through. Courtney gasped and knocked me in the arm playfully.

"Yes, I got in. Thank you very much. I realize we weren't in school together that long, but I had a rather impressive GPA in high school and an even better one after my freshman year."

I laughed nervously at my misstep and held up my hands in contrition. "I believe you. You're a smart girl, Courtney. I've always known that part."

She shrugged. "Let's be honest, it also doesn't hurt that my father went there or that he still writes them a big fat check each year. In fact, I think that's the integral part."

"I'm sure it doesn't hurt, no."

"And you?"

Drum roll, please. "I go twenty minutes up the road. Not nearly as exciting, I'm afraid. Community college for my basics and then I'll transfer to the remote campus of UC Santa Barbara to finish my bachelor's."

She looked at me with warmth in her eyes. "You want to stay close to home."

"Something like that."

"It suits you." She crossed her arms, which left our shoulders touching. I remembered Clay's advice about little touches and smiled at the implication.

"What can I say? I'm happy here."

"Hey, I don't blame you for a second. If I had your setup, I would certainly do the same."

I pushed off the wall and turned so that I stood in front of her, meeting those clear blue eyes. I had to steady myself because the sparks were alive and well and our proximity put them on clear display. I just had to decide whether or not I wanted to acknowledge them this time around. "You would? I somehow can't see you in Tanner Peak for the long haul."

She balked and held up a finger. "No, I can't either. I just meant hypothetically."

"Oh." Somehow that stung. Wasn't sure why. "How's your mom?"

"Better. I wish I could say that every day was great, but depression can be complicated."

It was the first time I'd heard her use the word. "Please send her our best."

"I absolutely will. And now the reason for my visit."

"There's a larger reason?" Interesting.

"There's always a larger reason." Courtney pushed herself off the wall so we stood face-to-face. The heels gave her the advantage. I didn't mind. "I'm here to invite you to dinner."

I grinned. "As in?"

"With me. A date. If you're not busy."

While the concept had me singing "Here Comes the Sun" in my head, I made a point to play it cool. I'd never been asked on a date before. "Well, there is a Beatles profile on the History Channel tonight."

"That is tough competition." She passed me her most winsome smile. "And while I know it would be hard for you to miss a Beatles profile on the History Channel, I'm hoping you can record it for viewings well into the future. So what do you say?"

"I think dinner with you would be fun. We can catch up."

She nodded. Her eyes never left mine, an attractive display of quiet confidence. "Great. I was hoping you'd think so. Where should we go?"

"Well, there's the café if you're into burgers and fries. When I look at you today, I definitely think greasy spoon."

She laughed. "Don't be so sure about that sarcasm. I happen to adore a good, messy burger, but is there anywhere a little more, I don't know, quiet?"

I liked where this was going. "Well, there is a little place about twenty minutes outside of town. My parents took us there once for my dad's birthday. Gardell's."

"Perfect. I'll pick you up at seven."

"Except, how about I pick you up? I know the way."

She squeezed my hand. "Even better."

I watched her drive away with the top down and marveled at this new development in the saga that was Courtney. As much as I wanted to linger on those thoughts and let my imagination wander in anticipation of our date, I forced myself to focus on the day ahead of me first.

"Did you find your brother?" my mom asked when I returned to help out at the Pick-Your-Own.

"I did not."

She turned her face to the side and regarded me suspiciously. "Then why are you smiling?"

"No reason at all."

"You're still doing it."

I looked skyward. "Am I?"

True to my word, I picked up Courtney at her house at seven sharp and we made the drive to Gardell's as music played on the radio. I tried for tunes that were soft and maybe a little flirty. I'd worn a lime green sleeveless dress that I hoped came off dressy enough without going overboard, and a pair of simple sandals. Courtney had swapped the sundress for a belted purple number that looked like it had been designed specifically for her body. She'd let her hair down and had one strand tucked behind her ear. Our conversation didn't come as easily as it had the last time we'd traveled together. I pretended to focus heavily on the beat of the music, letting my head bob slightly. Courtney stared at the passing farmland. Perhaps we were still getting used to each other again, finding our rhythm.

Once we settled into dinner, however, everything seemed to change. The quiet one-room restaurant provided an intimate ambience, and the conversation flowed easily once we were face-to-face across the white tablecloth.

Courtney shook her head at me as we ate. "Wow. So you're saying that you and Travis are—"

"Friends now. Pretty good friends, actually."

"Who would have guessed?"

"I know. No one is more surprised than me. He's a lovable dope."

"He is." She sipped delicately from her water glass. "And that's a good characterization, from what I remember."

"In fact, someone that I know once thought he was pretty handsome."

"Well, he is," Courtney said, smiling and gesturing with her fork. "Objectively. He could grace centerfolds."

"I will give you that. This steak, by the way, is shattering all my preconceived notions, which were already favorable. What kind is it again?"

Courtney laughed and I relished the melodic sound. She dabbed her mouth with her napkin. "You're a breath of fresh air, Maggie."

I felt my cheeks redden. "Thank you."

She nodded to my plate. "It's a filet."

"This *filet*," I amended, "is a thing of beauty."

"And here I was hoping you'd think that about me," she said casually and sat back in her chair. Well, there it was. A declaration if I'd ever heard one. "I'm kidding, by the way." Whether she was or wasn't didn't matter; I felt the butterfly parade and focused on the fancy green mashed potatoes on my plate. The ones I'd yet to touch.

"Do we know why the potatoes are green?" I ventured.

She peeked over at them on my plate. "I have no idea, and I'm a little afraid for you."

The wide-eyed look on her face had me laughing. "You're the sophisticated one here," I whispered, trying to keep it down. "You're supposed to know this stuff. Here, you try them first."

She shook her head and whispered emphatically, "No way. I draw the line at leprechaun mashed potatoes." That did it. My eyes filled and I took a moment so as not to burst into out-loud laughter in the small restaurant of very conservative diners. Deep breaths. Deep breaths. Courtney leaned in conspiratorially. "Maybe it wasn't a pot of gold at the end of the rainbow, but a kettle of mash."

And I lost it. I leaned sideways in my chair and fanned my face, an attempt to regain control and tamp down my laughter. Courtney was laughing now, too, and the other diners looked with curious amusement in our direction.

"I believe the mashed potatoes are infused with root vegetables," the man from the table next to ours whispered with a smile.

I nodded to him, feeling the heat on my face. "Thank you, sir."

"I don't like the color either," his wife whispered to us aggressively. "Reminds me of a witch!"

And I was off again in peals of laughter, tears streaming down my face. Courtney covered hers with her napkin, and the nice couple also enjoyed a decent chuckle. I was having fun, so much fun that I felt my nerves fall away. We moved on to dessert: salted caramel gelato topped with hot fudge and nuts and delivered with two spoons. After much sighing over the wonderfulness of the gelato, Courtney looked over at me.

"So how is your family? How are the strawberries?"

"The berries are red and mature this season. We're in the midst of the last third of the summer harvest. My mother just started a new book and is currently fascinated with corsets, which means she's dabbling in historical romance again. The Regency period, to be more specific."

"I love that! And your dad?"

"High cholesterol, but he won't listen to anyone and eats whatever he damn well pleases."

"Salt is important."

"Don't tell him that! He wholeheartedly agrees with you."

"My lips are sealed." She rested her chin in her hand. "And your brother?"

"Clay is Clay. Hard work and hard play. He's dated every girl within ten years of his age in Tanner Peak, and what I can't quite wrap my head around is that they all still adore him. Whose ex-girlfriends still adore them? They bring him pies!"

"That is pretty rare. He's a nice guy who must treat them with a great deal of respect. That's why he gets a pie."

"I think that's it. I want to be like that," I said, ruminating on the concept. "Not the serial dater thing, but the nice person part."

"I'll let you in on a little secret."

"Okay."

"From what I've seen, you're well on your way."

"Thank you." The compliment landed, and I fought the urge to argue the point, still maneuvering through the whole compliment paradox. "Tell me about the last two years."

She took a moment to stack her spoon neatly on our empty dessert plate. "It started with a divorce."

"Right." I grimaced. "I'm so sorry."

She shook her head. "I'm not sure I am. My parents rarely spoke to each other, and there was something about my father's presence that kept my mother…I don't know. Down on herself, as if her only window into who she was lived in his disapproval. He had all the power."

"That's got to take a toll. What about your relationship with him?"

"That's harder to pin down." Her gaze fell to her napkin as she said it, making it clear that the topic was a difficult one.

"Did you know my parents went to high school with him?"

She regarded me, eyes wide. "No way. They did? So they knew each other? You have to tell me more."

"I get the feeling that my dad is not a fan of your dad."

She blew out a breath. "Is it awful that I don't find that surprising in any way, shape, or form? I'm not expecting him to win any personality competitions. He's a cutthroat businessman who tries to run his household the same way."

"It's not bad at all. You have a right to your feelings about your father."

The waiter arrived with the check, and though I offered to pay, Courtney refused. "I did the asking. It's on me." There wasn't a lot I could say. She seemed determined.

"Thank you for dinner," I said as we walked to the car. "Green mashed potatoes and all."

She laughed again and met my eyes. "Now, that's one that I'll never forget." Her smile dimmed, and I picked up from the silence.

"Confession time. I've never actually done that before."

The side of her mouth quirked as she leaned against the car. "Ordered the filet?"

I laughed. "Gone out to dinner with someone. Just one person. Like this."

Understanding sparked and her smile softened in warmth. "I'm happy to have been the first." Cue the stupid blush. I hated how transparent I must have seemed to her. "You're adorable, you know that?"

"Yeah, well, sometimes I wish I wasn't," I told her.

"Tell me what you would rather be."

I looked up at the sky to form my list. "Exciting, alluring, mysterious. Take your pick." I brought my gaze back down to hers and watched as her eyes darkened. They carried a hint of something unnamed.

"Trust me when I say that you, Maggie, are all of those things. Now drive me home. I have to be at the store by six a.m. tomorrow, which is just, you know, unfair."

I opened the door for her. "That I can do."

The drive home felt so much shorter this time, and I honestly didn't want to say good-bye. The night had been fun, and new, and exciting. As we pulled into the driveway of her father's home, I turned to Courtney. "It's not that late. Are you sure you have to go now?" She nodded but was nice enough to look sad about it. I leaned my head against the seat wistfully. "What if you're gone again tomorrow? You were last time."

"This time I can guarantee a reappearance. Come on, Maggie. Walk me to my door, the way one does at the end of a really great date."

I smiled at her characterization and exited the driver's side. Staring up at the big, dark house, I wondered what Mr. Carrington did with all that space, day in and day out. Courtney slipped her hand in mine and I realized that on the other hand, darkness came with definite perks.

"Did I tell you how off-the-charts beautiful you look? I can't get over it," Courtney said when we arrived at her door. The sentiment made my stomach flip-flop in the most wonderfully torturous way. In response, I swallowed and willed myself not to sidestep or stammer or fall into the patterns of Margaret from two summers ago, and that would have been easy to do. In fact, I didn't even allow myself to so much as think. I pulled Courtney in wordlessly and caught her mouth with mine. Her murmur of surprise shifted quickly into one of appreciation as her lips relaxed into mine. I took my time kissing her, something I'd been dreaming about doing for two years now. I took in the feel of her lips, the way she tasted like tangerine lip gloss, and the little sounds she made when my tongue stroked hers. I knew inherently that I was standing on Courtney's porch, but it sure felt like I was hovering somewhere off the ground. I relied on Courtney to set the pace, but when she pressed me against the stone wall that lined the porch, I used it as an anchor. A variety of sensations hit me fast and furious. Nothing like I'd ever experienced. Courtney grasped at the material of my dress as our mouths moved in a dance every bit as sweet as it was decadent.

Her hands dipped beneath the edges of the fabric and brushed the backs of my thighs. I gasped, pulling my mouth from hers in search of air.

"God," was all I could say as intense need descended, hot and powerful.

"It's like I just have to touch you," Courtney whispered against my neck, and placed an open-mouthed kiss there. "I've wanted to since stupid Abraham Lincoln." Her hands eased up the backs of my thighs and I trembled.

"Really?" I asked.

"Really."

Her fingers crept around from behind, tickling the insides of my thighs. I steadied myself against her shoulders. The darkness acted as some sort of permission slip for our exchange and I longed for her to go further. I ached for it all over. She claimed my mouth and kissed me with authority. I was lost and helpless beneath the skimming of her hands across my skin. Delicious shivers moved through me.

"You're so soft," she murmured, and traced the spot where my skin met my underwear, inching my dress up my thighs for better access. The porch light lit above us, shattering the spell. I flinched at the garish beams, and our heads swiveled in tandem as the front door flew open. Courtney's father appeared, wearing khakis and an untucked dress shirt, his stare hard. He was an average-looking guy, balding, with the blue eyes I recognized as both Courtney's and Netta's. Only his were smaller, colder somehow, and piercing—a major difference. Courtney straightened and let go of me slowly, as if any sudden movement might call more attention to what we'd been doing.

"Dad," she said, calm, in greeting. While I was mortified and praying for some sort of invisibility cloak, Courtney held her ground. Mr. Carrington's gaze moved from Courtney's face to mine. "This is my friend, Margaret Beringer. Maggie, meet my father, Mitchell Carrington."

I took a step to the side, disentangling myself from his daughter and smoothing my dress. "Hi, Mr. Carrington. Pleased to meet you."

Some sort of recognition flared, and he focused on my face. "You're Henry's daughter."

I nodded. "Yes. And I should apologize. We were out to dinner and were just— "

"Saying good night," he finished for me in a commanding voice, and opened the door wider for Courtney to enter the house. "Courtney."

"Good night, Maggie," Courtney said quietly. Gone was the confident, gregarious girl I'd just spent the evening with, and in her place stood a meek and terrified version. She reached out and gave my hand a squeeze and without a word headed into the house.

"I'm sure your parents are missing you," Mr. Carrington said to me once we were alone.

I nodded. "Yes, sir. I should head home."

His voice followed me as I descended the steps. "Send Evie my kindest regards."

I paused and looked back, not liking the smile now plastered across his face or the way he said my mother's name.

"Yes, sir. I will."

He stood on the steps as I pulled away, either to see me safely out of his ridiculously long driveway or to make sure I actually left the premises. One thing seemed to be clear: Mitchell Carrington knew his daughter and I had been on a date. He'd seen her hands on me, our lips pressed together, and seemed none too happy about it.

CHAPTER SEVEN

The fact that I didn't see Courtney for most of the following week left me unsettled and restless. She'd been working around the clock and hadn't had time to get together before falling into bed exhausted each night. I wondered if there'd been fallout with her father from the night he'd walked up on us. I wondered if she was all right with all of it. I wondered what she was doing. What she was thinking about. But instead of asking, I gave her space, hoping we'd have a chance to reconnect at some point soon.

I could be patient.

As I fell asleep each night, I replayed the moments on her porch before we'd been discovered. Pulling her to me. Kissing her. Her body pressed to mine up against the wall. The tantalizing sensations of her hands under my dress, owning me.

To distract myself, I put in extra hours at the Pick-Your-Own, giving my mother a break and some free time to write. Currently in the midst of novel forty-two, she was lost in a world of high-society London.

"How are Theodore and Elmira today?" I asked as I passed through the dining room, also known as her office, on a break from work. I'd knocked off for the day after starting early with Clay and his guys, laying tarps for the new crops. My mother sat at the table tick-tacking away on the keys of her laptop.

"He's apologizing."

"What did he do this time?" I grabbed a purple Gatorade and placed it against the back of my neck, nearly keeling over at the cool relief it provided from the summer scorcher under way.

"He called her a spoiled, uptight little rich girl."

I came around the table. "Well, isn't she?"

"Without a doubt," my mother said. "That's why it's sexy. The room is filled with all this underlying tension. They could rip each other's clothes off at any moment. They're quite literally longing for each other."

"I see." I popped the top of the Gatorade and took a long drink.

"Do you think he should top her or the other way around?"

"Mother."

"Sorry. So I hear Courtney Carrington's back in town."

I froze. Why was she mentioning Courtney on the heels of our conversation about her romance novel? How much did she know exactly? Was this some sort of Jedi mom trick? "Oh yeah? Where'd you hear that?" Nonchalant—that was me. Courtney was *so* not a big deal. Except that she was.

"I ran into Netta at the produce section of Klein's. She said Courtney will be staying with her father for the entire summer, but I imagine you already knew that."

"I did know," I said cautiously, and headed for the stairs.

"Just wondering why you didn't tell me yourself is all. Are you embarrassed because I'm your mother or because Courtney's a girl?"

My hand froze on the banister. More like embarrassed because Courtney scared the hell out of me in a way I didn't have answers for. Embarrassed because I was entirely out of my depth. However, those weren't things I was prepared to admit to other humans. I faced my mother dead on and shrugged. "Just didn't come up is all."

She stared at me all wise and intuitive. "Sure it didn't. Would you mind doing me a favor?"

"What do you need?"

"It's Helen Dudek's birthday luncheon tomorrow, and I need a gift. I was thinking a pair of nice gloves from Carrington's. Would you pick up a pair? Maybe have them giftwrapped? I can't leave Theodore and Elmira hanging this afternoon. It would be cruel."

I sighed. "You're a little transparent. I mean, I feel like you didn't even try to be subtle this time."

My mother blinked at me. "I don't know what you're talking about." Oh, yes, she did. My mother was a very driven woman indeed, one who enjoyed playing matchmaker in her off time.

"Sure you don't," I said sarcastically, and headed upstairs to put myself together.

After a quick shower, I selected my slim-cut jeans and a navy blue pullover, hoping I looked maybe the tiniest bit sophisticated. I ran my fingers though my newly dried hair, making sure the layers fell gently around my face. How was it that I now cared so much? Regardless, I did.

Soft jazz music and a cool burst of air-conditioning greeted me as I walked through the automatic doors to Carrington's. I took a deep breath and inhaled the crisp new clothes smell that Courtney had once described to me. The store was relatively busy that afternoon, but then again, it always was. I made a lap through the clothing department, taking in the new arrivals on the mannequins. There was a short-sleeve black top with a V-neck that caught my attention. I contemplated the depth of its neckline, unsure I could pull it off. For fun, I thumbed the price tag and resisted a low whistle at the news. It turned out I wouldn't have to worry about that neckline after all.

"That would look killer on you."

I met Courtney's eyes and relaxed into a smile. She wore a black skirt and jacket combo, topped off with a stylish pair of red heels. She looked like she belonged in the midst of the opulence. "I'm confident you compliment all the customers."

"Believe me when I say I don't. Looking for anything special? It would be my pleasure to help."

"My mother is in need of some gloves for a friend. They're a gift."

"Right this way, ma'am."

I followed Courtney behind a nearby glass counter and perused the options. As I scanned my choices, I couldn't help but marvel at how grown up Courtney seemed, dressed like she was and behind the counter in such an official capacity. I couldn't help but feel proud of her. It was impressive. And…a little sexy. Okay, a lot. It was a lotta sexy all wrapped into a smokin' blond package, and my cheeks heated just thinking about it.

"Anything jump out at you?" she asked.

I swallowed. I had sadly not been focused on the gloves. "I'm sorry?"

"Do you see anything you like?"

"Maybe," I said, stalling. As I browsed, I felt her eyes on me, amping up the pressure. Ready to admit defeat, I leaned in and lowered my voice so the nice woman shopping next to me wouldn't think I was a total idiot. "Look, I think you might just have to tell me which pair to go with. This is all a little beyond me. Farm kid, remember?"

She smiled serenely. They must train them to do that, the serene smile. Courtney just so happened to rock at it. "Why don't you give it a try? I think you're selling yourself short."

I shook my head and focused. "Okay, well, these seem to be nice." I gestured to a pair of gray gloves with white cuffs.

"An excellent choice." She reached into the counter and retrieved the gloves, my confidence now bolstered. Impressive.

I followed Courtney to the register. "Why do I feel like you're programmed to say that?"

"Because I am. In your case, however, it happens to be true." She lowered her voice. "Besides, I wouldn't let you pick out a bad pair. Your mom's friend is going to love them. If she doesn't, bring them back."

"You have yourself a deal." I paid Courtney for the gloves and accepted the bag she handed me across the upscale-looking desk. I paused and made a decision to check in. "Hey, about the other night. Is everything okay? With your dad, I mean."

Her smile faltered, then rebounded. "No need to worry about him. I can handle it."

"I don't. I worry about you."

She met my eyes and smiled sincerely, as if the concept were foreign. "I'm fine, Maggie. I promise."

I smiled back, somehow feeling closer to her. "When do you get off?"

Her eyes flashed to a clock on the wall to my right. "In about twenty minutes."

"Tell me you don't have plans tonight." Courtney hesitated, and I theorized why. "Is this about your father? I could tell he was pissed the other night."

She raised a shoulder. "Yeah, well, what else is new?"

"Does he not want us to see each other?"

She shot a glance to a nearby coworker and directed me a few feet away. Her voice was noticeably quieter when she said, "Can we talk about this later?"

"Yeah, sure. No problem." I knew when to back off.

"I'll come by the farm later, if that's okay."

Or maybe not. "I'll be there. See you then." I turned to go but paused. "Courtney, is everything all right?"

She smiled, but it didn't quite extend to her eyes. She seemed wary. "Everything's good."

Somehow, I wasn't buying it.

❖

"So what's the best way to pick one of these guys?" Courtney asked a couple hours later as we walked the western portion of the farmland. Gone were the sophisticated work clothes, and in their place were denim cutoffs and a pale blue T-shirt that brought out the color in her eyes. God, I enjoyed this version of her just as much.

"As in, the proper technique?" I asked.

"Exactly that. I'll need it. This is strawberry country, and I can't have random people making fun of my novice strawberry aesthetic."

"And they would. Rene from the café would have it on Facebook in no time. Did you know they started a new page dedicated to the town?"

"I can't tell if you're joking or not."

I shot her a sideways glance. "Best not to risk it, then. A formal lesson might be in order. Allow me." I knelt next to a plant that looked moments away from its full potential. The fruit was bright and robust, just the way it should be before harvest. Courtney joined me and peered down at the row of plants, close enough so that her hair tickled my shoulder. I blinked purposefully and concentrated on the task at hand, hard as that was. I met her gaze, ensuring I had her attention. "So what you'll want to do is put the stem between your fingers like so. I usually go with the middle of my hand."

"Like this?" she asked, placing the stem between two of her middle fingers.

I smiled at how earnest she seemed to be to do it correctly. "That's perfect. Next, just pull the strawberry toward you, flicking your wrist as you go." I flicked my wrist and lifted the perfectly picked strawberry. "A clean break, see?"

She nodded with determination and gave it a shot, smiling at the equally clean result. "Look at that! He's beautiful!"

"Excellent. This method is also the quickest way to pick a strawberry, and at harvest time, that part is everything." I noticed her admiring her charge. "Are you going to eat that one?"

"I was thinking about gifting it to you, my own personal strawberry mentor, as a token of appreciation." I smiled as she carried the strawberry slowly to my mouth. This wasn't going to go well. I just knew it. As I bit down, the juice from the berry trickled down the side of my mouth in predictable and embarrassing form. I quickly swiped at it, but not before a drop hit my shirt. "Shit," I muttered, dabbing at it.

"Oh my," Courtney said, enjoying this series of tragic events way too much. I only seemed to make the spot worse, and she eventually gave into the laughter altogether, covering her mouth. "I am so sorry," she said through her glee. "I honestly thought that was about to be a really sexy moment."

Now I was laughing at my own damn self. "Yeah, well, have you met me? There was zero chance of that happening."

"Oh, come on. There was *some* chance. It's you, and you happen to be very sexy, in my experience."

"Don't lie to me. I think we can both agree that sexy is your lane. In fact, I'll prove it." I dangled the strawberry I'd picked just out of reach of her mouth. She eyed it and smiled, never one to shy away from a challenge. The result of Courtney's lips meeting the berry was swoon-worthy at the very least, the type of visual that fantasies were built around.

"See? Now that was sexy."

"I'll take it." She stole the rest of the berry from me and ate it slowly, only proving my point further. "You guys grow good strawberries out here."

"Now *I'll* take it."

We walked along the row of plants as the sun gently floated to Earth, the last little bit of daylight clinging to life. "So who's in charge of picking the strawberries with this impressive technique I now have?"

"Professional pickers, of course. Hired specifically for harvest. We need hundreds at a time, which is hard to come by."

"Hard to hire?"

I nodded. "Lots of farms, and only so many pickers."

"So what do you do to make sure you have enough?"

"We make it a priority to pay the highest wages of any neighboring farm. That way, we get not only enough workers, but the best."

She nodded thoughtfully. "I admire those standards. I hope to adopt them as my own one day when I'm at the helm of Carrington's and take care of my employees."

We walked on. "And how has that particular endeavor evolved since we last talked? You're employed now. That's something."

"Well, my father hasn't handed me the company just yet, but it's a start. I have, however, been able to engage him more on the important details surrounding the business. We've gone over regional sales reports, customer surveys, and buying trends as they pertain to seasons. It's a start."

"It sounds like more than a start to me. I think you might be well on your way to department store domination after all."

She sighed and lightly grabbed hold of a tree branch as we passed. "Don't be so sure. You know, I actually get the distinct feeling that he not only values women less than men in business, but is actually opposed to them."

"So no progress on that front."

She shook her head. "I don't know what it is, Maggie, but he talks about his female executives as if they were secretaries. It drives me insane."

"God." How did those things still happen?

"I have to figure out how to break through his preconceptions and show him that I'm every bit as capable as he is, if he will just give me the chance to learn more." She shook her head and studied the horizon. "I get that he probably always dreamed of handing this company off to a son, but that didn't happen."

"And he's the only one who has a say?"

"Not entirely. When I reach the executive level, hopefully after college, it will be out of his hands. The board will make those kinds of calls."

I gave her hand a squeeze. "You'll get there. It's just gonna take time."

"Time is one thing I'm willing to put in." She gestured to the sun setting behind the big red barn in the distance. "Can we sit and watch?"

I smiled. "We can. Let me grab a—hang on." I made the short

walk to one of our freestanding supply sheds and found a blanket I deemed clean enough.

"You're prepared," Courtney said, as I laid it out for us where the soil met the grass.

"Thank you for noticing." Courtney took a seat on the blanket, her legs stretched out in front of her. She was tan, I now realized as I joined her there. Really tan. "Someone's been in the sun."

She nodded. "I've been working on some landscapes when I have downtime."

I thought back to the time I found her sketching in front of Klein's and felt the lazy smile that crossed my face.

"What is that look?" she asked, turning her body toward mine.

"That would be the very first time I noticed you. As in, *noticed*."

She laughed and relaxed onto her back, staring up at the remaining clouds as they swirled. "Do you know when I first noticed *you*?"

I looked down at her and shook my head.

"Goddamn Abraham Lincoln."

"Really? You mentioned that on your porch, too." How was that possible? "That stupid speech?"

"Absolutely. You were all passionate and polished and hot."

"I was not hot," I said emphatically. "There is no way I was hot."

She pushed herself into a seated position. "You so were. And then and there I knew I had to get to know you. That you were going to be important to me somehow."

Important. I let the compliment wash over me. "And now?"

"Even hotter." She ran her index finger the length of my arm, and I felt the goose bumps hit. I closed my eyes and swallowed as she did it again, and again. "I love the effect I sometimes have on you," she murmured.

"Sometimes?" I asked. "Because it feels like a little more than sometimes."

"I have such a crush on you, Maggie," she whispered. "Do you know how I know?" I shook my head and met her eyes. "Because I very much want you to kiss me right now."

Those words were all I needed. I slowly touched my lips to hers and melted, because this was all I had been thinking about since that night on her porch. I kissed her once, tentative yet deliberate. And then again. The third time I found my footing and sank into the kiss, reveling.

There was that freshly baked cookie scent. I'd never get used to that. Courtney slid her hand into my hair and gripped the back of my neck. A burst of heat like I'd never known rocketed through me. I skimmed my hands up her newly tanned legs, amazed that I was allowed to do this, marveling at how smooth her skin felt. Courtney's tongue was in my mouth, and it was all I could do to keep myself anchored to steady ground.

"Do you remember that night at Melanie's?" she gasped between kisses. "When we had to lie next to each other all night? And behave." With a hand to my shoulder, she eased me onto my back and followed me down, settling her weight on me.

"That was hard. Torture is a good word. I don't think I slept more than thirty minutes all night."

More kissing ensued. Lots of kissing. Heavenly kissing. Her hands circled my waist and crept down to my ass, and she pulled me against her. I gasped at the intimate contact. There was so much I wanted to do but wasn't sure exactly how. Not that I didn't have ideas, definite ideas, and was ready to put them in action.

"You are so sexy," she said against my neck, kissing up its column. Courtney touched me with the confidence I craved. It was exhilarating and only encouraged me further. I knew this was where I was supposed to be. I'd never been more sure of anything in my life. This girl made my world spark into color.

The pull between us was undeniable. Intense. Electric.

I didn't have a ton of experience in the chemistry department, but this wasn't normal, right? These off-the-charts fireworks that only grew with time. I'd seen movies about this kind of thing, but never thought it actually existed in the world. And as much as I wanted to follow this decadent road where it led us right there and then, a reminder of our surroundings tapped me on the shoulder like an ambitious Girl Scout. While we were tucked away in the far reaches of the farm, any number of people could technically stumble upon us. Kissing was one thing, but losing my virginity in plain view of the employees who worked for my father—or worse, my dad himself—was quite another.

"Courtney," I managed to say. God, I didn't want to stop.

"Mm-hmm," she answered. Her hands caressed my stomach and inched upward.

"We should slow down. We can't do this out here. I really, really want to, but we can't." Her hands landed on the outside of my bra and I took a moment to steady myself, the ache between my legs almost too much. She nodded against my neck and paused to gather herself, her breath coming every bit as quick as mine.

"You're right," she said finally, and pulled her lips away. I rested my forehead against hers and took a moment, because my head was spinning and I wasn't sure which way was up. We simply stared at each other as cognizant thinking floated back to us. Finally, I smiled and she returned it.

"Nothing has been the same since you," I said quietly. "Where did you come from?"

"Chicago," she whispered back, smiling at her own joke.

I chuckled and brushed the hair from her forehead. "I will never look at that city the same way again."

"I will never look at a strawberry the same way again," she said, glancing around us. I watched as Courtney fluffed her hair and walked a few feet from the blanket, hands on her hips, staring out at the expanse of farmland. "I just about lost myself there for a moment. You make me completely lose myself."

"I just didn't want people, my family to—"

"God, me neither." She turned back. "Like we need to complicate this any further."

I caught the edge in her voice. She was hinting at something beyond this afternoon. "Is this about the other night? Your dad?"

She looked skyward. The glance-away tactic when I mentioned her father had now become predictable. "He was less than thrilled about what he walked up on."

"I could tell. Can I ask a personal question?"

She stared at me in amusement. "I think we blew way past personal over there on that blanket, don't you?"

She had a point. "Does he know you're gay?"

"We haven't discussed who I'm attracted to. No." She inclined her head as she considered the question. "I don't actually think of myself as gay."

"Oh." Okay, so what did that mean? "So how do you think of yourself?"

"I'm just a person. I'm Courtney."

I replayed the last ten minutes in my head, and my confusion hit its peak. "But you are attracted to girls, right?"

She sighed and sat across from me. "Yes. I have been."

I was trying to follow the thread. "But you've been attracted to boys, too?"

"It's happened. Yeah."

"I see."

She must have picked up on my confusion and attempted to explain further. "If I had to describe it, I would say that my attraction to another person doesn't seem to be tied to their gender. It just doesn't, and I can't fully explain that. For me, attraction is about everything wrapped into one. What the person looks like, how they make me feel, how we connect. All of it. At least that's what I've experienced so far."

"Okay." I drew the word out, unsure how I felt about this whole thing. "So you're saying you're bisexual?"

"Maybe. I don't know. And do I really have to? I'm saying I'm just Courtney and I'm fine with that. I love to sketch with pencils on a big white pad. I've lived in twenty-one different states and one other country. I love Starbucks and am crushed there's not one in town. And I very much like you, Maggie Beringer. You're the star of all of my thoughts lately, and confession time, a few of them aren't so pure."

It made sense. It did. But the lack of a label had me grappling to understand and a little nervous. "I've never been into boys," I said. "Ever."

She threaded her fingers through mine. "Good news for me." A pause. "Does it bother you? The fact that we're different in that way?"

I didn't know the answer. "I'm not sure. I don't think there's a rule that we have to be carbon copies of each other."

"I completely agree."

While I didn't fully understand Courtney's particular outlook, I could try to accept it. There was another issue looming, however. I could tell. "But about your father."

She nodded, waiting for the question. "He's upset because you were kissing a girl?"

"Well, it's not the picture-perfect Christmas card he was planning on for me." She paused briefly and seemed to make a decision to say more. "But he was more upset that I was kissing *you*."

"Me? What? Why?" I pulled my hand away slowly, because the words felt like a slap. Parents always liked me. They were cosmically ordained to. I was *that* girl: the one parents loved more than teenagers did. This had me thrown.

"Let's just say that the name Beringer turned out to be more of a hot button than we first imagined."

"Okay, so he was upset. What happened?"

"There was some yelling on his part. Some door slamming on mine. A few threats."

"Threats?" I shook my head. This was bad. "Why would there be threats? What were they?"

"The threats are stupid." She placed a hand on my knee. "Don't worry about them."

"How can I not? What are we talking about here?"

"Oh, that if I want any kind of future at Carrington's, I'll stay well away from you. That kind of thing. Relax, he's leveraging the store because he knows it's something I care about."

"Well, yeah."

Her eyes blazed. "I'm not going to let him control me, Maggie. I'm not a child."

"It's that rift with my dad, isn't it?"

Courtney nodded. "I think so. I found an old yearbook in his study that offered some insight. Get this. Apparently, your mother and my father were a thing when they were younger."

My mouth fell open. My mother and Mitch Carrington? Really? As in, that happened? I tried to imagine a scenario in which my parents were not a hot-and-heavy item, in which my mother had a thing for another guy. A horrific thought descended. "If you tell me we're related, I'm going to die."

She laughed. "I don't think that math adds up, but your dramatic side is hilarious."

"So I'm on the forbidden list?"

She traced her finger along the neckline of my shirt. "In more ways than one."

I closed my eyes as a shiver ran through me. "You can't do things like that to me when I'm trying to problem solve."

"I'm sorry. I'll behave."

"Maybe just for a little while," I said, taking a deep breath to clear my head. "A temporary embargo on flirtatious behavior." Courtney nodded in amusement as I ruminated on our predicament, tucking a strand of hair behind my ear.

She pointed at me. "Are you trying to make this hard?"

"What did I do?" I asked, grinning.

"The hair behind your ear. That dimple. You're making me want to—"

"To what?"

She opened her mouth to answer, and I could already tell it would be saucy.

"Forget it. We have to focus, because I've never been on the forbidden list before. It's kind of…exciting, if it weren't so horrible."

She shrugged. "Maybe we should just focus on the exciting."

"Does that make me the Montague or the Capulet? I want to get this right."

"You're definitely more of a Capulet," Courtney said, studying me.

"Right? I thought so, too. So, let's see what we've learned today." I leaned back on my hands. "You don't like labels, but you like me."

"True."

"But if you spend time with me, your entire future is at stake."

She scrunched up an eye. "Also true."

"And we're not related."

"Thank God that's not true."

I whistled low. "So there you have it. That's a lot to take in."

She smiled apologetically. "I can be complicated."

"Yeah, well, I don't mind." Things felt infinitely heavier now, but in spite of it all, I still didn't want to see the evening end. If anything, I wanted Courtney close. I had no clue what we were or were not to each other, and I had no clue if she'd be gone again tomorrow, which made the time we spent together all the more important. "Proposition," I said.

"I'm listening."

"Why don't we not think about any of that and just chill under the stars for a bit. I promise we can keep it PG." I instantly regretted that. PG-13 would have been a much better compromise. She hesitated before eventually joining me on the blanket. We lay there for several long minutes, looking at the clear sky, now a very dark shade of indigo, signaling that night was only moments away. The crickets had already struck up their chorus, and cooler temperatures were drifting in.

"Have you had sex before?" I asked. I was thinking out loud apparently and more than a little shocked about it.

She lifted her head and looked down at me, then nodded. "For the first time at sixteen with a boy named Elliot. He was popular and convinced me he was madly in love with me." She laughed.

This was new and interesting information. "Did you love him back?" I asked.

She thought for a moment. "I masqueraded like I did and took it all very seriously. It's what you do when you're sixteen and think you have the world figured out."

I smiled and picked up her hand, playing with it. "That was only three years ago."

"Feels like longer. Doesn't it? What about you?"

"What about me?"

She reclaimed her hand and ran it soothingly across my stomach. Only in the state I was in, it was anything but soothing, and my skin vibrated with the electricity that always seemed to flow between us. "How old were you your first time?"

I closed my eyes in preparation for the brutal honesty. Here went nothing. "There has not been a first time, actually."

She pushed herself onto her elbow and took a moment with that one. I had her full attention now. "Really?"

"I know. I'm lame. Let's not harp on it."

"You're not lame." She kissed me. "You're the opposite of lame. What made you wait?"

"I haven't wanted to until…"

She smiled and ran one finger across the waistband of my shorts. "Until?"

I caught her hand. "I met this girl."

She glanced around the empty fields in disdain. "Who is she? I'll find her. Does she know the proper way to pick a strawberry?"

I laughed and pulled my buzzing phone from my pocket and flipped it open. "Hi, Mom."

"Are you on the farm?"

"I am. The eastern side, chatting with Courtney."

"We're starting Pictionary, if you're interested," she said. "Berta's on her way over."

This was fantastic news! I adored game night. I turned to Courtney, who stared at me questioningly. "Oh, we'll be right there. Set a place for two."

CHAPTER EIGHT

"A spotted dog. A goat. A hamster," my brother said in rapid-fire succession as Berta scribbled furiously on a notepad. She shook her head and continued to draw. "A hydrant. A man on top of a hydrant. Mussolini!" Berta shot him a what-the-hell look just as the timer buzzed.

"Mussolini?" She bopped him with the back of her pad. "It's a fireman, you idiot!"

"Yes, clearly a fireman," my mother said, calmly examining the drawing.

"What?" Clay asked and motioned to the pad. "Looks like a man in charge. A dictator."

"Of a *hydrant*?" Berta asked, incredulous.

"A fireman," Courtney said quietly to me.

"A total fireman," I concurred.

Berta slid the box of cards to us in resignation. "You're up. No point for us."

Courtney selected a card, glanced at it, and picked up the pencil. I'd never felt more confident in my entire life. We'd already made it across the board in record time. This had to be some kind of Pictionary record, which I found thrilling. She began to sketch.

"A sidewalk," I said calmly. She nodded. "A man on a sidewalk. A runner. A runner carrying—torch! It's a torch." She set down her pencil and smiled at me in triumph. I moved our token to the finish line and regarded the table. "I'm sad to say this, but I believe that's the game."

"I hate them," my father said to my mother, though there was a grin on his face. He pointed at us across the table. "I demand a rematch at some point, young lady."

Courtney smiled. "You're on."

"I'm not partnering with Clay anymore," Berta said and stood from the table. "He's a lost cause."

Clay responded with a headlock and ruffled her hair. "Yes, you are, little cousin. We're the dream team unrealized. Just you wait." She rolled her eyes.

"We're going to wind down for the night," my mother said and wrapped her arm around my father's midsection.

"It's not even nine thirty on a weekend," Clay pointed out.

My father smiled proudly. "We are the definition of proud old fuddy-duddies. Give me an old episode of *Bonanza* and a couch and I'm a happy camper. Oh! Anyone want to watch *Bonanza*?"

Berta shook her head apologetically. "Uh, I think I'm gonna stop by Bag of Beans."

"Headed to Lonesome's," my brother said of the town's only bar.

"Coffeehouse sounds fun," Courtney said.

I smiled. "Three for the coffeehouse."

My mother stared at my father. "We've officially been ditched by the youngsters."

He shrugged. "It's a date, then."

As hard a time as I gave my parents, their relationship was also something I aspired to have for myself one day. I gave them one last look and felt the warmth wash over me as we headed into the night.

Bag of Beans was just as popular at night as it was in the morning, given that there weren't a ton of spots in town for teenagers to hang out. Throngs of youthful townies dotted the porch as we approached. Spotting us ascending the steps, Louis glanced up from his game of chess with Martin Timmons, the retired and much-revered AV club president of our graduating class.

"Hi, Berta," Louis said, beaming.

"Hey, Louis," she said with a smile, and touched his shoulder as we passed. She'd struck up a new appreciation for the guy, and his feelings for her seemed to have calmed down to a normal rumble, though they were noticeably alive and well. "We're gonna grab a spot inside. Come hang out later."

He nodded back at her. "I will do just that. Thank you. Hey, are we still on for that indie flick tomorrow?"

"Yep. I'll meet you there at three."

"I look forward to it. Hello, Maggie," he said to me. His gaze then shifted to Courtney, and his eyebrows bounced up. "Well, hello to you as well. You're back!"

"I am. For the summer," she told him politely. "It's awesome to see you."

"Likewise."

Courtney was met with similar hellos as we moved through the Tanner Peak crowd. Inside, I easily located Travis in a group of his old football buddies. He went still when his gaze landed squarely on our group, and I had a feeling which one of us had captivated him.

"Hey, there, Travis," Courtney said, moving to him and wrapping her arms around his neck for a hug. She hadn't hugged Louis.

His eyes twinkled as he pulled back, his hands still holding her shoulders. "Heard a rumor you were back in town."

She nodded. "Sometimes rumors are true." They stared at each other and I had to jump in.

"Hey, Travis. Did you get a chance to talk to Clay about the job?"

He turned to me. "He didn't tell you?"

"He did not."

"I snagged a part-time slot at your giant berry farm. If it goes well and I impress him, could be full-time by fall. I plan to impress him."

"That's great. I suppose I'll be seeing you around a lot more."

"Lucky you," he said and bounced his eyebrows.

"What will you do on the farm?" Courtney asked.

"Clay wants to get me set up on the machinery first and we'll go from there."

She nodded. "Impressive."

Yep. Super impressive. Ridiculously so. Dammit.

Travis stood a little taller at the compliment. "Hey, let me get you a coffee to say welcome back."

I buried the sigh on my lips and smiled instead at Berta. "I'll take a dry cappuccino, thanks. Decaf."

"Coming right up."

Courtney excused herself to the ladies' room and Berta turned to me expectantly.

"What?" I asked her innocently, knowing exactly what.

"You and Courtney. Are you a thing again? Because I'm picking up on some vibes." Berta had been a good friend to me when Courtney had left town. I'd been up front and honest with her about my feelings for Courtney and she'd been my rock, helping me pick up the pieces of what had been my hopeful little heart. I thanked God for Berta.

She followed me to a small conglomeration of mismatched chairs, away from the masses.

"It might be a thing again. I think it is. We went out the other night."

"Out? On a date?"

I nodded.

She dropped her voice. "And did anything...happen?"

"I kissed her." I sank back in my chair at the not-so-distant memory. "And it was even better than the first time."

"Maggie, listen. I like Courtney, I do. I just don't want to see your heart broken, because it's a pretty amazing heart. Be careful, okay?"

"I promise. I think our goals are similar, and thanks, Berta, for... being there. Everything."

She placed her chin on my shoulder. "That, my friend, is something you can always count on. Even after August. I'll only be a phone call away."

I winced. "Stop that. I'm operating under the pretense that August is never coming. Anything you can do to enhance this delusion will be heavily appreciated."

She laughed. "I'll see what I can do."

"What about you?" I asked. "I can't help but notice that you're spending more and more time with Louis. You sure you're just friends? He's done a lot of growing up."

She glanced to the front of the shop, where we could see him playing chess on the porch. "He really has. The answer is I don't know. I'm not sure it's there with Louis, but I do have fun with him. He's a good friend."

"I'm just saying, don't rule the guy out. Maybe he's the dark horse we never saw coming."

She shook her head. "Can you imagine?"

"No, not entirely. I'm just saying, it's possible. The world feels very possible lately."

I eyed Courtney up at the counter, chatting with Travis, laughing at the goofy things he said, just like back in the day. She caught my stare and winked at me. I smiled back and did my best to pretend I wasn't the slightest bit worried.

Because I wasn't.

Except for this little thing called reality that I heard knocking quietly in the recesses of my mind. I shook my head to clear the doubt.

Deep breath. I could do this.

❖

"And two fifty is your change," I said to the nice couple who'd visited the farm on their honeymoon.

"Have a good one," the man said, and hefted both buckets of strawberries for his new bride. I glanced around the Pick-Your-Own and blew out a relieved sigh that the crowd had finally dwindled.

"Where's a dude supposed to eat lunch around here anyway?" I turned at the sound of Travis's voice and regarded him with hands on my hips. He wore dirt-streaked jeans and a muscle shirt that fit him tighter than necessary. This look was totally lost on me, unfortunately.

"Did you mistake today for a calendar shoot or something? I can see how you would have confused the gigs. Farmhand, underwear model. Same thing."

He glanced down at his outfit. "Come on. I look good. Check out my rugged features and come-tear-my-clothes-off stare." He rolled his shoulders forward and smoldered.

It was actually remarkable. I'd give him that. "No one is disputing the handsome. Can you even lift your arms in that shirt, though? Try. I'll watch."

He feigned injury and took a seat in the grass next to my checkout stand. "Eat with me. Make me feel better after what you just said."

"Give me five and I will." After checking in on my mother, who declined lunch in order to push through Tad and Elmira's reunion scene, I joined Travis on the grass along with my homemade chicken salad sandwich. For good measure, I brought one for him, which he caught in the air once I arced it to him.

"So what's new, Beringer?"

I took a bite and studied him as I chewed. "Pretty steady stream of folks through the Pick-Your-Own this summer. That's been wildly exciting."

"Saw the cars. Surprised you snagged a sec to eat."

"Notice I'm not getting too comfortable."

"Hey, if you're about to jet, can I run something by you?"

Oh, man. Really? I had a feeling I knew what this was about. "While I think the world of you, Trav, I doubt I'd be much help. I mean, I don't know that I'm your girl for that."

He pressed on, undeterred by my clear lack of enthusiasm. "I have an issue or whatever." Fine, we were gonna do this.

"Is this about a girl?"

He flashed the million-watt smile before it faltered. Something was definitely on his mind. I braced myself.

"Here's the deal. I've been hot and cold with this chick, right? But I'm ready to turn up the heat."

I shook my head. "I'm not sure I like this metaphor. Can you just give it to me straight minus the *Days of Our Lives*?"

"It's been casual between us, but now I have these, I don't know, feelings." He made an awkward circular hand motion around his midsection to illustrate.

I did my damnedest to remain objective, but I felt like we were right back to square one. Total déjà vu of the nightmare variety. There was no way I was helping him on the Courtney front. Nope. I'd rather bathe in lava on live television. It was that simple. "You know what? I think it's better if you deal with this on your own, champ. I have every confidence in your ability to communicate with girls."

"Right. About that. When she's around, it's different. I get all tongue-tied. Say stupid stuff, jokes that make no sense, even to me. I was hoping you might step in and—"

"Okay, no. I'm not your own personal Cyrano here."

"Who?"

"Not going to happen, okay?" I began gathering what remained of my lunch and throwing it into the bag angrily.

"Beringer? You mad?"

"Not mad. Just in survival mode, struggling for air, and needing space. Got it? Space!" I headed to the big house where I could finish my lunch in the air-conditioning and with my sanity intact.

"What's that mean?" he yelled after me. "Who is Cyrano? Is he new to town? Do I need to fight him?" I didn't answer because any further contact would be detrimental to my well-being and his safety. "Beringer!"

❖

I didn't ask Courtney about Travis. Maybe I should have, but I didn't.

Due to her intense work schedule at the store, we had limited time together, and I wanted to enjoy every moment of it.

We relied on the couple of hours after Carrington's closed and before her father would expect her home, just to avoid any further drama in her house. The fact that she had to lie to him about who she was spending time with still gutted me.

Before I knew it, we'd landed smack in the middle of summer, and I had a precious few weeks before she left for Northwestern and I went back to the blander version of my life without Courtney. Until then, I planned to soak up every minute.

"What are you thinking about?" Courtney asked, as she played with my hair. We sat along the bank of the creek, her arms around me from behind as I leaned back against her. Nearby a cricket chirped.

"The summer is half over."

I felt her shake her head, her hair tickling my shoulder. "Yeah, how did that happen?"

"No idea. I'd give anything to slow down time."

"Me too." She kissed my temple and we sat there in silence, enjoying the night and the gentle sounds of the water as it lapped against the bank. The stars shone brightly overhead and Courtney ran her hands up and down my arms.

"What are *you* thinking about?" I asked, turning the tables. She hesitated. The silence prompted me to turn in her arms so I could fully see her face. "You don't have to tell me. Sometimes you like to keep things to yourself. I get that about you."

"I don't know why I'm like that. But it's true."

"Because you don't let a lot of people in. You're friends with the entire world, but you keep the people in it at arm's length. At least when it comes to anything too serious."

She stared off into the distance. "But you're different, Maggie. Everything is different with you. I don't want to hold you at arm's length."

"Then don't." She kissed me gently and then held my gaze. "Why don't you start by telling me what you were thinking?"

"I could try that." She nodded a couple times as if gearing up. "Okay. So I was thinking about how much I enjoy these nights. Our nights."

I smiled because I did, too.

"I look forward to them all day, actually. Talking or not talking. You always want to hear about my day, and I'm always dying to hear about yours."

I shook my head and turned back to face the creek. "I still don't think it's fair that you had to stay late and fold those boxes. That Wally guy should have done it."

She laughed and wrapped her arms around me. "See what I mean? You care. About something as trivial as boxes. I'm not used to having someone like you."

"Well, of course I care." Because we were doing well, I pushed a little further. "Tell me one thing you're afraid of."

"Flying roaches. They should be banned in all fifty states."

I laughed but recognized the deflection as standard Courtney. I squeezed her arms. "Let's go for two, just for kicks."

She blew out a breath, and took a moment to think. "You don't let me off easy, do you?"

"I'm pretty much the Barbara Walters of Tanner Peak."

She took a moment, then turned me around and met my eyes. The vulnerability on her face crossed every feature. I was struck. I hadn't seen it on her before.

"I am afraid of...being alone," she said quietly. The words hung in the air, and their meaning tugged at my heart. Because for the most part, Courtney did walk through life alone. She was smart, and independent, but solitary.

I laced my fingers through hers. "Well, you're not anymore. Even when you leave here, you take me with you. Here." I placed my hand over her heart and she blinked back tears before losing the battle. "Please don't cry." I wiped them from her cheeks with my thumbs.

"That's the best part of all this," she said, placing my hand back over her heart and covering it with hers. "The world feels very different now that I know there's a you."

"Good. It's only fair, because my world's been totally rocked since you walked into it." I pressed my forehead to hers and just lived there for a moment. We shared a kiss, and as our lips hung on, my heart squeezed in that recognizable squeeze that only Courtney could inspire.

"Drive me home?" she whispered.

"Of course." While I didn't want to say good-bye to her, she'd had a long day, most of it on her feet, and she probably needed to rest. "Let's go."

As I turned onto Legend's Lane, every house glowed with the soft illumination of a porch light, signs of life. Some flew flags or displayed the occasional yard gnome. Others ran sprinklers or sat on their front porches, waving at us as we drove past. The Carrington house stood dark as always, the lawn neatly trimmed but devoid of any other evidence that people actually inhabited the large house. I didn't want to send Courtney in there to be alone yet again. I turned off the car and sat back, prepared to draw out this good-bye as long as possible.

"Why don't you come inside with me?" she asked.

Well, that was new. "But your dad—"

"Is in New York."

Understanding settled. I was, then and there, awash with butterflies inspired by excitement about what I thought she was insinuating, and terror…about what I thought she was insinuating. Didn't matter. "I would love to."

I followed Courtney to her door. With a quiet click, her key granted us access to the house. She turned on a lamp in the two-story entryway, and when the warm glow hit her face, a shiver moved through me. I could literally feel her gaze move down my body and answering any lingering question about what she had in mind.

She wanted me.

The quiet in the room amplified the tension.

My lack of experience now screamed at me. Gone was the nineteen-year-old version of myself and here stood the immature twelve-year-old one. "Want to make pancakes together?" I asked like an idiot.

She shook her head and the side of her mouth tugged upward. "Nope."

"Take in a marathon of all five Beatles flicks?" The nerves skipped just beneath my skin.

Her smile grew. "No."

"Are you going to draw me like one of your French girls, Jack?"

She full-on laughed at that one.

Yep. My self-edit button had taken a vacay as my brain struggled to cope with what I knew Courtney was proposing.

"Maybe at some point." She didn't say anything else. She didn't have to. Courtney walked toward me, biting down on her lower lip and looking very much like my fantasy come to life. Up until this point, we'd only kissed and maybe made it halfway to second base, but there was so much more I wanted to do, had imagined doing for well over two years now.

Don't think. Don't think. Don't think.

She kissed me once and met my gaze. I nodded, answering the question she didn't actually voice. The longing that had been pent up inside me for so long now came rushing to the surface in an overwhelming wave. My lips were on hers again and moving insistently. My hands slid around her waist, up her back, and then down again. I walked her backward as we kissed, bumping into furniture and walls and who the hell knew what else in a house I was unfamiliar with. Courtney took the reins and grasped my hand, leading me through the living room to a bedroom tucked away at the back of the house. Hers, I decided distantly as I waited to kiss her again. She walked to the far side of the room, turned on a lamp, and dropped a scarf over it, dimming its effect a great deal. Next, with a turn of her wrist, what could best be described as modern-day-angst-ridden music filled the room. I couldn't have named the artist, but I'm guessing she could. She was a pro at this, I realized. She had all the right moves.

Don't think. Don't think.

Courtney turned back to me and undid the top button of her shirt. Then the second. The third. And then the final button. The confident look in her eyes alone had me undone, and I watched, captivated, frozen to my spot as she slid the shirt off her shoulders. She unclasped her bra and let it fall to the floor. The sight of Courtney topless in front of me was something I'd never get over.

"You're beautiful," I said quietly and went to her. I reached out slowly and traced the outside of her breasts in awe, lifting them, pushing my hands against them as she closed her eyes against my touch. This was heaven on Earth. I let my hands explore, moving slowly, tentatively against her skin. When she opened her eyes again, they blazed with desire.

Courtney dipped her head and paused, just before her lips touched mine. She was so close that I could feel the energy crisscrossing between us. The only sound was Courtney breathing; I had completely stopped. Finally, she crushed her mouth to mine and kissed me thoroughly, urgently. She slipped her hands under my T-shirt and caressed the skin at my waist, causing it to pebble and shiver in the most evocative way. She lifted the shirt over my head and immediately leaned down, kissing just above my bra, the space between my breasts, and up the column of my neck. My knees felt weak and I thought I just might combust before my clothes were even off.

Don't think.

Her eyes found mine, and she smiled, though her breathing was shallow and quick. "Lie down," she said gently. That's when I noticed it: she was nervous, too. I did as she asked, and she followed me down. I reached for her and blazed a path from her shoulders to her stomach, obsessed with the way she felt beneath my fingertips—her curves as they filled my palms, the softness of her skin.

"Have you done this with a girl?" I whispered.

She shook her head. Her only other answer was to kiss me. I slid my hands into her hair and gripped as our mouths danced. Her lips trailed down my jaw to my neck, her hands moving over every inch of me, making my toes point. She adeptly worked the front clasp of my bra and sighed reverently. "Oh, wow," she said, dropping her head to my breast and pulling my nipple into her mouth. I gasped. Her tongue ran across it and I bucked beneath her, feeling it harden instantly. "Oh my God," she said again, voicing my own wordless wonder. "Your body is amazing, Maggie. I knew it would be." She returned to my breast and sucked torturously on one nipple and then the other as I squirmed beneath her, wondering how I'd gone this long without Courtney touching me this way. When she was ready, she pushed my jeans-clad legs apart and settled her hips between them. When she pushed her hips against me, I saw white, moaning at the little shock waves that sparked through me and the need that she had yet to satisfy. She ground into me again.

"Fuck," I said breathlessly, tossing my head back. I rarely swore, but this moment warranted it. The sensations were too much. Way too much. Reading my signals, Courtney unbuttoned my jeans and slid them down my legs. Lying there in nothing but my underwear, I watched raptly as she stepped out of her shorts, sliding her bikinis off with them. The song shifted to some sort of loud and aggressive rock song as the most beautiful girl in the world eased her body on top of mine. How did I get here? We started to move. Soulfully. Purposefully. Urgently. I was no longer in control of myself when Courtney slipped her hand between us and into my underwear. I was wet, I could tell, and strained against her hand desperately searching, silently begging. She didn't delay and pushed her fingers inside me, the feel of it burned into my memory for all eternity. I cried out at the new sensation and clung to her shoulders. I moved my hips against her hand, but it didn't take much before the fireworks hit and I came fast in a blurry and powerful tumble. I lay there, becoming intricately familiar with the patterns of the light across the ceiling as I attempted to come down from the high. Courtney lay alongside me, that much I knew. With just her fingertips, she traced little circles across my stomach and breasts.

"Hey. You okay?" she asked quietly.

I nodded and turned my head to her. "Yeah. I'm good."

"I can't believe I finally got to do that. Do you know how long I've wanted to?"

I shook my head and met her eyes, still not quite verbal. I knew one thing, however. I wanted Courtney and I wanted her now. I slipped my hand between her legs and watched her eyes widen, then close, melting into my touch. I slid on top and watched her face as I explored, memorizing each gasp, each murmur of pleasure and what had inspired it. I hovered somewhere close to heaven, and though I never wanted to stop, her breathing had turned ragged and her eyes searched mine helplessly. When I entered her, the air left my lungs. I'd never felt closer or more connected to another human in my life. She arched her back and moaned. Suddenly, it wasn't enough for me. I crawled down and touched her softly with my tongue. Daring to explore further, I did it again and again, loving the sounds it pulled from her, lost in the taste of her. With a final flick of my tongue, Courtney went still and clenched tightly around my fingers, crying out and clutching the sheets. I couldn't take my eyes off her. Blond hair tossed against bare shoulders, her back arched, and her face awash with pleasure. *Beautiful* was the only word I had.

"Was that okay?" I asked as I moved up the bed.

She blinked at me and cradled my cheek with her hand. "I've never felt that before. At least, not from another person. No one's ever made me do that."

I understood her meaning and felt a rather pleasant blush beginning. "Beginner's luck," I murmured and kissed her shoulder. She wrapped her arms around my neck and we lay there, tangled up, staring at each other, lost in a world I never wanted to leave.

"You are so not a virgin anymore," she said. "How does that feel?"

"I feel like I'm a million miles away from who I was an hour ago."

Courtney smiled. "Me too."

I met her gaze. "But I wouldn't go back for anything. Courtney, this was…indescribable. So many things at once. I feel like I'm overflowing."

She pulled me closer. "And it was only the first time." Her words enveloped me in a promise that there was so much more to come. There would be *more*.

Courtney closed her eyes, and as the music played, I watched her drift peacefully to sleep. It was well after midnight, and I would have to leave her soon and creep home. I still lived with my parents, a detail I was now rethinking, and as such needed to respect reasonable hours.

For now, I enjoyed the serenity of the moment and basked in this new level of our relationship. Being with her like this felt so good that it almost hurt.

I was falling in love with Courtney, and each day, those feelings only grew. I didn't know if it was the same for her. The uncertainty felt like a free fall without a net.

All the same, Courtney was a risk I was ready to assume.

CHAPTER NINE

The next morning as I blinked against the welcome sunlight, memories of the night before floated back to me languidly. I'd had sex last night. With Courtney. I was a person who had sex now. Would other people be able to tell? How could they not? Should I strut? Pay dues to a new sexually active club? Hell, I'd volunteer to be treasurer. A smile touched my lips and I snuggled into my pillow feeling rather excited about life.

Bang, bang, bang.

Someone was at the front door, I realized distantly, getting back to my rather entertaining daydreams. There were surely other people around who could get that. I turned onto my back and gazed through the window at the sky above, my arm up over my head like a silly little dreamer. I could own that.

Bang, bang, bang, bang, bang. And now two rings of the doorbell.

Okay, maybe no one would be answering the door after all. Triple sigh of despair. I tossed the covers off and padded my way downstairs. As I swung open the large wooden door, I was mystified to find Berta staring back at me. Her eyes were red rimmed and her cheeks tearstained. She looked like she hadn't been to bed.

"What's going on?" I asked as she whizzed past me into the house.

"I have to tell someone." I followed her into the living room, where she plopped herself down hard on the couch. My mind was still a little sleep drunk, so I took a second to catch up. Berta was clearly upset about something. "I don't know what I'm going to do."

I ran my hand through my hair. "Okay. Slow down. What's going on?"

"If I say it, it's going to be real. If I don't, the weight of this is going to kill me."

I took a seat next to her on the couch. "You're starting to scare me."

"It was one night." Berta said tearfully. "And it was fun, but it was one night. I just didn't…and he…but now this…and then I'll probably…"

"I'm gonna need a verb." I put a hand on Berta's shoulder to calm her.

"Pregnant. It's an adjective, but it's the truth. Margaret, that's what I'm trying to say. I'm pregnant."

No. Surely I had heard that wrong. "How is that possible?" I asked. She threw me a look. "I mean I know how it's possible, but *who*? When? I don't under…" But the words died on my lips because I knew. "Oh my God. Louis. I knew you were spending more time together, but I didn't realize it had gotten to…this point."

Berta jerked her face back. "What? No. God. I didn't have sex with Louis."

"You didn't? Then how did—"

"Travis."

The word hovered in the air for a long moment as I worked to assemble the pieces. No go. I needed help. Could I phone a friend? "Travis," I repeated.

"Yes." I gestured for further explanation. "Okay. I've always had a thing for Travis but never said so because, I mean, how cliché, right?"

"Right. Because *Travis*."

"But it's there all the same. I'm human." She stood up and began to pace random patterns throughout the room as she explained. "He's actually always been very nice to me. That's the thing. Smiled and held doors and walked me places when we ran into each other, especially lately. We struck up a friendship, I guess is the best way to describe it, outside of the friendship we all have."

"A secret friendship," I said.

"Yes, much like that," she said and pointed at me. "You've been so busy with Courtney."

"Still, you could have said something, dropped a clue at least."

She wasn't listening but seemed to have drifted off on a wonderful daydream. "And then there's the fact that he has those arms. And that hair. Chestnut and wavy with little blond flecks." He did have nice hair. "It was like I was in the middle of an Abercrombie ad, only the model was also a really great person."

I smiled because that was a really sweet characterization of Travis. "So when did this happen?" I asked.

"A few weeks ago. We had a picnic in the park one night. Just the two of us. We sat together and had a really nice time. We laughed, and ate, and then this." She gestured sorrowfully to her stomach. The weight of the situation settled over me. My heart broke for her, for what she was going through, and what she now had to face.

"Oh, Berta." I moved to her and pulled her into a tight hug, which didn't seem to help as she was now crying fully in my arms. "It's going to be okay. I promise. *You're* going to be okay. This is not the end of the world." Her only answer was a sob, so I held her. "Have you thought about what you're going to do?"

She pulled back. "I'm having it," she said automatically. "That's not even a question for me. Look, this is not what I planned on, but I can't not have it."

I nodded, understanding fully. "But college?"

"Not gonna happen. At least not now. I'll have to notify UC Santa Barbara and see if I can take some sort of break. My parents are going to die."

"They're not," I told her. My aunt and uncle would be floored, she was right. But at the end of the day, they were reasonable humans and they would be there for her. "Once they get past the shock, they'll help you. I know they will. What about Travis? Does he know?"

She shook her head. "You're the first person I've told. Margaret, I don't know how I'm supposed to say this to him. I'm sure he's regretted that night since it happened. Ever since, he's said the weirdest things to me. Like he hasn't been himself."

A memory struck. "As in, goofy things?"

"Yeah, like he became a space cadet overnight. He comments on things like the weather and the price of gas. Things he doesn't even care about. He tells jokes where the punch lines don't even match up, and it's because I make him uncomfortable and he regrets everything."

Wait a minute. Now I was the one up and pacing randomly, because

Betsy Ross sewing a flag! Travis hadn't been talking about Courtney several weeks back. He'd been referencing Berta! "He has feelings for you," I blurted rather loudly. "Legitimate ones."

She held up a hand. "No. He doesn't. Trust me."

I walked to her with purpose. "He told me, Bert. He didn't use your name, but it all matches up. You make him nervous because he's into you and doesn't know how to handle himself. It's classic. It's just not classic Travis, which explains the weird."

"Are you sure?"

I nodded. "Tell him. He's a good guy. A meathead, one hundred percent. But a good guy all the same, and he will be there for you."

A hint of a smile touched her lips, died, and sprouted again. It was the first sign of hope that I'd seen since she'd arrived that morning. "Okay, I will. Today, do you think?"

"I do." I squeezed her hand. "Do you want me to go with you?"

"No. I think this is something I have to do on my own." Hesitation crossed her features, and I could sense how nervous she was at the prospect. While I rooted for her wholeheartedly, I also regretted the complications this news brought with it. Berta's future plans would now be scrapped, demolished. A new baby should be something people celebrated, and maybe they would down the line. I decided to do everything in my power to make this part of the journey easier for Berta. I would be happy for this baby. I would give her that celebration.

"You're going to be okay," I said again. "And I'm here for you every step of the way. You know that, right? And when this is all said and done, there will be a tiny little baby for me to hold and love and be his or her favorite aunt."

She launched herself into my arms and held tight. "Thank you, Maggie. Thank you. I almost didn't come over here. I'm so glad I did."

❖

"Berta's pregnant?" Courtney asked, halting a grape midway to her mouth. "Oh no."

"She's pregnant. And it's Travis's baby."

She whistled low.

It was Thursday, and for the first time in a long while, she'd managed to get off work before the sun went down. We'd grabbed dinner at the café and now enjoyed the sunset from the far recesses of the berry patch.

Courtney shook her head. "That's a lot to take on at twenty."

"Berta's still nineteen," I pointed out. "So am I, by the way."

"I had sex with a teenager!" Courtney squeaked, which was ridiculous. She was only six months older than I was. "Berta and Travis, though."

"Shocking, right?"

"Yes, and no. Let's think about this." Courtney pushed herself up onto her knees and looked down at me where I sat on what had become our blanket. "Opposites attract, right?"

"I think that's true to an extent. Historically speaking, it's often the case."

"So it doesn't totally shock me," Courtney went on, "that levelheaded Berta fell for the town pretty boy. It's chemistry in a bottle."

"Okay. And how do we stack up?"

She grinned at me and placed a hand on my thigh. "Oh, we blew the lid clear off that bottle and shattered it into a million pieces."

She wasn't kidding either. It'd been ten days since our night at Courtney's house, and we couldn't keep our hands off each other. We kissed constantly. At the creek. In the strawberry fields. The front seat of her car. The backseat of my car. Anywhere and everywhere, we kissed. Slow and sensual, fast and furious, urgent and intense, we kissed.

"Does Louis know?" she asked. "I thought he had a total thing for Berta."

"He does." I felt horrible for the guy. He'd always been so sweet. "She told him yesterday, and he didn't take it so well. Berta says there were tears and lots of questions. Some of them angry."

"Oh, man. So what's going to happen with Travis?"

"She says he wants to marry her, and I think she's on board with that idea."

"Wow. Married with a baby. Good for them." She studied me. "You don't exactly look thrilled by the prospect, though. You keep staring at the ground."

"They're so young, you know?"

She nodded. "Yeah, but when you know, you know."

I lifted a hand and dropped it. "They're so young."

"So are we."

"We're different."

Her eyes sparkled. "We are, aren't we? Stand up."

I did as she asked and she followed suit. "What are we doing?" I asked.

Courtney lowered herself onto one knee and took my hand. "Margaret Eileen Beringer, marry me."

"You're insane. Get up." I pulled my hand back and turned away laughing. She was up and following me.

"I didn't get an answer."

"Courtney, you're not getting an answer because you don't mean it. Now stop."

"What if I was serious?" she said, facing me.

My stomach tightened at the prospect. "But you're not, so it doesn't matter."

She stared off at the horizon and then met my eyes, all jesting now gone from her demeanor. "I think I am, though."

I studied her, trying to find the words to explain. "We can't get married, Courtney. We're in school. You live across the country."

"Fine. But listen to me, Maggie, and listen very closely. I'm going to ask you again someday. I will marry you. Mark my words."

"One day I'll marry you right back." I smiled and kissed her, easing my hands under the back of her shirt so I could feel the warmth of her skin. "When you're a department store mega mogul."

"Exactly."

"Dressed in the latest fashions."

"Well," she said proudly. "I have to look the part."

I looked skyward and cringed. "Confession time."

She rubbed her hands together. "Oh, I love confession time. What do you have for me?"

I was blushing and feeling stupid, but I said it anyway. "I find you incredibly hot when you're all dressed up and put together for work. Like it does things to me. Major things."

Courtney gasped. "And you're just now telling me? I need to know all your sexy triggers so I can use them."

I shrugged, the heat from the blush still present. "I can't give away all my secrets just yet."

"I just proposed to you! I think you can." She seemed to be enjoying this new piece of information. "Business attire, huh?"

I nodded and took a seat on the blanket. "A big weakness. Gets me every time." I held out my hand for hers and she obliged, following me to the ground with a wicked grin. We made out until the sun was down, and under the veil of darkness made love under the stars, bucking my fears and taking the risk. We took our time with each other, still exploring and reveling in the newness of it all. I discovered how sensitive the skin was on Courtney's inner thigh; when I touched her there, she just about melted. Courtney loved how sensitive my breasts were and seemed to never tire of lavishing attention on them.

As we lay there, spent and happy, I couldn't help but ruminate on the proposal. Courtney had been joking around, yes, but it had me wondering about the future. What would happen when we did graduate? Courtney's father had been clear about his feelings about her seeing me. We were essentially sneaking around, ducking public venues and lying to her father about Courtney's whereabouts. If I wanted any kind of future with Courtney, I was going to have to find a way to change her father's mind about us.

But first I needed to know more.

The next day I found my mother tick-tacking away on her laptop at the dining room table and decided it was now or never. She'd welcomed pretty much any discussion I'd ever hoped to have with her in the past, including retreading the birds and the bees explanation fifteen different times to clear up my lingering questions about trajectory and mechanics.

This topic was different.

"You know, Margaret, this is not a subject I'm especially comfortable discussing with you," my mother said tersely.

She was never terse, so it was clear I'd struck a nerve. She went quickly back to her laptop and seemed to shake off the conversation. But I wasn't done. I came around the dining room table and sat next to her. "You'll talk to me in depth about characters in your books but not about your actual life?"

She eyed me once, twice, and then finally sat back in her chair and sighed. "It was a different time, and I don't like to think about it that often. Some things are best left in the past."

"But Courtney is very much a part of my present, Mom, and she's not going anywhere, as far as I'm concerned. She shuts down most any conversation having to do with her father, and he's pretty much forbidden her to see me. I need to understand why."

She turned to me abruptly, not looking at all like herself. "I want you to stay away from him. Do you hear me? He is not a nice man. If that means you can't see Courtney, then maybe that's an unfortunate consequence."

"I'm in love with her."

That had her attention. She walked to the window and took what felt like forever before turning back to me. "Maybe we should take a walk."

I nodded, but my insides churned. "I'll grab my shoes."

Ten minutes later, we walked the perimeter of our property under the shade of the giant oak trees. She didn't say much at first, and I didn't press her. Finally, she looked over at me. "I was sixteen and Mitch was eighteen. I'd never had a boyfriend before and he was an older boy, showing little old me some attention. It felt like a pretty big deal and all the girls were jealous of me. Everything was grand at first and I wondered how I'd gotten so lucky. We went to the movies, or for ice cream. But slowly things started to change. He had a temper. He was known for it, in fact, but it was rooted on the ball field as far as I knew. One day he turned it on me."

The fear churned my stomach. "What did he do?"

"I'd never been hit before in my life, but I'll never forget the feeling of the back of his hand across my face. I'd told him he sounded arrogant after he gloated about a baseball win. He didn't like that."

"He hit you? Mom, he *hit* you?" The anger started low and grew. The idea of someone hurting my funny, quirky, wonderful mother had my head spinning and my blood boiling.

She nodded sadly.

"So what did you do?"

"At first, I didn't say anything to anyone. I was embarrassed. I was the one everyone was jealous of, remember? I used concealer to cover up the mark he'd left and avoided too much time around my parents because I thought they'd take one look at me and know."

"You didn't break up with him?"

She continued with quiet control. "I didn't. He apologized and I believed him. But as time went on, he started telling me where I could and could not go, and who I could be friends with. It got to the point that I had to check with him before I made plans with my girlfriends."

"So he was an abusive control freak?"

"The labels were different then, but yes. He held all the power. An abusive control freak."

"Can I ask how you got away from him?"

She smiled wanly. "Your father was a big part of that. He was one of my very best friends, and the kindest soul I could ever hope to meet. I confided in him, knowing I could trust him, and he was there for me. Eventually, we fell in love."

"Thank God."

"But things got worse before they got better."

I sobered. "In what way?"

"Though he apologized for hitting me that first time, he did it again. And again. The last time was when I told him it was over. I came away with a black eye and broken eardrum."

"Mom," I whispered, tears filling my eyes. I stopped on the path and turned to her, my voice cracking when I tried to speak. "Why did you never tell me?"

"Some things a young girl doesn't need to know."

"Please tell me he went to jail. Why isn't he still there?"

"He was arrested after I visited the emergency room. But in the end, the charges were dropped, which was probably best for everyone. Me, my parents, Netta, who was devastated. She really did everything she could with him, but it was a losing battle." She ran a hand through her hair as if to clear away all marks from the past. "He left town shortly after that for Northwestern and built his empire over time. He was always very smart. Shrewd."

I shook my head, trying to understand. You hear about stuff like that happening to other people, but this was the first time it had touched someone I loved. "I'm so sorry that happened to you," I said, hugging her.

"I'm okay, sweetheart. I don't want you to worry. I've had a fabulous life since then, and the evidence of that is right here. This precocious kid in my arms who's not such a kid anymore."

I placed a kiss on her cheek and smiled until the very pressing present came rushing back to me like an alarm bell.

"What about now?" I said looking up at her. "Courtney and her mom."

She nodded, her brow furrowed. "We talked, Beverly and I. Once when I took her to lunch and several phone conversations after. She was unhappy in her marriage, and I think hearing my story may have helped give her the courage to finally—"

"Leave that bastard."

"Yes." She sighed. "Don't think I haven't worried for Courtney. I have. I keep an eye on her as best I can."

The idea that she would need to had my heart plummeting and an urge to do something raining down on me, sharp and pressing. "I think I need to talk to her," I said. "Is that okay?"

She stroked the back of my head. "It's okay. If she needs to talk more, let her know I'm here."

"I appreciate that more than you know." I headed off in the direction of the driveway, already jingling my keys.

"Margaret?" I turned back. "Did you mean it? You're in love?"

I smiled at her. "I am."

CHAPTER TEN

Courtney exited Carrington's at eight thirty that night in a matching navy blue skirt and jacket, and I resisted a full-on swoon. Instead, I smiled at the continued fashion strides she made in the role of fierce department store up-and-comer. But my admiration was cut short as I remembered the talk with my mother earlier. There was still so much about Courtney that I didn't know. She wasn't an easy nut to crack, but I had to give it a try.

I was leaning against the hood of my car when she approached.

"Now, that's a really sexy picture," she said, and paused a moment to study me. "A hot girl and car? I must have done something right today."

"Oh, good, because I've been posing like this for hours now, just hoping you'd stumble upon me." I pushed myself off the hood.

"And I was planning to text you, but now I don't have to. You're here and you're beautiful and I get to kiss you. Look at that!"

I sighed happily and looked skyward, accepting the kiss Courtney placed on my cheek and inhaling the vanilla wonderfulness. "And what would this text have said?" I asked.

"Something to the effect of, 'Let's get milk shakes together and forget all about today.'"

"Hop in. I know a spot."

She relaxed into a grin. "Thank God for you, Maggie."

We drove to the Berry Good Café and snagged a spot at the back. The cozy little throwback of a restaurant had a string of booths along the wall on the right and counter-style dining in the center of the room.

With the café closing within the hour, the patronage was sparse. I smiled at Carter Hill from the auto repair shop as he paid his check at the register.

"How's your brother?" he asked. "Haven't seen him around in a week or so."

"Probably at his place still reliving the day you caught his game-winning pass."

Carter laughed. "Favorite of mine, too. Say hey to him for me. Tell him to stop by the shop for a brew."

"Will do. You know he'll take you up on it."

Courtney turned to me. "You know everybody."

"Small-town syndrome. It's a gift and curse."

She set her menu down. "Do you think many people know about us?"

"At least a handful. I told Travis."

She grinned. "And how did that go?"

I thought back on the exchange…

He'd been doing some repair work on the smaller John Deere in the barn and I'd offered to help. "You're turning the wrench the wrong way," I'd told him with a smile. "You sure you don't want me to do it for you?"

"No, I'm not," Travis said, but took a moment to study the bolt in question. "Oh. Right. Gotcha."

"As long as you know what you're doing."

He passed me a look.

"Hey, I hear you have a doctor's appointment next week." Berta's first official doctor's visit since finding out. She'd withdrawn from UC Santa Barbara, sadly, but was beginning to compile other options for herself.

I watched him sink into a smile at the mention of Berta and the baby. "We're gonna get to see him or her on the big screen. Hear the heartbeat and everything."

"I'm happy for you two."

"Thanks, Beringer. Maggie." He seemed to be making every effort at maturity lately. "I hope I can make Berta proud of me, ya know? That's the only thing. I want to do right by her and this kiddo." He shifted uncomfortably and I realized just how much pressure rested squarely on his shoulders, and I felt for the guy.

"I'm confident you will, Travis." I decided to lighten the mood a bit. "So Courtney and I have been...talking."

"About what?" He grabbed an apple from on top of the toolbox and took a bite.

"As in, we've been seeing each other. Dating."

"Dating?" He tilted his head as if to let the new information roll around in there. "You guys are gay? How did I miss *that*?"

I smiled because Travis had never been the most intuitive of individuals. "I feel you're predisposed to imagine that every woman has the capacity to be madly in love with you. And that's an observation, not a dig. I swear. Side note, though, Courtney isn't into labels, so tread easy on the whole gay thing where she's concerned. She just likes who she likes."

"But you're—"

"Gay. Totally."

"Shut the fuck up. Seriously?" I nodded. "Congrats. Do you say congrats? I don't know the proper whatever it is to say here."

"Don't worry about the mysterious saying that goes here. Congrats is fine, too."

"Cool. Congrats, then. So you guys are—you know, that's kind of hot, now that you mention it." He smiled and made a big show of staring dreamily at the wall.

"Stop it."

"What?"

I smiled and shook my head at him. "Don't be that guy. The walking cliché." The funny thing was that Travis was one of the only people who could get away with that kind of thing with me. There was something about him that was so genuinely flawed, yet sincere. As such, I seemed to have developed a soft spot for the guy who would sooner rather than later be a part of my extended family.

"Fine," he said, holding up his hands with a stern look on his face. "Not hot at all. Girls kissing is blech. Won't give it another thought. Not even later."

"You suck at this," I'd told him affectionately and left him to do his work.

"Travis is a good guy," Courtney said, retrieving her menu and perusing. "He means well."

"Yeah, he does. Clay's already impressed with him on the farm.

Says he's an up-and-comer, which is great for Berta." I sat back against the booth. "So what's it going to be?"

She beamed. "A homemade chocolate milk shake. What about you?"

"I will have to settle for one of Rene's famous brownies with a scoop of vanilla."

Her mouth fell open. "You're trying to make me jealous."

"Is it working?"

"Yes!" She smiled at me and relaxed, dropping her tone. "Everything feels lighter when we're together, Maggie."

I opened my mouth to respond but was interrupted handily.

"Well, well," Rene said and sashayed up to our table. She'd owned and managed the café since its opening some twenty-five years prior. Blond. Plump. Friend to everyone. "This is a nice surprise! The two of you grinning it up at my café. Warms my heart." I smiled up at Rene, who was known for her no-nonsense demeanor but also her zest for life. Not to mention, she made the best cakes, pies, and ice cream I'd ever experienced. "Facebook says you two are thicker than thieves, and this seems to prove that true."

"Facebook says so?" Courtney asked curiously. Her gaze moved from me to Rene and back again.

"Tanner Peak now has a Facebook page, remember?" I explained. "It's full of sensationalized gossip. An unfortunate development."

"Our very own *National Enquirer*," Rene gushed proudly.

I had a feeling she was a regular contributor.

Courtney's smile dimmed noticeably and I knew why. We placed our orders with Rene, and I turned to Courtney. "You're worried about our forbidden relationship popping up on your dad's news feed?"

She shrugged. "I've never known him to troll social media, but I suppose anything is possible."

"On that subject, I did a little detective work into our families' history."

"Oh yeah?" Her interest was piqued. She leaned in. "And what did you find out?"

"You were right. My mom and your dad dated in high school. It ended badly." She closed her eyes for several seconds before opening them again.

"I can only imagine. What happened?"

I recounted the details my mother had shared and watched as Courtney seemed to shrink smaller and smaller in her seat.

"I'm really sorry he did that to her. You have no idea how sorry." She shook her head and stared at her hands, but said no more.

"You don't have anything to be sorry for." She nodded to the table numbly. "Did you see that side of him growing up?"

"Unfortunately, I did."

I felt like I'd been punched in the stomach, but I had to know more. The next question left my lips with terrifying calm. "Did he hit you?"

This time she didn't look away. She met my gaze square on. "A few times, sure. My mom had it worse. I'm glad she got away from him."

"God, me too. But what about now? I don't want you living there. You can move in with us. I'm serious. Pack a bag tonight."

"No. Absolutely not. I can handle my father. His temper's mellowed over the years. Though he still likes calling all the shots, even when they're not his to call. That part hasn't changed."

"Like him not wanting you around me?"

She nodded. "Notice it hasn't stopped me. I wouldn't let it."

"But there could be ramifications. You realize that, right?"

"I'll live with them," she said, lifting a shoulder.

"You shouldn't have to. Is it wrong that I can't wait for the day where you're as far away from him as possible? I know you love Carrington's, but have you considered opening your own store?"

"No."

"You could start with just one, something small, maybe after graduation, and see where it goes."

"No. Maggie. God." She stared at me incredulously. "I realize that you're not exactly sure what you want to do with your life, but that's not me. I've known from the time I was small that I wanted to climb the ladder at Carrington's, and I'm so close. I've put in so many hours, and when I graduate, that's where I want to be."

"That doesn't mean you wouldn't be equally happy doing something else, far away from your father. Put in the hours there."

"Do you even hear yourself? He's not far off from retirement. If I work hard enough, and stay the course, the board will see that. I know they will, and someday this company will be run by me."

"But at what cost?"

Courtney stared blankly at the milk shake Rene placed in front of her, the unanswered question echoing in the hollow space between us.

❖

Nothing felt right for the next few days. Courtney and I had chatted on and off, but since our disagreement, the proverbial elephant in the room made its presence known. She'd come to the farm after work three days later, but try as we might, we couldn't seem to get back on track.

I lay there next to her, staring up at the stars, trying to figure it all out.

"I don't want to fight with you," Courtney said quietly from her spot next to me on the blanket. "We have less than a week left, and I want to spend as much of it as possible with you."

I turned to face her. "I don't want to fight with you either, but I'm worried. About you. About us. About what's going to happen."

She crawled slowly on top of me and stared down into my eyes. "I love you."

I blinked up at her and replayed the sentence. "You do?"

She nodded.

"I know in my heart that this summer was meant to happen, that you're the person I'm supposed to be with forever. I want that. I want there to always be an us. Because I love you."

The ever-present voice of reason wanted to point out to her that we could be pulled in a thousand different directions by life or fate or who knows what else, but I didn't. Because I knew she was right. "I love you, too," I said simply.

I'd never been more sure of anything.

Her mouth descended on mine and she let out a tiny little murmur when our lips came together. "And you drive me absolutely insane with this body of yours," she said, before devouring my mouth once again. Luckily, I didn't mind at all. We kissed and touched and touched and kissed and moved against each other until I thought all the air had been sucked out of the universe. Slowly the clothes were subtracted one piece at a time. I didn't know if this would be our last chance to be together, but our time alone came with a measured desperation to memorize each kiss, each touch, each caress.

"I want to taste you," I whispered, and crawled down her body.

I let my breath caress her and watched as she squirmed beneath me in anticipation. With the first touch of my tongue, she moaned, a low and hungry sound. The intimacy of the contact was like a drug, and I couldn't get enough. With the flat of my tongue, I traced her perimeter and then kissed every spot for good measure.

"Maggie," she said softly, drawing out my name for literal seconds. God, I loved that sound.

In response, I let my tongue sweep across her center once, and then again. I dipped it inside and out, quickening my pace until her hips told me she was close. Hoping to satisfy her, I pulled her firmly into my mouth and sucked until she called out, twisting on top of the blanket.

"Oh my God. Oh my God," she breathed. "That was so good. Like beyond."

I smiled up at her and dipped my head. It had been over too soon. I wanted more. She jerked at the sensation of my tongue but softened to the delicate little touches, surrendering once again. "Maggie, I don't think I can—oh man." I smiled against her and slipped inside. She began to move, sexy and sure. That was Courtney, all confidence, and I loved that about her. She let her hands loose in my hair, holding on only for brief moments when she needed an anchor, a move I found incredibly hot. With a final push of my fingers, she tumbled for a second time, closing her eyes and arching her back in release.

Minutes later, when we came back to ourselves, she pulled me to her and cradled my face. "I don't want to say good-bye to you. I can't."

"Then don't," I said, tracing her breast. I never got tired of looking at her body.

She kissed me long and deep and held me tight up against her. "Maggie. Promise me it'll always be us."

I found her baby blues and held on. "I promise."

We made love until the sun came up, not caring about the wider world. I had her and she had me and the rest would sort itself out in time.

CHAPTER ELEVEN

The fourth summer

"Timothy, have you ever missed someone so much that you simply couldn't wait another moment to lay eyes on them? Because that is what I'm feeling right this very moment." My four-month-old little cousin cooed at me from his baby blanket on the floor. I touched his little tummy from my spot alongside him and made the funny faces I knew would pull a smile. Jackpot. His wattage didn't disappoint. "I bet that's how you're going to feel when your mommy and daddy get back from their date night, aren't you?"

Timothy giggled, which meant I had to die of cute overload, a recurring activity where Tim the Tiny Man Oakham was concerned.

"Where's Tiny Tim?" my brother asked, poking his head into my cottage.

"Do you ever knock?" I asked. "As in, ever?"

"I don't have to. I'm your older, wiser brother and have rights to do whatever I want."

"One day you're going to have to explain that logic to me."

For my twentieth birthday, my father and brother had surprised me with my very own place on the eastern portion of our property line. How they pulled it off so quickly and without me driving through that portion of the land had me stumped. I now had over two acres overlooking the farm all to myself, which was awesome. The one-bedroom house had become my personal project over the past year, and I never got tired of finding new ways to spruce it up. It turned out decorating was a favorite pastime of mine, as was figuring out how to make space functional, and eye-catching with color, layout, and light.

"How long do we have this little dude?" Clay asked.

"They should be back within an hour."

"Well, that's plenty of time," Clay told Timothy in a baby-talk voice, "for us to get into all sorts of bro trouble. Can you say 'kegger'? Repeat after me. Keg-ger."

I gasped. "Stop that. You're going to ruin his innocent wide eyes."

"Your Aunt Margaret is no fun at all." Clay shook his head at Timothy. "No, she is not. You don't like her as much as you do your handsome Uncle Clayton. I can tell."

"I don't know about handsome anymore, Clay. Your boyish good looks might be fading with age." I casually flipped through a brochure on California real estate, and Clay looked like I'd just put his beloved puppy in the basket of my bicycle.

"You wound me." Couldn't have wounded him too bad because he moved on quickly, stealing my brochure and flipping to the front. "Real estate, again?" It was an avenue that bore exploration. Because I'd taken extra hours each semester, I'd graduate early with a bachelor of business administration. I was beginning to wonder what that would look like paired with a real estate license. "You gonna do it? Become a broker? Make deals happen all over strawberry city?" Clay asked.

"Well, nosy," I stole the brochure back, "I'm starting to think I might. I would wait until I graduate, though. Not a lot of free time between school and the farm." The Pick-Your-Own operation had pretty much been turned over to me, and I'd run with it, doing what I could to turn us into the place you had to stop if you wanted the freshest strawberries in creation. As a result, we were more popular than ever. I'd convinced Clay to plant one of our empty fields with pumpkin vines, which had translated to tons of foot traffic in the fall. People loved pumpkins and even more so loved having their photos taken in a giant patch of them. As a result of the growth, I now had a couple of employees who manned the place when I was in school, and my mother, hotter than ever in the world of historical romance, pitched in on occasion when her hands weren't full with Luke, Sebastian, or some other alpha male du jour.

"I think you'd rock the real estate world," Clay said. "You've got a great head for business, Scrap."

"Can I quote you on that?"

"No. I will disavow all compliments. Can't have folks in town thinking I'm soft." He growled and I rolled my eyes. "When does Courtney get in?"

"Tomorrow," I told him, smiling at just the mention. "Late afternoon. Time hates me. It's crawling by."

"Kudos to the two of you, though, gotta say. The long-distance game is not something I'd be very good at."

I blew a strand of hair off my face. "Please, the short-distance thing isn't something you're very good at either."

"That's true." He smiled guiltily. "I'm getting to be an old man, though. Might need to start changing my skirt-chasing ways. What do you think?" he said to Timothy. "Does Uncle Clay need to find him a girl who can make an honest man out of him?"

"This little guy," I said, taking Timothy and planting a kiss on his cheek, "will never chase skirts. He's the tiniest gentleman on the planet." My phone buzzed from its spot on the coffee table. I read the text and smiled.

"Courtney?" my brother asked. "The love of your life? The reason you wake up in the morning?"

"Mm-hmm." I typed my response. "She says her plane lands just after lunch, but she shouldn't make it into town until midafternoon." I couldn't dim the smile on my face if I tried. It'd been there all week. I couldn't believe that this time tomorrow she'd be here, in front of me, after so many months.

"So what time is Pictionary?" Clay asked. "I want to give her a chance to set her bag down, the little artistic genius. I've been practicing up, though. She's in for a reckoning." He cracked his knuckles.

"There will be no Pictionary tomorrow night."

"You plan to jump right into the sack?"

I winced painfully. "Do not say the word 'sack.' Or talk about sex. You're my brother. It's weird." I covered little Tim's ears for good measure.

He stared at me like I was crazy. "You do realize I have sex, don't you?"

"I choose not to think about it."

"And if you ever need any tips, I'm just saying, let me know."

"Gross. You're a weird person." But I adored him and we both knew it.

He smiled at me genuinely and dropped the jokes. "Seriously, though, I know it hasn't been the easiest year for you. If you ever need to talk…or just complain a little. I'm here. You just gotta knock on my door or knock me in my head."

I had the warm fuzzies now because he really was a great brother. "I will remember that."

"That's all I ask." He pushed himself up off the floor and planted a loud, smacking kiss on Tim's cheek. "Be good to that baby. Don't go out drinking together."

"It's tempting, but we'll abstain. Oh, hey, Clay? How's Travis doing at work?"

"The kid's a natural. I give him more responsibility each month and he nails it every time. Gonna hold on to him."

I smiled, happy that the good reports continued to roll in. "Awesome. Berta will be glad to hear it."

"That Louis kid is another story, though. I've about had it on that front."

"Really?" This was an interesting development. "Why is that?"

"Been missing work a lot lately. Not calling in when he does, either."

"You still got him working the books?"

"Yeah, and he's a whiz at it, but I need someone I can count on. I put him on probation yesterday."

I winced. "Ouch. He's not used to that kind of thing."

"Hoping he turns it around. I know he's your buddy." He headed for the door.

"Don't worry about that."

Clay nodded. "Good to know. See ya, Scrap."

"See ya."

I made a mental note to check in with Louis, see if maybe he could use a friend in the midst of whatever it was he was going through. He would do it for me. Timothy babbled, and I pushed the thought aside because the cutest baby in the world needed my undivided attention.

❖

Phone calls, text messages, even the occasional package hadn't made up for the fact that I hadn't seen Courtney in close to nine months. As I sat on the steps in front of my cottage, I checked my watch for what must have been the nine hundredth time. I had all this extra energy moving through me, reminding me how nervous I was, which was silly. This was Courtney, the person who probably knew me best in the world, whose voice it was that I fell asleep to on the phone each night.

She'd had a good year at Northwestern and seemed to fit in the way she fit in everywhere—perfectly. She had tons of friends whose names I learned via posts on social media. There was Heather, Ryan, Bryn, Angela, Nathan, and a million other names and good-looking faces I'd seen splashed across my screen. Yes, Courtney seemed to be thriving at school and was even more of a social butterfly than ever.

This prompted a myriad of internal questions.

Would it be different when we saw each other again this time? How would I hold up against her more exciting friends from school, and would she still feel for me what she did last summer? I stood and walked the expanse of the porch, jamming my hands in my pockets as I waited, pulling them out again, willing myself to relax and squirming against the uncomfortable flutters in my stomach.

God.

A few minutes later, my breath caught. I saw the familiar blue Mercedes coast up the gravel drive to my cottage. She'd never seen the cottage, and I wondered what she'd think of the décor, the exterior, all of it.

I felt my smile start and grow as she pulled in. I caught sight of her through the windshield, her blond hair pulled back in a loose ponytail, tendrils falling out. She exited the car and I forgot to breathe, remembering now how beautiful she was in person, how heart-stopping. She wore denim capris and a white cotton button-up shirt. She paused for a moment, looking up at me, resting her head on the top of the car door and grinning. I met her gaze, and for a moment we just stared at each other. I tried to wrap my mind around the fact that she was actually here. And then she was on her way to me, taking the steps two at a time, and in my arms, her face nestled against my neck.

All was right with the world.

All was right.

I buried my nose in her hair and took a deep inhale of the vanilla, never wanting to be away from her for so long ever again. I refused to think about the fact that I only had her for a month before she headed back for the fall semester. She'd just completed a summer internship at Carrington's Corporate in Chicago and would continue with them for the remainder of the school year.

But I had a month.

"You're one hell of a sight for sore eyes," she said. There were tears in her eyes, and now I realized there were tears in mine, too.

"I can safely say the same."

Her lips were on mine and mine were on hers because there was so much time to make up for. The familiar tingles hit, and I welcomed them fully. When we came up for air, I rested my forehead against hers and smiled. "You're here. You can finally see my place."

On cue, Courtney popped her head up and looked around. "It looks just like the photos! You have a truly precious house."

I winced. "And that's what I was going for, precious."

She laughed. "Fine. How about attractive? Quaint. Rustic. Are any of those better?"

"I can get on board with quaintly rustic."

"Show it to me," she said and peeked in through the screen. "I know you've been putting in a lot of time."

I opened the screen door. "Follow me."

"If there's not Beatles memorabilia somewhere in this place, I'm going to be incredibly disappointed."

I looked back at her. "This tour comes with a lot of pressure."

I led her inside my new home and instantly saw it through her eyes for the first time. The door opened immediately to the living room, which was joined to the kitchen and the breakfast nook at the back of the house. The cottage's only bedroom and bathroom were down the hallway to the right. I'd done my best to keep the cottage rustic but modern, finding as much beige driftwood furniture as I could and then punctuating it with turquoise accents in the form of throw pillows, complementary art, and curtains that hinted of color. I wasn't into clutter, so the surfaces were mostly clean and sparse with only an occasional knickknack. I had an apple crisp candle burning in the kitchen and Courtney took a deep inhale as she looked around, moving through every inch of the space. I gave her time to explore all of it and enjoyed watching her take in each detail.

"It's fantastic," she said at long last, pausing in the center of the living room, turning in a circle. "Every detail is so very Maggie, which means I love it."

I felt the pink on its way to my cheeks. "I love it, too. I couldn't wait for you to see it."

"No Beatles, though," she said in disappointment.

"But wait!" I raised one finger. "The closet door was open. Follow me." She trailed me down the short hallway to my favorite room in the house. I'd gone with a fluffy white bedspread and pale blue walls. Hanging to the right of the bed and behind the closet door was a framed photo of the Beatles' *Abbey Road* album. I closed the closet door, revealing the artwork, and watched her smile take shape.

"Now I can rest easy. All is right with the world." She scanned the rest of the room and paused, her eyes landing on a familiar frame on the wall. She'd sent it as a Christmas present earlier that year, but I hadn't waited until Christmas to open it. When I did, I fell madly in love with the scene before me. A pencil sketch of Courtney and me sitting along the bank of the creek, the way we had countless nights last summer. The detail was so precise, so shockingly accurate that I had simply stared at it for days. I considered it my most treasured possession, and I'd hung it across from my bed so that it was the first thing I saw when I woke up in the morning and the last thing I saw before switching off the light.

She turned back to me. "I love that you hung it up. That means a lot."

I shrugged. "I mean, it's *okay*."

She laughed and it felt like us again. "Come here." I moved into her arms and we stood there for a moment. "Remember when I arrived last summer and couldn't believe how beautiful you looked?"

I met her eyes, and smiled. "Vaguely."

"Well, it's happened again. How am I so lucky that you're mine?"

I rolled my eyes playfully. "How do I know that's not a line, that you don't say that to all the girls?" And there were a ton of them in her life. Heather, Jorie, Tonie, Simone, to pinpoint just a few of the names she often referenced on our phone calls. Not to mention the string of guys that seemed to run with their group. The time apart had me feeling a little vulnerable, wondering if she'd met someone fabulous she could do fabulous things with and forget about tiny little Tanner Peak. About me. I wasn't sure I would have blamed her either. Courtney's life seemed pretty exciting compared to what I offered her.

"All of the girls," she replied, nodding. "All the time. Except the truth is so very different from that, Maggie." I shook my head and watched as she undid my top button and traced my collarbone. "For me, there is only you, and that will never change." She undid my second button, exposing part of my bra and running her finger across the top of my breast. I hissed in a breath. Another button.

"We have dinner reservations, remember? To celebrate?" My shirt hung completely open and Courtney tucked a strand of hair behind my ear. Her eyes dropped to the skin on display. I was starting to care less and less about that dinner.

"Don't take this the wrong way, because I love how much of a planner you are, but I would much rather order a pizza and stay right here, getting...reacquainted."

"Sold," I said, and looked around for the phone.

She took a seat and watched me call in a pizza order to the café. Danny, the delivery driver, would bring it our way shortly. I hung up and grasped my shirt, prepared to button it once again.

"Don't," Courtney said, her gaze beckoning me. I walked to her willingly, wantonly, and allowed myself to be pulled into her lap. I knew that look on her face, and I loved it. Her hands settled inside my shirt on the sides of my waist. She slid her thumbs up my torso to just beneath my breasts where she readjusted, allowing them to fill her palms. She looked up at me with eyes of wonder, and I ran my thumb along her bottom lip. She kissed it and squeezed my breasts through my bra. When I dropped my head back as the wonderful pinpricks of pleasure assaulted my senses, Courtney took the opportunity to kiss my collarbone and then sat up taller, kissing my neck, holding the back of it, as I pressed against her stomach with my hips.

"God, I've missed you," she murmured, unbuttoning my jeans.

I grabbed her wrist halfheartedly. "The pizza guy will be here in just a few minutes. Small town. Short distance."

"I'll be quick," she said, and silenced me with a searing kiss I could not argue with. The best kind of kiss, where her tongue stroked mine, leaving fireworks in its wake. At the same time, Courtney pressed with her palm against the seam of my jeans and I was hers, surrendering to anything she wanted. She smiled at the little noises I made and slid down the zipper on my jeans. When she eased her hand inside, I swore quietly and held her shoulders for support. Quite honestly, she didn't have to do much. It had been so long, and I was so far gone already. After a few quick strokes, I was ready to tumble over the edge. When she slid inside and pressed against me with her thumb, I did more than that. I shattered entirely, squeezing her shoulders and tightening around her. Powerful waves of pleasure hit one right after another, a pattern that seemed to keep giving.

"Fuck," I breathed, my forehead resting on her shoulder.

"Exactly that." Courtney chuckled and kissed my cheek. "It has been way too long since I've done that. And in a few short minutes, we can eat pizza."

Fifteen minutes later, that's exactly what we were doing.

Courtney sat cross-legged on the couch facing me, pulling off one pepperoni at a time and popping them in her mouth as soft tunes played from the radio in the kitchen. She held up a hand at my raised eyebrow. "Can I just take a moment to say how nice it is to be sitting here in front of you? Enjoying a meal as fantastic as this one and not counting down until we're together again because we already are?"

"It's surreal, though, at the same time."

"It is." We shared the moment, taking each other in.

I grinned. "So tell me more about the internship."

She nodded and took a moment to finish chewing. "Corporate was even more interesting than I thought it was going to be."

"So you started off in marketing and then rotated into..."

"Operations, which is what I'm most excited for. It seems to be what I excel at. Big-picture stuff."

"I had a sneaking suspicion you were going to rock at bossing people around." She tossed a pillow at me, which I caught handily. I smiled and swallowed back the disappointment that we now had so little of the summer left. She'd be heading back to Chicago in just a few short weeks. "What does your dad think?"

She considered the question. "He's been surprisingly hands off. Isn't talking to me much these days."

"Because of me, you mean."

She attempted a smile but didn't quite make it. "He knows I'm still seeing you, yes. I think he's also aware that he's not going to be able to stop me."

"So he's freezing you out?"

"A good way to put it. I mean, he picked me up from the airport, said a couple of words. We're living in the same house, but he's made his disapproval clear. All of my communication at Carrington's now goes through Jonathan Voorhees, the COO. He's really taken an interest in determining my strengths and how that translates to a future role with the company."

"Jonathan's your mentor, huh? Is he handsome? Are you in love with him?" God, could I be any more insecure? I hated that part of myself.

"Well, he's sixty, but I've always been into the older ones."

Now it was my turn to launch a pillow. "So would they ever give you control of your own store?"

She nodded. "Once I'm ready, yes. That's the goal. Provided my father doesn't put himself in the way of it."

"He would do that?"

"It doesn't matter. He'll have to come to terms with you and me sooner or later. I'm an adult and I will date whomever I want to. Which brings me to my next topic."

I set my empty plate on the coffee table. "And that would be?"

"Us."

Okay, this could go a lot of ways. It wouldn't completely shock me if Courtney was over the long-distance headache and maybe wanted to ease up on things between us. But judging from the earlier chair encounter, sex didn't seem to be one of them. My stomach dropped out beneath me and I asked myself if I was capable of casual sex, and honestly had no clue how I would—

"I want you to come back east with me."

I didn't follow. "Come back east with you where?"

She sat a little taller as if making a presentation. "I want you to move to Chicago. You could transfer to Northwestern. Finish school there."

I laughed. "I'm not sure it's that simple to get into Northwestern, Court."

"It's not as hard as you might think. Plus, there are tons of schools in the area. Take your pick. I just know that I want you there with me, and I will bend over backward to make you comfortable with the idea." I raised an eyebrow at the provocative visual, which pulled a grin from Courtney. "See? That right there, that sly sense of humor, is one of many reasons I can't be apart from you anymore. I don't just love you, I like you."

A long silence enveloped the room.

"You're serious about this?" I asked.

"I'm very serious." She took my hand, and that's when I noticed that she was trembling. When I put together everything I knew about Courtney, the girl who didn't let a lot of people in, it made sense that she'd be nervous. In fact, she was probably terrified. For once, she was putting herself out there. But at the same time, I wasn't sure this was a move I was prepared to make. What about the farm? School? Timothy? So many thoughts zigzagged across my brain that I needed a moment to process the whirlwind.

"While not having to say good-bye to you sounds like a wonderful idea," I squeezed her hand, "this is such a huge decision. Can I think about it?"

She nodded and I watched the color drain from her face. "Yes. Yes. Of course you can. I probably should have picked a better time, anyway. I didn't mean to spring that on you."

I placed a calming hand on her knee. "You didn't." But she wasn't looking at me anymore, and that stung.

"Good." She stood and collected our plates. I watched her walk into the kitchen, understanding that she now felt wildly off-kilter. Vulnerable, and she didn't like that. I decided I needed to help as best I could.

"Do you know how off the charts in love with you I am?"

She turned to me and smiled that perfect smile that got me every time. The one that had my heart. "It's nice to hear the words."

"Well, I'll say it again: I love you, and I will make sure you know it every day." I walked to her and took her hands in mine. "I will buy you flowers to say so."

"I do love flowers."

"And chocolate."

She looked skyward. "It's hard to beat chocolate."

"Then I'll hire a chorus of singers to follow you wherever you go."

She held up a finger. "That might get creepy. Flowers and chocolate are just fine."

"Gospel ones, and they'll sing really loud. Mainly just your name entirely in high notes."

"Probably not the wisest idea." But she was laughing, which was key. Mission accomplished. I followed her around the kitchen as she attempted to escape.

"And they'll all wear blond wigs in your honor."

"You've lost your mind."

"What about choreography?"

She turned around, walking backward now as I pursued her. "No."

"I'm thinking they could do the shopping cart dance move in homage to you." I demonstrated.

"I'm going to kill you."

I pulled her to me. "I'll die happy."

CHAPTER TWELVE

I started the next week off at Bag of Beans, where I laid out my notes and plans for streamlining the Pick-Your-Own. The checkout process had become too time consuming when we were in the midst of a busy afternoon, and I had some definite ideas about expediting the whole process.

"Aha, the Pick-Your-Own shuffle is in full effect."

I glanced up and smiled at Berta and instantly held open my arms for little Timothy, who didn't begrudge me. I loved that he recognized me and reached for me readily each time he saw me. "Good morning. Yes, the rumors are true. The Pick-Your-Own is in need of some restructuring. How are you two?" I asked, referencing her and the baby.

"One of us is a little less frustrated than the other and hasn't had their hair pulled eighteen times, but we're both here."

"I don't know how you can beat not having your hair pulled," I said to Timothy. "You've got the good end of this stick, buddy."

"Hold him while I grab a coffee?"

"Just try wrestling him from me." As I cooed at Timothy, I caught sight of Louis through the window sitting on a curb across the street. He looked awful and wore the clothes I'd seen him in the day before.

"What's with Louis?" I asked Berta when she returned, gesturing out the window to where he sat.

She followed my gaze and shook her head. "He's been so distant lately. I've tried to talk to him, but he doesn't seem to want anything to do with me. I still don't think he's forgiven me for Travis."

"His heart is still broken. That makes me so sad." I watched as he got up and walked away and decided, then and there, that I needed to be his friend. Go out of my way to show him that his life still had meaning even if he didn't have Berta. There were so many great girls out there for him to go and meet. Given, Tanner Peak was small, but he needed to realize that there was a life out there for him. He just needed to reach out and grab it.

"I just want him to be happy, you know?" Berta said wistfully. "I can't stand that I'm the reason he's not. He's too sweet a person." Timothy squirmed in my arms, and Berta took him from me. "Someone wants his breakfast. Say good-bye to your Aunt Maggie." She looked to me. "It was nice having a conversation with someone who is verbal. Thank you."

"Likewise," I told her. With a wave, Berta was off and I was back to work in the gritty world of strawberry procedures. Courtney had some phone appointments scheduled, so I had most of the morning to work at my own pace. I was only a few minutes in when I felt that awkward sensation one gets from being stared at. I threw a glance to the front of the store and saw Melanie tear her eyes from me instantly. *Weird.* I shook it off and went back to work, only to jump five feet out of my skin when I discovered her standing right next to my chair.

"Oh my God," I said, grabbing my chest. "You teleported yourself from the counter."

"I didn't mean to sneak up on you," she said, and took a seat next to me. This was odd. What was happening? I was still in the same body, right? Why was Melanie seeking me out? "Do you have a second to chat?" She forced a smile.

"Sure," I told her, glancing around the relatively empty shop to see if there was anyone else around to witness this rare event. Melanie Newcastle was approaching me for an actual conversation.

She paused a moment and then jumped right in. "I don't want to seem nosy or like I'm prying into your personal business…"

Oh, this was off to an interesting start. I braced myself.

"But you and Courtney Carrington are an item, right?"

"We are," I said slowly. I wasn't sure where this was going or how I felt about it.

"I just thought you should know that people know about it," she said ultra quietly.

"And I'm totally cool with that," I whispered back.

The concerned look on her face was wiped clean with that answer. A perplexed one took its spot. "You don't care that people...*know*?"

I shook my head. "Look, Melanie. I'm not trying to hurt anyone. I've not done anything wrong, so that's correct. I have no problem with people knowing about me and Courtney."

That seemed to bowl her over. She ruminated on the information for a moment before moving on. "How have people treated you?"

"Because I'm in a relationship? Well, I would say the long line of people waiting to date me has quelled." I was making ridiculous jokes because her questions had me on edge. They were strange. Was she about to invite me to church to save my soul? Was that what was happening here?

"No. Not because you're in a relationship. Because you're..."

"Gay?" I finished for her. She didn't seem able to on her own.

"Right. That. And I'm wondering if I might be."

Whoa.

Halt the presses. Did Melanie just say what I think Melanie just said? I decided I needed to be sure. "You think you might be in a relationship?"

She shook her head and her gaze dropped like lead to her hands, folded in her lap. My heart tugged at the gesture, because it was clear that Melanie was really struggling here.

My voice was quieter this time. Gentler. "You're wondering if you might be gay?"

Finally, after a long silence, she met my eyes and nodded. "I'm starting to think I am. No. I know I am." Well, color me shocked. I was no longer the only lesbian under the age of twenty-five in Tanner Peak.

❖

"I don't think I believe her," Courtney said over lunch at the café the next day. "Melanie."

I held up a hand. "I hear you, but I've been thinking on it. Pass the ketchup?"

"Well, I'll need three fries as payment." Courtney held the bottle like she was protecting an important hostage. I handed her the fries.

Courtney grinned and I grinned, because that's how we worked. I loved us. "Proceed. You were saying?"

I looked sideways at her. "Before I was extorted for food?"

"Before that."

I shook my head to clear it because she looked hot today in her cutoffs and Beatles T-shirt, also stolen. "Okay, so Melanie."

"Right."

"She's always been a little too Regina George for my taste, you know? Mean. And maybe that's because she was dealing with some internal stuff of her own."

"Meaning, she took out her unhappiness on others?"

"Right. Exactly. It's hard to be nice when you're miserable and hating yourself."

Her bottom lip came out. "Well, that makes me sad."

"Me too."

"Is there someone in particular she's interested in? Because if it's you, I might have to go to war."

I grinned at her proclamation. "I don't think that will be necessary. There was a woman who came into the hair salon who captivated her in a manner she'd never really experienced. She's thought about her ever since. She coupled that wake-up call with her lackluster interest in guys her whole life and bam, there she was next to me at Bag of Beans, her terrified heart in her hands."

"Well, good for her." Courtney's phone buzzed and she glanced at the readout and smiled. As she began to type, I hated myself, but I had to ask.

"What's so funny over there?"

She flashed the phone at me briefly. "Nathan. Everyone's left Chicago and he's bored out of his mind." Nathan was a name I'd heard more than a handful of times. He ran in the same crowd Courtney did back at school.

"Let me just finish this answer so he doesn't think I'm ignoring him, and then I'm all yours."

"Cool."

I ate in silence while Courtney texted back and forth a few extra times with Nathan, who I came to find out was a senator's son. Fancy. I didn't want to be that person, so I pushed any feelings of unease aside.

These were her friends. It just so happened they were from a world I wasn't a part of. That is, unless I wanted to be. I hadn't discarded Courtney's invitation to Chicago. In fact, I'd thought on it religiously since she'd mentioned it the week prior.

The offer was there for the taking. But did I have the courage?

Courtney stayed over that night. We'd made out for what felt like hours before ravishing each other appropriately. Lying there, happy and spent, I ran my fingers through her hair slowly, lifting one strand and letting it fall, something I'd learned she loved.

"Okay," I said into the darkness.

She looked up at the sound of my voice and kissed the underside of my jaw. "What is okay?" Her late-night voice was quiet and raspy. I loved it.

"Okay, I'll come to Chicago."

She went still in my arms before popping up on her forearms. "You're serious?" She straddled me and placed her hands on my shoulders, grinning down at me like it was Christmas morning.

"It's going to take a lot of work and planning, but I figure if I start now, I can have at least the important details ironed out in the next couple of weeks." Her answer was to kiss me into next month, which meant that she was pleased. I laughed when we came up for air.

"I can't believe that this is happening," she said, smacking both of my shoulders. "We're going to need a plane ticket for you, and your transcripts from Santa Barbara. Oh, and we need to shop!"

I was still laughing, my heart stolen by how excited she was. "Shop?"

"For stuff you like. It can't just look like my place that you've moved into. It should look like ours." I was touched by the sentiment.

"Well, we'll need a Beatles shrine. Preferably in the living room." My hands went to her breasts as she lowered herself on top of me.

"Keep talking."

"And probably an Abraham Lincoln alarm clock."

"This is sounding more and more dubious. What does this alarm clock do?" she asked, placing an open-mouthed kiss on my neck.

"He wakes you up with the Gettysburg Address, Courtney." I felt her smile against my skin and she moved lower, kissing my breasts. My eyes fluttered closed. "We'll also need strawberry everything."

Her teeth skated my nipple and I hissed in a breath. "Oh no. Like?"

"Plates, cups, calendars, and of course, the patterns on any and all furniture. Guests will eat it up. Get it?"

She lifted her head. "I do."

"Well, you want me to feel at home, don't you?"

"That is the goal," she said pushing my legs apart. The decorating session had to be put on hold as other glorious things took priority. But once the words were out of my mouth, I was 100 percent on board to make what would be a very scary leap in the trajectory of my otherwise safe life.

Love, I was finding, was more than worth it.

My heart had never before been so close to bursting, and I couldn't wait to begin what would be a new and exciting chapter in my life. That night, each touch felt different than ever before, as each caress now came with a promise. We would take on the world together. Courtney had chosen me and I had chosen her right back. It wasn't sex that time, it was an expression of love. I grew up that night, embracing adulthood fully for the very first time—scary, daunting, exhilarating, and wonderful. I looked forward to all that lay ahead.

CHAPTER THIRTEEN

"It feels a little too sudden for my liking," my father said, as he sliced up a carrot for the salad my mother tossed next to him. I would miss their tandem dinner preparation.

"Why does it have to be *this* semester?" my mother asked. "We're not opposed to you moving if that's what you truly want. In fact, we'll even help, but what's the rush?"

It had taken me a few days to work up the nerve to explain my new plan to my parents. "I wholeheartedly understand your concern," I recited from the prepared list of answers in my head. "It probably could wait, you're right. But if I'm able to work it out now, why not take the leap and go back when Courtney does?"

"When would we see you?" my mother said sorrowfully, shifting into maternal mode. "You've never been away from home for more than a week, and now you're setting off across the country? I don't know how I'm going to do with all this."

"I'll be okay, Mom. I promise. I'll call you every week, every day if it would make you feel better. How else am I going to keep up with all the Tanner Peak gossip?"

She abandoned the salad and cupped my chin in her hands. "This terrifies me, you realize this?"

"I do."

"And I love you more than peanut butter and chocolate, do you realize that?"

I laughed at the humongous declaration. "That, too."

Another sigh from her, as my dad looked on. "We like Courtney, but why can't she move here? We can have Pictionary Thursdays."

The question was valid and I did my best to explain, following her back to the salad. "Because Carrington's corporate offices are in Chicago, and if she wants to learn the business, that's where she needs to be. At least for now."

My father stepped in, the lines noticeable across his forehead. This was his worried face. "I would be less than truthful and not doing my job as your pop if I didn't tell you that her last name concerns me. I know that's not something that you want to hear, but it's the truth."

"It's not fair to punish Courtney for that." I looked from him to my mother. "Please. You guys have been so wonderful to her. Don't judge her for something entirely outside of her control. As for her father, she feels about him much the way you do."

"Well, that makes me very sad for her," my mother said.

He sighed. She sighed. Suddenly the room felt heavy.

My parents exchanged a long look. They always amazed me with their flawless system of nonverbal communication. I'd been trying to decode it for years. With a nod from my mother, my father turned to me. "We'll support you if this is what you really want, but know that you'll always have a home here if it doesn't work out. Call us and we'll come get you."

I hugged him hard and then my mother harder. This was the last major stop in regard to the move, and I had trouble holding back my smile. The idea of life in the big city had my imagination in overdrive. I loved Tanner Peak, but I was beginning to imagine myself closing real estate deals in Chicago, going to restaurants, theatre, and art galleries. Of course I'd come home as often as possible. Holidays, special occasions, all of them. How could I not?

This would always be my home.

Courtney had spent the day at Carrington's, acquainting herself with a new floor plan as rolled out by corporate, designed to help the stores flow better, a concept I found rather intriguing, because I thought it flowed fine. We had plans to head to Lonesome's for a drink, so I swung by her house to pick her up, excited to share the news. I dodged the next door neighbor's rotating sprinkler and climbed the steps with extra energy but paused at the partially opened front door. Interesting. I glanced around the property for signs of life and decided that Courtney must have forgotten to close it on her way inside. As I raised my fist to knock, the sounds of angry voices drifted out onto the porch.

I froze.

"Have it your way," her father's snide voice echoed, "and see how empty that bank account of yours starts looking. All over a farm girl, and the dime-a-dozen type. I should know."

"Don't say that," Courtney shot back. She sounded like she'd been crying. "You don't know what you're talking about, first of all. And second of all, this isn't your decision." I pushed the door open a little farther, battling guilt for eavesdropping and the need to protect Courtney at the same time. "I don't need your money. I'll do it on my own if I have to. I have a job."

"Best of luck, little girl. Last I looked, interns made close to minimum wage." He was right. Courtney didn't make a ton for the work she did at Carrington's. "What a disgrace you turned out to be. Have fun with your whore."

The air fled my lungs at the word. I felt like I'd been sucker-punched and tried to imagine a universe in which either of my parents spoke to me that way. I jumped at the sound of a door slamming, then heard footsteps on the stairs. I stepped back and there she was. Tearstained cheeks, red-rimmed eyes, and a shocked expression to find me standing there.

"Are you okay?" I asked immediately, taking Courtney's hand and leading her down the walk.

"Did you just…" She gestured behind her, embarrassment coloring her cheeks.

"Hear? Yeah, I caught the gist."

The tears were back in her eyes. She looked horrified. "Maggie, I'm so sorry. What he said—he's angry."

I met her gaze. "Wanna get outta here?"

"Please."

I took her hand and we hopped in the car. She was silent on the drive to the bar, lost in a world of her own as she studied the passing scenery.

Once I parked the car, I turned to her. "Do you want to talk about it?"

She met my eyes. "No."

I cringed internally because she'd rebuilt the wall around herself. It was what she did when she felt exposed. "Don't shut me out."

She rested her cheek against the seat resolutely. "He's cutting me off if I move in with you. He says a summer fling was one thing, but real life is another."

I nodded. "A farm kid from a loser family."

She sat up fully. "You and I both know that's not true. Don't listen to him. He knows he's not in control, and it kills him."

"I care a lot less about what he thinks and more of what you do."

"What I think is that we're going to be in Chicago in two weeks and all of this will be behind us." Somehow I had my doubts. "I also think we could both use a drink." I followed Courtney into the dimly lit bar, a little nervous about the fact that I was not legally allowed to be there. I nodded obligatorily at an old mascot head on the wall. I always thought the Tanner Peak Beavers to be an unfortunate choice. Courtney ordered a sophisticated-sounding martini and I the generically titled "white wine, please."

We settled into a table to the right of the bar and I did my best to tolerate the noise from the rowdy group of Clay and his friends, crowded around the dartboard. We shared a wave and Clay went back to his game.

"So what did your parents say when you told them?" Courtney asked. She'd sent me a "good luck" text earlier in the day.

"They voiced concern, but they support my decision."

She relaxed back into her chair. "Finally, some good news! We should mark this moment." She raised her martini and I joined her in a toast. "To my awesome girlfriend and her powers of persuasion."

I grinned, really enjoying that word, "girlfriend." "I love you," I mouthed. She mouthed it back, which was even better than the girlfriend thing.

"I'll get a second job if I have to, and I'm sure my mother will help supplement me. She gets a big fat check from him every month."

I nodded. "We'll make it work."

"I want you to know how seriously I take this."

I smiled, enjoying the take-charge attitude she now brandished. It looked good on her, and I saw how it would translate to the corporate world, and that gave me a little shiver.

"You guys doing anything fun tonight?" I turned at the sound of the slightly slurred sentence.

"Hey, Louis," I said, smiling up at my disheveled friend. "How are you?"

The question was all he needed. Louis plopped into the chair next to Courtney and set his drink down with an equally jarring thud, causing it to slosh onto the table. His short red hair stuck out in several directions. "I'm bored as fuck."

"And drunk," Courtney said quietly to me. I nodded.

"You guys wanna…you guys wanna…you wanna go somewhere?"

"I don't think so," I told him. "You doing okay, Lou? I'm worried about you."

He raised his gaze, abandoning his intense study of the swirling pattern in the knotted wood of the table. "I've had better moments, but you gotta take 'em as they come. Life has never been, you know, easy."

"What's been the problem?" Courtney asked delicately. "Can we help? We're your friends."

"We're worried about you."

He stared at me, as if translating what I said before responding. "Nothing ever works out for me. S'all." I'd watched him spiral over the course of the year, and my concern was that he hadn't seemed to rebound. At all. It had started with Berta marrying Travis, but alcohol was definitely accelerating the situation, like gasoline on an already burning fire. I hated what was happening to him.

"Everything okay over here?" Clay asked.

"My boss," Louis said, and pointed sadly at Clay. "That guy doesn't like me, like, at all."

"I like you fine, buddy," Clay said, patting his shoulder. "You need a ride home?"

"We can take him," Courtney said, and looked to me. "Right?"

"Yeah, we got it, Clay." By the time we settled up, Louis's eyes drooped. Keeping him awake on the ride home was a losing battle. Courtney sat in the backseat with him and kept him company, which seemed to cheer the guy up a bit. He seemed lonely. We made it to the apartment I knew he rented. I got his front door open via the keys he'd surrendered, then Courtney walked him in.

"There you go, Louis," she said, depositing him onto his bed. "Drink this water." He accepted the fresh bottle from her and chugged it down. "We're gonna let you take it from here. Get some rest, okay? We'll check on you tomorrow."

"Oh, this is nice," he said, snuggling into his bed. Once he systematically began taking off all of his clothes, we snuck out.

"You were really good with him," I said as we descended the steps in front of the building.

"Yeah, well, I have the caretaker thing down pat." She looked more than a little weary, and I remembered her mother and the depression she struggled with.

"Come here. You've had a rough day." I opened my arms and she moved into them, crushing herself against me. "Want to go to my place and lie on the couch and do nothing?"

"If I go to your house, you know we'll do way more than nothing."

"We could have ice cream and try."

She stepped back. "As tempting as that is, I think I just need some alone time tonight. Is that okay?"

"Of course." She kissed me and headed to the car, looking like the weight of the world rested squarely on her shoulders. My heart clenched as I drove her home in silence.

"Are you going to be okay?" I asked her, when we arrived back at her house.

She placed a hand on my cheek. "If I have you, Maggie, I will always be okay."

"Well, that's a promise I can make you," I said, and covered her hand with mine.

"Good night, Maggie. I love you," she said and placed a tender kiss on my lips.

I smiled at her. "I love you, too."

She climbed out of the car, and just before closing the door, she paused and looked back at me. "Do you ever think back to that first day? To Abraham Lincoln?"

I laughed. "I do, actually."

"My life was never the same. From that moment forward, you've made everything better. Brighter. I'm very lucky."

I looked up at her. "Nope. That's my line." And because I just didn't want to say good-bye, "You sure you don't want to come home with me?"

She laughed. "Not at all sure. Good night, Margaret Beringer. I will see you tomorrow."

❖

Boxes stacked, and ready to ship? Check. Suitcase packed for the short term? Check. Last-minute admission to DePaul University? Barely. Transfer of all my credits? Not exactly, but we'd work that out.

With three days left before Courtney and I were set to head to the Windy City, I slipped into a simple black cocktail dress and checked my reflection in the mirror. I lifted my hair away from my face and then let it drop again, deciding to go with it down tonight. I added the Northern Star necklace that my mother had given me for Christmas and struggled with the fastener.

I was looking forward to tonight. My parents were taking us all out to Gardell's as a farewell meal. I realized regretfully that this might be the last time I saw my family all together before we left.

"Hey, there, beautiful girl. You have that faraway look in your eye," Courtney said from the doorway of the cottage. I turned and grinned at what I saw. She radiated, wearing a blue dress that was surely from a well-known designer I'd never be able to name but would bet a million dollars she could.

"And you are gorgeous," I said back.

"Thank you. But I'm afraid we have to make eyes at each other later. We're already late."

"Right behind you, just as soon as I get this necklace—there. All set." I followed Courtney onto the porch.

"I just came from the big house. Your parents and Berta are ready. We're just waiting on you and Travis."

I raised an eyebrow, realizing now with Travis also being MIA, we had a moment. I grabbed her hand and gave it a little tug. She looked too good to resist in that dress. "I hear it's fashionable to make people wait." I stole the kiss I'd been longing for, and our lips lingered for an extra perfect moment or two.

"It is," she whispered. "Unless they're your really nice future in-laws."

I shook my head. "There you go with the early proposing again."

"I'm a determined woman." She kissed me soundly. "I told you I'm going to marry you, and I am. But first, dinner."

"Fine," I said in mock exasperation. "We can go out for a fancy dinner."

We drove the short distance to the big house and found Berta waiting out front with Timothy. She shrugged at us apologetically. "I don't know where Travis is. He was supposed to meet me here twenty minutes ago. I apologize on his behalf."

"Boys are trouble," Clay said, and scooped Timothy from her arms. He wore a sport coat and tie, and I had to admit, my brother cleaned up nicely. I snapped a photo of him and Timothy. "Want me to see if I can rustle him up? I saw him near the barn an hour ago. Might have lost track of time."

Berta smiled. "If you don't mind, Clay, that'd be great."

It was a nice night out and my parents joined us in front of the house. We laid down a blanket in the grass for Timothy and watched as he attempted to demonstrate his ability to roll over. I took a million photos because everyone was dressed up and looking sharp. That's when we heard the yelling. It was one voice at first, and then several. My father took off in the direction of the barn. I was hot on his heels until he turned back to me.

"Stay here."

"No, I'm coming with you."

"Did you hear what I said?" He turned back and pointed authoritatively, his voice loud. "Stay put. I mean that." It went against every instinct I had, but he was my father and the final word at Beringer's, so I stayed. I looked back at my mother and then Berta, who had lost most of the color from her face.

"I have a bad feeling," she said to me quietly. "A very, very bad feeling."

"I'm sure it's fine. Dad will help, whatever it is." There were still sounds of a commotion, but the voices were so far away it was impossible to make out the words.

Berta shook her head. "No. Something's definitely wrong. Look." She held up her arm, displaying the goose bumps that had formed.

Then the yelling stopped. All of it.

An eerie silence emerged, and it felt like time ticked along at an excruciating pace as we waited for some kind of information. It must have been five minutes. Then seven. When we heard the sound of a siren in the distance, my blood went cold. I exchanged a worried look with my mother, who stood with her hands on Berta's shoulders. When it grew louder and then louder, I knew it was headed our way.

"Travis," Berta whispered. I took her hand and she gripped it with everything she had. Courtney put an arm around her. My mother took the baby. I couldn't stand it anymore. We needed to know.

"Mom?"

She nodded at me. "Go."

By the time I reached the barn, there was no sign of anyone. The big doors had been slid open, but the dusty structure stood uncharacteristically empty. I ran around to the back, and that's when I saw a cluster of people, and the ambulance approach from the perimeter street. It cut across the field and stopped near a ditch. That's when I saw it, my breath catching in my throat. An overturned tractor, one wheel exposed from the ditch. My father stood with both hands in his hair. Louis was there. His eyes were bleary and he was apologizing over and over again as he staggered from person to person. I tried to piece together what had happened, but it was like my brain was two steps behind. Louis made a beeline for me when he saw me there. His shirt was torn and there was blood coming from his nose. "Maggie, I just wanted to take it for a drive. They never let me."

I seized the chance for clarity and grabbed Louis by the arms. "What happened?"

"He tried to pull me off, but I fought him."

"Travis wouldn't let you drive the tractor?"

He nodded. "I should have listened to him. I didn't know what I was doing and then it flipped over, so I got out." He continued to ramble, no longer making much sense. I turned to my father.

"Dad?" I asked. "Dad, what is it?" But he stood there wordlessly, staring at the ditch, his eyes haunted like nothing I'd ever seen. "Dad, is Travis okay? Do we know?" Two of the paramedics jumped into the ditch. My father turned to me as if not expecting to see me there but said nothing, turning back to them, walking to the ditch. I felt a hand on my shoulder and I turned to see Travis looking down at me, which had me confused at first and finally flooded with relief. "Oh, thank God. Thank *God*." He wrapped his arms around me tight.

"I'm sorry, Maggie."

"Why? Why are you sorry?" I glanced around. "Travis?"

Travis shook his head, choked up now. "He was just trying to stop Louis from hurting himself."

"He who?" I asked. I whirled around in the direction of the tractor, and I knew. The world came to a stop and all sound drained from the movie playing in front of me. It had to be a movie because this wasn't real. I couldn't have moved if I'd wanted to, my body now completely paralyzed with abject fear. *Please don't let it be.* In that moment, I knew for certain who had gone down with that tractor, and I knew that from this moment on my life would never be the same again. While I'd held out hope that Travis was going to be okay, I understood in my heart that Clay, my big brother and best friend, would not be.

I was screaming, or trying to, but no sound left my throat. I watched the workers assessing the scene. I watched someone pull Louis away and sit him down. I thought of my mother and watched as my father was physically pulled away from the edge of the ditch by a police officer. But it all happened as if I were underwater. Until, that is, it all came rushing to the surface and the guttural, bone-chilling scream filled my ears. It was mine. I screamed until my throat was raw, until I had nothing left in me. I fisted the dirt, clenching it in my hands as I continued to scream and scream and scream until all was quiet.

I'd taken a photo of him just minutes before.

Just minutes.

CHAPTER FOURTEEN

Sometimes you just go through the motions. You have to because they're the only part of your life you recognize.

I did that. Was still doing it.

It had been two weeks since the funeral when I decided to sit on the front steps of my cottage. Up until that point, I avoided looking out over the farm for any longer than it took to travel to and from the cottage. The farm made me think of Clay and how much he loved it, and when I did that, it was hard to come back.

Today felt different.

Today, I needed the farm.

The rain that hit shortly after Clay's death had finally stopped after a never-ending string of pretty intense downpours. It was as if the Earth knew, and mourned his loss right along with the rest of us.

But the sun broke through that September morning and beckoned me out of the house. I padded barefoot with my coffee out onto the front step and just stared. The feelings, the opinions, the hopes, and dreams I had always carried inside me were noticeably absent now. In their place was a hollowed-out numbness. A void. I took in the expanse of the land all around me, the plants that would soon hold the robust fall fruit. It didn't seem possible without Clay. It somehow was.

The air was cold all around me, but then I wore only a T-shirt and running shorts. I couldn't have cared less about the uncomfortable chill.

I didn't care about anything.

Courtney was back in Chicago. She'd stayed in town an extra three weeks. She'd tried her best to be there for me. I just wanted space.

From everyone. And really, what could she have done to help? Nothing would bring my brother back at this point. There was no rewind button. So when it was time for her semester to begin, I told her to go. I thought the time on my own might help.

"I don't want to leave you," she said and ran her finger across my temple, then tucked a strand of hair behind my ear. "I'm going to take the semester off. I think that's the best decision. I can work at the store here."

"Honestly? That sounds like a horrible idea. What are you going to do? Sit around and watch me try and exist? I don't want you here for that."

She looked crushed. "I feel helpless. I don't know what to do for you. I'm so, so sorry, Maggie."

I nodded. "I know. The one thing you can do for me is go back for the fall semester. Give me some time on my own, okay?"

Her eyes were sad. There was nothing I could do about that. "If that's what you want."

"It is."

Needless to say, I didn't go back to Chicago with her. My parents needed me and I needed them. I couldn't imagine being anywhere else. Plus, there was a lot that had to be done. So while Courtney didn't take the semester off, I did. With the breakthrough of sunshine that morning came a breakthrough in my resolve. New plan. I'd take up the slack on the farm. Keep myself busy. Jump in and help any way and every way I could. I'd work until my brain and my body were so worn down that I'd fall into bed each night and drift away without a moment to think or feel or remember.

It was a good plan.

It worked for a while.

Thanksgiving came and went with little fanfare. Thank God for Timothy, who gave us all something to focus on instead of what was so obviously missing. My mother ended the day in tears and my father in silence, sitting in his chair, staring at the wall.

I was beginning to understand that things weren't getting better or easier or simpler. Instead, we were all fractured humans struggling to hold it together on our own, when in fact, maybe we should have been helping to prop each other up. With Christmas looming, Courtney returned to Tanner Peak and brought with her a sense of lightness that I so desperately needed, but I still kept her at arm's length, where I kept everyone.

She wore a Santa hat and carried an armful of presents when she arrived at the big house her first night back. I'd heard her enter and walked from the kitchen where I'd been putting the finishing touches on the garlic mashed potatoes for the dinner we would share with my parents.

"It smells amazing in here," she said to my mom, who pulled her tight and held on. She released Courtney but kept her hands on her shoulders, marveling.

"Look at you. More beautiful than the last time I laid eyes on you."

"You doing okay?" Courtney asked.

She nodded, the light dimming from her eyes. "I hope to get back to writing soon. Occupy my thoughts more."

"I think that's a fantastic idea."

Courtney turned and saw me standing in the doorway. She didn't say a word. She didn't have to. I moved into her arms and closed my eyes at the safety and warmth they provided, even if I knew the feeling was temporary. I'd missed her more than I'd even realized. The warm scent of vanilla took me back to simpler times, and the tears hit fast and hard at the memory.

"No crying," she whispered, though tears now pooled in her own eyes. My mother stepped away to give us a moment alone. "So hey, you," Courtney said, and wiped my tears away with her thumbs. "And what's the deal with dodging all my calls, huh? You're too important for me now? Too busy?"

The truth was that I hadn't been up for talking much and I'd dodged the world, not just Courtney. "I'm sorry. It's been really rough lately. I haven't been on my phone much."

She smiled. "It's okay. I understand. But I'm here now, and it will be so much harder to ignore the live and in person version," she said adjusting her Santa cap as if reporting for duty.

How was she able to still make me smile? I didn't think it was possible, but I did just that. "I'm glad you're here."

"Good, because I need to kiss you."

I sank into warm and wonderful and tried to remind myself what life *could* be like if I could just figure out how to let it. It was a tall order. Courtney was caring, and sophisticated, and funny, and stylish, and wonderful, and that made her seem a million miles away from where I was.

But I decided to try and let her in. *Just try.*

Over the next few weeks, however, it proved harder to reach right out and grab her, to ask for what I needed. Our nights together, while familiar and comfortable, didn't come with a ton of conversation like they used to. My fault. I caught her watching me a lot, making sure I was okay. It was equal parts endearing and unnerving, as I felt like I was falling short. Sex was a welcome distraction that I clung to, as it allowed me to pretend that everything between us was as it always had been, when how could that be the case?

"Hey, Maggie?" she asked one night as we lay in bed, my back to her. "You awake?"

I turned. "What's up?"

"I just wanted to tell you about something that happened at the store tonight."

"I'm kind of tired. Can you tell me later?"

She nodded and stared at the ceiling. "Sure."

I turned back to the wall. The sound of the clock was my only comfort. That sound meant that life was moving forward. One day, maybe I'd be able to jump back on.

Tick. Tock. Tick. Tock. Tick. Tock.

I drifted off clinging to its predictable melody.

CHAPTER FIFTEEN

The fifth summer

The month of May brought with it the promise of an unusually hot summer. Forecasts had me worried and wondering how much of our crop we'd be losing to the toxic hot and arid temperatures. In response to the forecast, my father had invested in the latest technology, a motorized tractor that would expedite the summer harvest and take the pickers off their feet, eliminating exhaustion and a great deal of missed berries.

After a long day, I'd just finished taking my nightly shower and fell into an exhausted heap on the bed. Courtney had been back for the summer for only a few days, and we hadn't really been afforded much time together. I threw most of my time into the farm, which left us the evenings. I watched from the bed as she riffled through my dresser for a T-shirt of mine to sleep in, which had long become her tradition.

"So you're telling me that this tractor is going to drive twelve people, who will all lie on their stomachs and pick strawberries? I'm trying to picture it."

I shifted onto my back. "Think luxury strawberry picking. It's supposed to really cut down on worker fatigue." I watched as she unbuttoned her shirt and laid it out on the dresser. I never tired of the way Courtney looked in a bra, especially this particular red and black one. It was my kryptonite.

"Well, let's hope." Now the bra was gone and my eyes feasted as she pulled my blue and white tie-dye shirt over her head. "Are you too tired?" she asked, crawling across the bed and settling on top of me.

My hands were immediately under her shirt and on her breasts. She chuckled low. "Is that a no?"

"I'm sorry, were you speaking?"

"God, I miss your hands on me when we're apart."

"Me too," I murmured, pulling her down for a kiss I knew wouldn't end there. We'd been away from each other too long. In fact, our relationship had never been without these continuous separations. I hated them as much as Courtney did but at the same time couldn't quite comprehend leaving Tanner Peak after everything that had happened. My sense of adventure had dimmed considerably, and I couldn't fathom leaving behind everything I knew. I needed the familiarity and clung to it.

She killed the lamp next to my bed. "Have you talked to DePaul about enrolling for the fall semester? They know you're accepting this time, right?"

I hesitated, as I had not quite pulled the trigger on that one. Instead, I employed my go-to stalling tactic. "It's on my to-do list."

She sighed at my answer and pulled her lips from my neck. I couldn't fully make out her features in the darkened room, but I had a pretty good concept of what the disappointment looked like. "You said that four weeks ago. And the month before that."

I removed my hands beneath her shirt and turned my face to the side, taking a moment for myself. I didn't know what to say, how to say it. At my silence, Courtney slipped off me and turned the lamp on.

"Can we take a minute to go over the plan, please? I know you've had a horrific time, and I didn't expect you to leave behind your home, but it's been a year. I just need to know that this is going somewhere, just some sort of indication that we will take that next step forward, that I'm not some summer fling on repeat year after year."

I bristled at the characterization, annoyed she would even go there. "Don't say that. You know you're not."

"But that's the thing. I don't, Maggie. That's what I'm trying to articulate to you. I have this whole other life. Friends, my job, school, and I hate that you're not a part of it, and it kills me that you show no interest in wanting to be."

I didn't know where the anger came from, but it flashed hot and instant. "Oh, you mean *that* life. The one with Heather and Nathan and Bryn and all the other Northwestern upper crusts? I know how important they are to you." My tone was patronizing, but I couldn't seem to stop now. "As are the wine-and-cheeses you attend like it's your job. I just have trouble getting excited about that kind of thing, okay?" I heard how it sounded out loud and didn't recognize myself, but this version of me just didn't care.

The light dimmed in her eyes noticeably, but she maintained control. "Those are my friends. Good friends, actually. I would love it if they were your friends one day, too. I'm just starting to understand that maybe that's not what you want anymore. Be straight with me, Maggie. Is it?"

I stared at the floor and let the emptiness of the last year consume me, the darkness descend. My defenses flared and I turned off my feelings, a trick I'd picked up when the pain became too much. "I don't know. Maybe it's not."

"Maybe it's not," Courtney repeated blandly, and when I raised my gaze, it looked like she'd been slapped. "You don't know if you want to meet my friends, or you don't know about you and me?"

I shrugged, barely giving her anything, but it felt like I had nothing to give. The well was empty, and it was all I could do to keep myself together, much less hang on to another person who was asking for so much.

"You lost Clay, Maggie, and it's awful and I am so sorry, but don't lose yourself, too. Don't forget who you are and what you once wanted out of life. Remember your real estate license? Your plans? Us? You can still do all of that. But you're so damn focused on the day-to-day details of this farm now and—"

"And what? What do you want me to say to you, Courtney? That I'm going to leave this place, the only thing that makes me happy, and run away with you to the land of flashy and exciting? I think we both know I'm not going to do that." Hearing her use Clay's name to argue for what she wanted, for the future she envisioned for us, set something off in me. Whether it was fair of me or not, she somehow became the enemy.

"You lost your brother a year ago, and my heart is broken for you. Crushed. If you need more time, tell me. I can live with that, but I just have to know that there is a someday in the not-so-distant future where you'll be ready to take that leap with me."

I didn't say anything.

"Maggie, please. Is there a someday?"

I couldn't answer her.

"So what?" she asked, her eyes searching mine. "I float into town every few months and we have sex and—"

"Apparently you leave again. It's what always happens, and we've been fine."

She stared at the ground for a moment, compiling her thoughts. "Yeah, well, I'm afraid that's not enough for me anymore. I need to know that I mean more than that." She shook her head in defeat and looked around for her jeans on the floor. She dressed in silence while I stared at the bed, hating what was happening but seeing only one way to stop it.

"Then move here."

"What?"

"If you want this to be something more, move here. We have a store."

She turned to me, her eyes sad. "And work right under my father for the rest of my life? Do you know what you're asking?"

I did know. I shrugged. "You know what? Forget it."

"Maggie."

"Just forget it. All of it."

She was crying now, the tears ran in streams down her cheeks as she shook her head. "The thing is that I would have actually done that for you. I would have."

She finished dressing. From the doorway of my bedroom, she turned back to me. "You know, my whole life I've been perfectly fine not mattering that much in the scheme of things. I was okay with being an afterthought or a detail to sort out. But I needed it to be different with you. I thought it was, and that's on me. I love you, Maggie, which is why my heart just can't do this anymore. I want nothing but good things for you, but it's clear that's not me. So I'll go."

I didn't say anything but closed my eyes so I wouldn't have to see her leave. I didn't want to have to live with that image. I pulled the covers tight around me so I would have something to grip when I heard her tires against the gravel. When I was alone and enveloped in the silence, I cried. The world that once felt like my own happy playground was now a vastly different and very scary place.

Courtney came with way too much to be afraid of.

❖

With May turning to June and June to July, summer slid into its prime, and Tanner Peak blossomed to life. People were outside more, spending time with their neighbors and soaking up the sunny days. There were car washes, baseball games, and cookouts. Peak of Berries had come and gone, bringing in record numbers this year.

Yet I'd never felt more alone in my entire life.

"Louis called last night," Berta said, toeing the water in the creek. Travis had agreed to watch Timothy so Berta and I could steal a little one-on-one time. But at the mention of Louis's name, I went still from my spot along the bank. I didn't hate Louis, I had come to realize after a long bout of soul searching. What he did had not come from a place of malice. At the same time, it was still incredibly hard to think about him without thinking about the accident. About Clay. Berta, on the other hand, had gone out of her way to reach out to Louis and had been a steadfast friend. She'd always been a better person than I was.

"And how is he?" I heard myself ask. I only allowed myself to be partially present for these kinds of conversations, the goal being self-preservation.

"He sounds more like himself than he has in a while. He's been out of treatment for a few months now, and mentioned maybe coming to town for a visit." She was gauging my reaction, that much I knew.

"Oh, yeah?" While I wasn't jumping at the chance to see him again, it wasn't like I could keep the guy out. He'd not been charged. There was no law that he couldn't come back to town.

"Yeah." Berta studied me as a cool breeze hit and lifted my hair. "You can be honest with me, you know."

"What am I supposed to say, Berta? It's a free country." What happened had been a horrific accident of the worst kind. I knew that in my heart. But at the same time I understood that none of it would have happened if Louis hadn't behaved recklessly. How was I supposed to reconcile those two things?

Berta raised her arm. "You're supposed to say 'Hell no, I don't want to see that guy,' or 'You know what? It might be therapeutic to actually have a conversation with him.' Whatever it is you feel. There's no wrong answer here."

I shook my head because she was wrong. "There's always a wrong answer."

She turned to me in exasperation. "Maggie, I'm lost here. I'm trying to be your friend, but I don't know how to pull you back from wherever it is you've gone."

"I'll be fine. I don't need to be pulled back." I hopped in the creek and lost myself in the feel of the cool water, sinking in up to my chin. Unfortunately, Berta wasn't done.

"Courtney went back to Chicago and none of us understand why. You've barely said two words on the topic, and everyone's worried about you."

"She's in Chicago because that's apparently where she would rather be."

"And that's okay with you?" she asked in disbelief. "Since when?"

I didn't have the words to explain that I felt in control of very little and was held together by a string at this point. I gave it a shot anyway. "It's not okay with me, but I don't know what else to do anymore, Berta. I didn't have it in me to fight. We want different things, and I can't be who she needs me to be anymore."

She shook her head, not comprehending. "So that's it. You've just thrown in the towel on someone you love?"

I winced internally and realized I couldn't shut everything off. "Yep."

"That's horrible."

I nodded numbly. "I think that's my line."

"Well, why aren't you saying it, then?" Berta asked, practically yelling. "Who are you? Why aren't you feeling *anything*?"

I turned in the water, and faced her. Raw. Exposed. Feeling more than she realized and more than I wanted to. "You know what I think? I think Louis should definitely visit regardless of the pain he's caused everyone. I think Courtney was right to go back to Chicago. I think that everybody should do whatever the hell it is that they want to do and leave me alone. And you know what else? It turns out I'm not really in the mood for a swim after all."

I hopped out of the water, gathered my things, and stalked away home. I'd let my warring emotions fight it out without me and notify me later of what they decided. I was taking the rest of the damn day off.

Two weeks later, I sat with my father in his office, which was surrounded by the large cooling tanks that would keep the strawberries cold and fresh until the trucks arrived to haul them off into the world. We'd watched as the crew transferred a new portion of the summer crops into the tanks by the thousands just an hour before. With the place now cleared out, we stole a moment to down our sandwiches across from each other at his desk.

As I unpacked my brown bag lunch, my father did what he always did at precisely noon: cut his tomato on wheat sandwich in half with his pocketknife. He always had been a creature of habit, and I found comfort in that kind of dependability. We ate in silence for a few moments, the comfortable kind. Finally, he looked over at me. "Got folks around here talking about you, ya know. Concerned."

"You get that impression, too?" I attempted a laugh. I don't think it landed.

He shrugged. "Well, I'm not worried."

I looked up at him. "That's refreshing."

He pressed on casually. "You're too smart a kid to throw your life away, watch it circle the toilet like a used tissue."

"Geez, Dad. That's some potent imagery."

"Well, it's true. I was blessed with two great kids. One who was led around this world by his heart and another who was smarter and wiser than I thought possible for her years. But you know what I also found out? She was a lot like her brother, too."

I was touched by the sentiment and took a moment to gather my thoughts. "It's been a year now."

He nodded.

"I often ask myself what Clay would do when I find myself in a tough spot. Sometimes I know the answer, but sometimes I have no clue. Those are the times that are the hardest." I swallowed. "When I don't know."

"That makes a lot of sense," he said. "He was your big brother. I wonder what he would think about what we're all doing now. If he would want us to stop living the way you have."

"I haven't stopped living."

He shrugged. "You walked away from all your big plans for yourself. Lost your girlfriend."

"Logistically, it wasn't working out between Courtney and me."

He looked at me like I'd just laid an egg. "Logistically? You're gonna have to decode that one for your old dad, because you two got on like white on rice. She made you smile."

"Okay." I stared at the ceiling, blew out a breath, and tried to explain. "This is the thing. She wants Chicago and Carrington's Corporate and I want Tanner Peak and the life I have going here."

"And what life would that be?" he asked.

"Ouch. The farm. You and Mom. This town."

"Listen, to me, Scrap." I felt the lump in my throat at the use of the nickname. "You love the farm, but it was never your dream, what you'd envisioned for yourself."

"Maybe it is now."

"Because we lost your brother? That's your way of feeling close to him, sure, but don't trade in your life for his."

"It's so far away," I said of Chicago, the fear rising in me again.

"It is far. But you think I wouldn't have followed your mother to the ends of the Earth? Of course I would have. I love that gal of mine." He looked at me long and hard. "We're all wounded here, Margaret, and we're all paying a very steep price."

"I know."

"I just don't want yours to be any bigger than it has to be." With that, he stood, slowly collected the trash from his lunch, and exited the office.

Rattled.

That's how I felt.

I sat there for a long while as the words he'd just imparted chiseled away at the barriers I'd erected between myself and the rest of the world, rocking what I thought I knew and making me question my choices all over again. My dad had a way of getting through to me, and as a result my throat was tight, my stomach felt weak, and regret washed over me in a horrifying chill.

Because what if he was right?

Days turned into weeks, and in that time, the truth gradually revealed itself to me. I missed Courtney. I missed our late-night conversations and our teasing. I missed the subtle touches when we were in public, and the intimate ones when it was just the two of us. I missed her laugh, and her wonderful cookie scent, and her unmatched ambition that I admired no end. I missed making love to her and kissing her and telling her how much I loved her, because I did love her. There wasn't a world where I could not.

But it had been months since she'd left my cottage, and I'd hurt her badly. I reflected back on the shock of pain in her eyes and the finality of the click when she'd closed the front door. She'd called me once a few weeks later. I hadn't picked up and she hadn't left a message.

I knew now what I wanted.

As time marched on, I gathered my courage and began to make a plan, one building block at a time. I wasn't sure how to undo the damage I'd done to our relationship, but I had to try. A phone call felt cheap. Actions spoke louder than words, I decided.

I booked a ticket to Chicago, needing to talk to her face-to-face. To find the right words to let her know how wrong I'd been and how much I valued our relationship, how much I valued *her*, no matter what I'd said months before. I was prepared to move to Chicago and had already begun taking steps in that direction. The more I planned, the more the fear turned to excitement. To my amazement, I was able to recapture the enthusiasm I'd felt just over a year ago. The smile that took up residence on my face was authentic and frequent. And while it's strange to say, I felt like my brother was with me, ushering me along on this new adventure, and that was everything.

As I wasn't sure exactly how long I'd be in Chicago, I grabbed several extra outfits and went about organizing them into my suitcase as "Ticket to Ride" appropriately blared from the speaker in my bedroom.

Through it all, I heard my cottage door open after a very brief knock. I peered down the hallway to the living room and smiled at Berta. "Hey, you. Wanna help me pack?"

Since she didn't answer, I killed the music, deciding to take a break and chat for a bit. Berta didn't get a ton of time without a toddler tugging on her for something, and I tried to make myself available when it happened. I joined her in the living room and plopped down on the couch, a little winded from my busy morning. She studied me. I made a lighthearted show of studying her back. "You're being weird," I finally said. "What's going on?"

She took a deep inhale and covered her eyes. "I have to show you something and I don't want to. God, I *really* don't want to."

My curiosity piqued, I crossed to her. She held out a copy of that morning's paper folded in half. I took it from her and read the headline out loud. "Tanner Peak Fire Chief to Retire." Berta took the newspaper from me and flipped it over, revealing the secondary headline below the fold.

Hometown Department Store Heiress Elopes with Senator's Son

Sometimes shock camouflages pain.

Not this time.

My heart moved into my throat. It felt like my stomach filled with ice water. Displayed beneath the headline was a photo of Courtney in a modest white suit, a bouquet hanging at her side, kissing Nathan, her friend from school. I carried the paper to the couch and took a seat, scanning the details of the article for explanation. It was short and to the point. Courtney Carrington had married Nathan Vaughan before a justice of the peace in Nantucket, Vaughan's hometown. The couple would honeymoon in Niagara Falls.

I played that part back. *They would honeymoon.*

I set the paper down and felt sick, my body revolting against what I'd just learned. My instincts told me to shake it off and finish packing, but then there was nothing to pack for anymore, was there?

Instead, I just sat there, staring.

"Maggie, I'm so sorry," Berta said, her tone stricken.

"Yeah, me too." I scratched my head and gazed at the floor, trying to decipher it all, attempting to connect the dots in a world I no longer understood.

Berta snatched the paper from me in disgust. "You know who made sure the paper covered this particular story? I could kill that guy." Of course I knew. Mitch Carrington couldn't wait for me to find out that Courtney was off the market and married to a senator's son, no less. It had to be like his own personal Christmas morning. He was probably patting himself on the back as we sat there.

Honestly, I didn't care about any of that. "It doesn't matter where it came from," I told Berta. "All he did was report the facts."

Who I more than cared about, however, was Courtney. I didn't understand how she could do something like this. We didn't work out, so she ran off and married Nathan What's-his-name? Just like that?

"You know what? What do you say you and I go stuff our faces with ice cream and count all the ways you're going to be better off?"

I glanced up briefly. "I think I'm going to just stay here, if that's okay."

She sat next to me on the couch. "Fine. Then I'll sit here with you." She placed her hand on top of mine, and that's what we did. We sat for what felt like forever. One at a time, each emotion took its turn with me. Sadness, regret, anger, sense of betrayal, and finally desolation. I felt it all and let it all wash over me in an overwhelming tidal wave.

The smile was gone and so was the girl I loved.

I was drowning and didn't know how to get air.

CHAPTER SIXTEEN

Now

It was after six, and I sat behind my desk in my office with Berta and Melanie, who'd walked over from the salon. The space was petite and consisted of a small lobby that led into the singular office I used to meet with clients.

Of course, Berta had updated Melanie on just who we'd run into in the square. The two of them were vibrating with questions. Luckily, they'd come with a bottle of wine and three glasses. I added my secret stash of old-fashioned peanut butter cookies to the cause.

"So how'd she look?" Melanie asked, kick-starting the conversation. I resisted an eye roll while Berta considered the question.

"Beyond good. The years have been kind to Courtney." I passed Berta a look that said *really?* and she held up her hands in defense. "Are you saying you disagree?"

"No." I turned to Melanie. "She looked great. There. See? I can say it."

"But so do you," Berta said.

Melanie nodded. "You know me. I'm rarely nice, but Berta's right. You've grown up to be a knockout."

"Thank you," I said, sitting a little taller. I'd needed that. "It's not like I wanted her to look horrible, but it couldn't have hurt."

"Right?" Melanie tore off a hunk of cookie. "And you all haven't seen each other or spoken in—"

"Over five years," I supplied.

"Wow," she said, and sat back in her chair. "*Wow.*"

"It's not that big a deal," I said, waving off the concept with a flick of my wrist. "A lot of time has gone by. Water under the bridge, you know? Courtney and I are both adults."

"Who used to be in mad, passionate love," Berta pointed out. "She's not wearing a wedding ring, by the way."

I'd noticed that, too, but was not about to point it out. "Some people choose not to wear them."

"When they're divorced," Melanie said.

I shot her a look and she shrugged.

"What? I Googled them, okay? If you want to know the backstory, she dropped the name Vaughan three and a half years ago."

Well, this was new information, not that it mattered. While I also had easy access to Google, Courtney was on the "no fly" list as far as my thoughts went. Now that she was back, it shouldn't be a big deal to make the adjustment. If I had to see her occasionally, I could be an adult. I'd just keep our time together short and polite.

"I wonder where she's staying while she's here," Berta said, sipping her wine.

"Facebook says she's at Sugarberries B-and-B for the time being."

This time I did roll my eyes. "Is this a town Facebook page or the *Tanner Peak Enquirer*? I see no reason why our every move is reported online for the masses to consume."

"To be fair," Melanie said, "it's kind of fun to know everyone's business."

Berta patted her shoulder. "Says one of their top content providers."

"What can I say?" Melanie said unabashedly. "People get chatty in the salon."

"Oh, I can attest to that," Berta said, nodding. She'd taken over ownership of the salon, and business had practically doubled since. "I've found that folks tend to really open up when they're trusting you with something as critical as their hair. But we're off topic, and I have to pick up my kids in twenty minutes, so let's get to it."

I looked from Melanie to Berta. "Get to what? You're going to have to be more specific." I flipped absently through my planner, detailing my appointments for the next day.

"What is your plan for maneuvering the situation? For maneuvering Courtney Carrington-minus-the-Vaughan?"

I looked up at them, perplexed. "I'm just going to go about my days normally, you guys. Was it weird running into her? Yes, damn it, and awkward as hell. Is it going to change my world in any way? No. I've moved way beyond Courtney."

"Excellent plan." Melanie folded her hands in her lap and smiled sweetly. "What could possibly go wrong with that?"

After closing up the office for the day, I stopped off at the big house on my way home to pick up Ernie, my three-year-old Weimaraner, named for the great writer himself. While Ernie lived with me at my cottage, he had easily become the tried and true Beringer Strawberry Farm mascot.

He leapt to his feet from his spot on the porch when he saw my car approach and spent the next two minutes peppering me with sloppy dog kisses as I asked him about his day. He'd become a favorite around the farm, sunning himself between the rows of plants on good weather days or following Travis around the barn when it rained. He had the prettiest blue eyes that, I swear, communicated his every emotion with unexpected accuracy. Ernie was a soulful boy, and I was lucky he was mine.

"What do you think, pal? Should we go home and rustle up dinner for the both of us? Binge-watch something dramatic on Netflix and discuss it in detail?"

His response was a swipe of his tongue across my hand. Because I couldn't resist, I scratched behind his ears and watched him drift to his own personal heaven, inclining his head to get even closer to my hand.

"He stole three slices of roast beef off your father's plate tonight." I looked up to see my mother standing in the doorway, an amused grin on her face. "I smiled, but your father was not impressed."

"Tell Dad I'm sorry about that, and I'll have a long talk with Ernie when we get home." My dog had always been a bit of a food whore, stealing from anywhere and everywhere he could. He'd stolen more hot dogs on their way to my mouth than I cared to count. To his credit, he had the decency to look sorrowful in the aftermath, but it didn't stop the thieving lug from making his move in the first place.

"You want to come in for a slice of your father's flawless flourless fudge cake?"

"There are a lot of Fs in that sentence."

She fluffed her hair. "Well, I *am* a writer."

"As tempting as that alliterated offer is, I'm going to pass. Too many showings today to count, and I'm exhausted."

"And you also ran into Courtney, which must have been a bit of a jolt."

I paused. "How did you—" But I didn't have to ask. The stupid Facebook page had seriously outdone itself of late. "I ran into her in the square. We said hello."

"Your father invited her to the farm. He's always had a bit of a soft spot for her. I guess both of us do."

"Well, that makes two out of three." I winced, because I wasn't supposed to care anymore, and hostility meant caring. I had forgotten the stupid plan already. "I'll talk to you tomorrow. Let's go, Ern. Night, Mom."

"You okay, Margaret?"

I turned back a little exasperated. "I'm fine. Why does everyone think I'm some breakable little china doll?"

"We just love you is all."

"Well, I appreciate that, but all is good. See?" I pointed to my face and offered my most winsome smile.

"I do see. Good night, Margaret."

❖

"Ms. Beringer," eighty-two-year-old Mr. Noriander began from his spot across from my desk.

I smiled and held up a hand. "You can call me Maggie, remember?"

"Yes, I do." He nodded and began again. "Ms. Beringer, I know you've been keeping an eye out for hot little places for me to scoop up, but I was wondering if you've seen any houses around here with a red door?"

As I quickly gathered my paperwork for my ten a.m. closing, I squinted back at Mr. Noriander. It had already been a hell of a morning. I'd overslept, kicked over the dog's water, torn my pants on a loose screw on the beam of my porch (hence the fantastic, but uncharacteristic skirt now in its place), and now I was late and losing more ground, as my most talkative client had chosen this very morning to discuss his real estate prospects. I liked Mr. Noriander and his rounded little old-man-face, but I so did not have time for him.

"A red door? No. Nothing comes to mind." My folder slipped from my grasp, and documents flew. Perfect. "Why a red door?"

He leaned down to help me reassemble my pages. "I read on the Yahoo internet that red doors were back in style, so I thought I should pick me up some."

"I had not heard that," I told him. "But go you for being in the know. Have you thought about maybe just painting the door on whatever house you fall in love with?"

A lightbulb seemed to appear over his shiny, bald head, and he held up a finger. "Brilliant!"

"It is rather ingenious," said a familiar voice from behind me.

I turned in surprise. Courtney stood in the doorway, attaché in hand. Her hair was up today, some kind of twist I would never have known how to execute.

Mr. Noriander pointed at me in full-on testimonial. "She's a smart one, Ms. Beringer is. You'd do right to hire her." He stood and turned to go. "Let me know if you find that red door, Ms. Beringer. Or a good one to paint. I'll get out of your way and wait to hear from you."

"Will do," I said weakly and waved as he exited.

"Ms. Beringer," Courtney said, borrowing the name. "I hope this isn't an inconvenient time."

I stood. My documents were now completely out of order, but at least they were back in the stack. "I thought we'd decided I'd let you know about that coffee. Busy, remember?" I focused on my desk, trying desperately to remember which things I needed to take with me for this appointment, but now my brain didn't seem to be working. I was rattled.

"I'm not here about the coffee," she said simply.

"Oh? I thought you were—because yesterday—you know what?" I made a gesture as if to erase it all. "Never mind. What are you here for, then?" It sounded rude and I hadn't meant it to. Okay, maybe I did a little.

Regardless, Courtney seemed unfazed. "Funnily enough, I need a Realtor."

"For what?"

She paused and suppressed a grin. "For real estate. I'm staying at the bed-and-breakfast, but it's temporary. I'd much rather a rental."

I scratched my cheek. "What are we talking? A week? A couple weeks? Have you tried Airbnb? I can give you their website." I reached for a sticky note.

"A few months, at least. Furnished would be ideal, but if not I can arrange for furnishing."

I swallowed. It was one thing to put up with Courtney sightings for a handful of days, it was quite another for an extended sentence. "I'm kind of swamped right now, though…is the thing. You might talk to Patterson's Realty in the, uh, office building next to the courthouse. First floor."

Courtney scrunched one eye. "Mrs. Patterson is blind as a bat and has horrible taste. We used to make fun of her outrageous outfits."

"Yeah, well, I hear she's killer when it comes to closing a deal, and I'm late." I reached around her, hit the lights, and waited in the hallway to lock up after her.

She met my eyes as she passed. "Somehow I think you know what I like a little better than Mrs. Patterson."

With my hand still on the knob, I let my head drop. "No. See, that right there is why we're not working together." I turned and headed for the parking lot, bristling at the fact that I heard the click-click-click of her heels on the pavement behind me.

"I'm sensing a modicum of hostility, which I certainly understand."

"No, you're not," I said, without looking back. "You're not sensing anything."

"You don't want to take me on as your client because of our… history. You can say it."

Now, that did it. I whirled back to her, car door open and in my hand. "That's laughable. In fact, nothing could be further from the truth. I wish you only the best in life."

"Great. Then when could we check out some houses? I promise to be respectful of your time."

I sighed. I was later than ever and just wanted to be far, far away from this conversation. In response to my frustration, I felt something give way. "Stop by tomorrow morning and we can go over the specifics of what you're looking for."

"I will see you then. Have a good day, Margaret."

I nodded and closed the car door, gripping the steering wheel in frustration until she click-click-clicked away with a gentle sway of her hips. Whether I wanted to admit it to the rest of the world or not, seeing her again was doing a number on my head.

I just had to figure out what in the world to do about it.

❖

One-year-old Ellie smacked my cheeks with her little chubby palms and laughed gleefully when my mouth popped open as a result. She did it again. And again, and again, throwing back her blond head of curls, a genetic gift from Travis. It was her favorite game in all of the world and she never got tired of it, even if my cheeks totally did. I'd agreed to watch little Ellie at my place for Berta and Travis so they could enjoy Tim's T-ball game without the extra added pressure of chasing a toddler around the bleachers or keeping her from building mountains made of dirt.

"Mote," Ellie said, grabbing my remote from the couch next to me.

"That is, in fact, a *remote*," I said. "You are correct. That is the contraption we use to turn on the TV. You are a brilliant child." To demonstrate, I turned on the television and set her on the floor. "Want some dinner? Your mommy says fish sticks are your favorite. Let's have those."

Behind me, the female newscasters brought us the latest headlines. "Police made a key arrest this afternoon, just outside of Santa Barbara. Con man Grant Tranton, wanted in several states for fraud and embezzlement, was taken into custody at a local Pizza Hut."

"Hear that?" I said to Ellie. "Crime doesn't pay. And you lose out on your pizza. You heard it here. Don't make me bail you out of jail in twenty years. Not that I wouldn't." She waved at me in response and I decided she would make a lovable criminal. I tossed a handful of fish sticks onto a cookie sheet and set the oven to preheat.

"Tanner Peak residents welcomed home department store heiress Courtney Carrington, who told us she has big plans for the small town's own branch of the store." I turned to the screen. No way. But there she was, her flawless face flashed across the television in my living room.

"We're excited to strengthen Carrington's connection to this community, the very community where my grandmother still lives."

Courtney smiled at the reporter, and I braced against it. This was the smile she called on for the public, her polite smile. As dazzling as it was, it wasn't the smile that lit up her whole face, the smile I used to live for. "We'll be donating ten percent of every purchase made at the Tanner Peak store this weekend to the building of a new auditorium for the high school."

"The very high school you once attended," the reporter pointed out.

"That's true. I have fantastic memories of that time."

I flashed to the girl in the plaid skirt and boots walking through the door of my history class, and the twists and turns my life would take from that moment forward. Given the way it had all ended, it was hard to admit that I had fantastic memories from those days, too. But I did. I just chose not to think about them too often. I shifted back to Courtney.

"Carrington's wants to give back, and this weekend is a definite start."

Her face faded into a commercial for in-ground pools, and I turned back to Ellie. "Don't fall in love. It never goes the way you want it to."

"Man, Beringer. When did you get so dark?" I jumped a foot in the air and Travis laughed from where he stood in the doorway. In the midst of my diverted focus, I hadn't noticed him arrive.

"First of all, don't sneak up on me like that. I might have killed you. And second of all, it's best to prep her early."

"No need." He turned to Ellie. "You're gonna be the heartbreaker, aren't you? Little boys won't know what hit 'em." She clapped her hands in total agreement.

"Or little girls. You never know." I held up the frozen fish sticks. "We weren't expecting you for another hour. I've been slaving away over dinner."

"I can see that. Game was called for rain." Ellie made a beeline for her father who, as the coach, was dressed in a blue baseball uniform of his own. Travis scooped her up and kissed her cheek nineteen times, which only made her giggle. "Berta took Tim the Champion home and I'm here for the munchkin." He turned to her. "You and Aunt Maggie go out on the town?"

"We did," I told him. "She's the consummate socialite."

"Reminds me of a certain blonde from high school."

I stared at him blandly. "I have no idea who you're referencing."

"Yes, you do. You were just captivated by her on your TV screen."

"Pshhhh," I said, drawing the sound out extra long. "Captivated or merely tolerating? Because there's a distinct difference."

"You're mad at her. Would have called that, but I say this as a happily married and very content man—"

"It's cruel to brag about your sex life, Trav," I said, whispering the word "sex" for the benefit of the toddler.

"Courtney's looking hot. Smokin'."

"She's always been very pretty. That hasn't changed."

"Yeah, but this is other-level hot. I don't know what she's been doing since last we saw her, but—"

"Okay, I get it. I get it," I said, holding up my hand like a traffic cop. "Yes, she's hot. Just don't regale me with the details."

"Given the way you were looking at that TV, Beringer, I don't think I have to. Why don't you take her out on the town? See if you can find that old spark."

I scoffed, because for him, it really was just that simple. "I think there's a little more to it than that. And Courtney and I will definitely not be going out."

"All right. Be a girl if you want. Gotta take this one home."

"She still needs dinner."

"Then I'll rustle her up some grub." He strolled to the door and I followed him, kissing Ellie's cheek.

"Night night, kiddo."

"Night night," she said in her tiny voice. My hand moved to my warmed heart.

"Hey, Maggie," Travis said. "I didn't mean to act like your feelings don't matter or whatever. I just think Courtney is a cool chick. And I also think you're a cool chick, so—"

"I know, Travis. You mean well."

"You sound like my wife."

I placed a hand on his shoulder. "That's one of the nicest things you've ever said to me. Now get out of here, and knock your son in his head from his Aunt Maggie. Remind him I'm taking him to the movies next weekend."

"Will do."

Once Travis, Ellie, and Ellie's entourage of stuffed animals had left the building, I turned back to my empty cottage and pondered whether I'd heat the fish sticks after all or maybe settle for a sensible salad.

My life was thrilling.

CHAPTER SEVENTEEN

W̲e need to work on being more exciting.

That was the text I sent to Melanie as I dressed for work. I knew she'd be up because her claim to fame at the salon was her early-morning appointment slots, which were known to go like hotcakes with the elderly crowd. As the only out lesbians in our age group in a fifteen-mile radius, Melanie and I relied on each other for sojourns to the wider world in search of a social outlet. We'd found little successes here and there. We were dedicated members of a lesbian book club that met two towns over. We'd also made the occasional trek to a lesbian bar on the outskirts of Santa Barbara. For me, it was a good time out. I'd met a couple of women over the years, had my fun, but stayed on the perimeter of anything resembling an entanglement.

Best decision ever.

No drama. No headaches.

Just two people sharing an evening on occasion, with no messy strings to slice and dice them with later.

Melanie was different, though. She was looking for the love of her life and had come away with some decent candidates. Just not "the one" quite yet. The fact that she'd mellowed into an actual human over the past few years had certainly helped her cause.

My phone buzzed in my pocket as I locked the door to the cottage. I checked the readout to find a text from Melanie.

What are you talking about? We have book club next week.

This served as an excellent reminder that I needed to read that damn book. Something about a very lonely well. Regardless, it looked depressing. I typed back.

This weekend. You. Me. Dancing.

I was a horrible dancer but had mastered the art of the head bob to roaring success.

You're on. It's been too long!

Perfect, I thought as I descended the steps with Ernie. While I'd planned to drive him down to the big house, he lumbered off into the fields instead. He had an adventurous spirit, a trait I admired. "Have a good day," I yelled to him. The spring in his step seemed to amplify at the sound of my voice. "Be kind to others!"

I was in a good mood, and there was no denying it. I didn't even mind the consult with Courtney scheduled for that morning. I blared some Stones on the short drive to work and arrived at my office feeling like a rock star, not a woman who'd eaten fish sticks alone the night before. New leaf time, people.

I took my spot at my desk, returned a couple of phone calls for a listing I'd just landed, all the while bopping along to the song in my head.

"Looks like you're having a fun morning," Courtney said as she entered.

"What can I say? I love my job."

She smiled warmly. "Then I've come to the right place."

"Have a seat." See? This was going well already. Look how professional I could be. She settled into the chair across from me, looking a lot less businesslike today. Jeans, a black and maroon striped V-neck, and she'd worn her hair down. "So you're looking for a rental," I began.

"Right. Something modern. One or two bedrooms. The part of town is less important, but they'd have to be willing to agree to a month-to-month, just because my plans are so up in the air."

"Gotcha." I went to work on my computer, pulling up the listings I knew would fit her profile. "While there are more than a few contenders, I've got three that might really work for you."

"Great. Can we see them?"

"Oh." I paused. "You want to go today?"

"No time like the present." She raised a shoulder. "I took the morning off."

"Okay. No problem. Let me make a few calls." While I did that,

Courtney stood and perused the office, picking up knickknacks and setting them back down again. The whole practice had me a little distracted. I hung up from my first call and she turned to me.

"No Beatles memorabilia."

"Nope," I said distantly, and began dialing again.

"How come?"

"That was years ago." The metaphor was larger than the Beatles, and the meaning didn't seem lost on Courtney. I saw the shift behind her eyes as she turned away from me.

"It definitely was," she said. The office felt smaller now and the air heavier. I focused on the small task of dialing the phone, though my eyes followed Courtney's progress as she took in the rest of the space. I couldn't help but see it through her eyes and somehow wished it were sleeker, more pulled together color-wise. Was I trying to impress her with my success? If so, what was that about? *Old habits.*

"It's perfect," she said of my office, once I'd booked the final showing. "Very you."

"Thanks."

"You're welcome." She held my gaze for a beat past comfortable, and I remembered how the different blues of her eyes swirled together in a startlingly attractive combo. I heard Travis's voice in my head. *She's looking hot, Beringer.* I shook it off like a parka in the summer sun. Not gonna happen.

"Shall we go?" I asked.

"Yep. I'll drive. You navigate."

I wasn't going to argue.

The Mercedes we climbed into was an updated version of the one I'd once known her to drive, though this new one had all the fancy bells and whistles designed to impress. Soft leather interior, fancy cameras, and a large touch screen probably capable of launching us into space with the stroke of a button.

"Nice car," I said to fill the silence.

She kept her eyes on the road. "It gets me there."

"I'd say it more than gets you there." The sentence came with judgment, and I had no idea why I was being judgmental about a stupid car. Courtney had done nothing to deserve it. Well, nothing *today.* If she'd picked up on my tone, she'd didn't show it.

"Oh, wow. When did they rebuild the town library?" she asked, gesturing to the new two-story structure with a playground off to the side.

"Last year. Mrs. Rolando retired, and a fund-raising big shot took her place. It's been great for the library, though. Tons of new after-school programs. Reading challenges."

She passed me a melancholy smile. "That makes me happy and sad. I adored Mrs. Rolando. I'd hang out there for hours during the hot summer months."

"You like her because she used to let you sketch the patrons through the stacks."

She held up a finger. "As long as I promised to read a book a week. There was payment involved, and I followed through."

"I guess Mrs. Rolando was pretty shrewd herself. Turn left up here."

We pulled into a modest two-story, set back from the street a bit. Quaint. Charming. And with a considerable amount of space between the house and its two neighbors. With any luck, it'd be a home run and Courtney and I could go back to our regularly scheduled lives, shelving this uncomfortable trip down memory lane.

She looked up at it through the windshield. "Unacceptable. I can't live here."

I followed her gaze. "Why is that?"

"There's no red door."

I smiled and shook my head. "Come on."

I let us in and followed behind a few steps as Courtney moved about the house. I generally tried to give each client room to explore and get a feel for each place before offering too much insight or information. Courtney was giving me very little in the way of signals, however, and I had no idea whether it was a home run or not. Regardless, I thought the place was perfect for her, and I did have at least some knowledge to draw from.

"Well," I asked, when she finished the initial walk-through.

"It's really charming. I like that the kitchen is open to the rest of the living room."

"All new finishes, too. Top-of-the-line appliances."

She made a circle through the living room. "Something's missing, though."

I cocked my head, ready to make a note. "And what is that?"

She shrugged. "I have no idea. I'm just not connecting to the space."

"It's a temporary situation, though, right?" That was Realtor code for *this is good enough for what you need*, but Courtney didn't seem to care.

She winced as if there were an annoying pebble in her shoe. "It's important to me that it be the right fit, you know? Even if it's short term. Can we see the others?"

I nodded, ready to do my job if it killed me. And in this case, it might. "Of course. Let's head to the second house." Only that one wasn't friendly enough. It could also do for more natural light, according to Courtney.

"This is fun," she said, as we drove to the third and final house on our list. "I'm a little jealous that you get to do this all the time."

"It is fun. Especially when you find the house, which I'm guessing is about to happen to us in three, two, one. Welcome home." We arrived at a petite but stylish garden home with a Spanish tiled roof and off-white exterior. Courtney hopped out of the car eagerly, bolstering my already good feeling about the house. My hopes and dreams were shattered when she went on to criticize the small master, insisting that she needed more space.

"Well, this is the last house I'd lined up for us."

"So what's the next step?"

I went into professional mode. "I set up some more showings and we revisit this soon."

"Perfect. When can we go?"

"Give me a couple of days to make the arrangements. There's also a pocket listing on the outside of town I could probably get us into if I pulled enough strings."

She bit her lip. "I like the sound of that. In the meantime, let me buy you lunch to say thanks."

"Can't," I said automatically. "I have an afternoon appointment to prep for."

She stared at me. "You have an appointment this afternoon?"

"I do."

"It's a little early in the day for lying, don't you think?"

I scoffed. "You don't know I'm lying. I have no reason to lie."

"Except you are, because you're scratching your head each time you say it. It's what you do when you lie. You're horrible at it. Always have been."

I drove my hands to my sides and balled my fists to hide any and all evidence. I'd forgotten about the head-scratching thing. Damn it! I really needed to work on that and maybe try to lie more for practice.

"Come on," Courtney said. "We can catch up."

Right there was the problem. See, I was in the business of self-preservation, and sitting across a table from the "really hot" Courtney Carrington didn't lend itself to that plan. I'd already caught and chastised myself for staring, because there was something about the way her clothes fit that made me a little bit warm. I was going to hell.

"What are you afraid of?" she asked. "That we'll actually get along? We always did, you know."

"I'm not afraid of anything. It's just...weird." There. I'd said it. "We don't need to hang out together to find you a rental."

"It's not weird if we don't make it weird. Have a harmless lunch with me." She raised an eyebrow in playful challenge, and because I'm competitive I caved.

"Fine. But I have less than an hour. Thirty minutes is more like it. I'd be surprised if anywhere could get us in and out that quickly."

"Luckily, Rene likes you."

I sighed and forced my most laid-back smile. Totally breezy, that was me. "The café it is."

The Berry Good Café, as always, smelled fantastic. BLTs, burgers, and the best fried chicken ever had the place bustling with lunch crowd fans. I followed Courtney to a booth and heard a shriek, turning to see Rene herself racing over to our table. "Am I hallucinating or is that Courtney Carrington patronizing my establishment?"

"Your eyes are not deceiving you. Hi!" Courtney stood and hugged Rene warmly.

Rene shrieked again and I winced. "I saw you on the news, young lady, but needed to lay eyes on you myself to believe it was actually true. And it is! Welcome home!"

"Thank you."

With hands on her hips, Rene shook her head, giving Courtney the once-over. "More beautiful than ever. You're getting a free slice of chocolate cake. No arguments." She turned to me and then looked back to Courtney. "It's like a time machine, you two sitting here in my café."

"Oh, I wouldn't go that far," I said evenly.

Almost as if she didn't hear me, Rene clasped her hands together in celebration. "This must be my lucky day or something. You're getting cake, too, Maggie! It's a chocolate cake kind of lunch."

I held up a hand. "Oh, that's not necessary."

"It most certainly is," Rene said, fussing at me. "Don't kill my fun. I rarely have any at my age. I lost my boyfriend to a hussy with a mustache and a D cup." Courtney widened her eyes at me and I held up my hands in acquiescence.

"I wouldn't dream of it."

We placed our order and I sat back in the booth, because now what? I wished there were some sort of guidebook for navigating the waters of an ex-girlfriend who'd once ripped your heart out, never looked back, and then somehow managed to get you to have lunch with her.

"So how have you been?" Courtney said finally.

I laughed at the breadth of the question, and once she heard it out loud, she did, too.

"Okay. So, that was lame."

"I've been fine," I told her anyway. "No major complaints. In fact, life is grand."

"I was happy to see that you pursued the whole real estate thing. I knew you'd be great at it."

"And when did you hear about my chosen career path?" I asked, hating myself for wanting to know if she'd been paying attention.

She closed her eyes briefly. "Not until I got back into town, actually."

Oh, so she hadn't thought about me at all. Wonderful. Not at all ego slamming. I sipped from my water glass. "I guess you've been busy."

"Yeah."

We glanced around the restaurant, each pretending to be ultra interested in the décor, the other patrons. I swallowed back my discomfort and refocused. "Congratulations on the whole vice president thing." The news had come the year prior, splashed all over town and Facebook.

She sat a little taller. "Thank you. It wasn't an easily won position."
"Why is that?"

She seemed to choose her words. "I think the board wanted to make sure I was ready and wasn't riding on the Carrington name. Plus, my father, in his last year, didn't exactly champion my cause."

"Shocker." It seemed I still carried my basket of bitter. "I take it you two didn't mend any fences before he passed."

"No, and I have mixed emotions about that. Sometimes I wish we had. He wasn't a good person, but he was my father, you know?" She had that distant look in her eyes again, and I was jolted back to a time when it would have made me hurt for her. Hurt *with* her.

"I'm sorry."

She forced a smile and shook her head. "Don't be. I'm fine." A pause. "I know you don't have any interest in discussing it, but I feel like there's something I need to say to you."

"We don't have to—"

"Just let me say this, okay?"

I bowed my head and gestured for her to continue.

"The last time we saw each other, the circumstances were pretty awful." I nodded as she searched for words. "Sometimes you hurt the people you care most about. It's my hope that we can find a way to move beyond the events of the past. I would love it if we could be amicable, Margaret. Life is too short to walk around with ill will. People break up. It doesn't mean we have to hate each other, or even," she referenced me, "feel weird around each other."

My gaze drifted to the wall just beyond Courtney as I took in what she'd said. It was a huge request. Friends? While the goal was beyond lofty, in my opinion, carrying around the anger was exhausting. A respite from that didn't sound so horrible. I met her gaze. "It was a pretty awful time, and I'd rather not dwell on it, if you don't mind. I did that for a while." I couldn't believe what I was about to say. "So, sure. We can give the friends thing a shot. I stand by the weird, though, because that's how it's going to feel."

She laughed. "Already does a little." That's when I realized that I wasn't the only one totally at sea. Our sandwiches arrived, along with two plump slices of chocolate cake with double chocolate frosting, and offered a nice respite from the need for conversation.

At least, for a short time.

That's when I decided to tackle the elephant in the café, so to speak. "So you were married."

Courtney set down her French fry. "I was, yes. For just under two years."

"I would say congratulations, but it seems a little ill-fitting given—"

"The divorce? Yeah, I'd say. It's fine, though." She waved it off. "We're still on good terms, all very harmonious in the scheme of what it could have been."

"So…"

She eyed me, attempting to fill in the gap. "Why the divorce? Is that what you want to know?"

I hesitated. "Is that something a friend would ask? I'm trying to learn the rules."

She smiled. "It is."

"Okay. Then why the divorce?"

She inclined her head side to side. "I think it became clear that we both wanted different things out of the relationship. He's a great guy. He just wasn't the person for me, at least in the long term."

"But in the short term?"

"He was what I needed."

"Fair enough." I didn't push for more, as much as I wanted to know the whole story. But what comfort would those details possibly bring me? Nathan Vaughan hadn't been the one for Courtney. That didn't mean that I had been. Things happened the way they did for a reason, and I should embrace that.

We finished our lunch in a wash of small talk. Finally, Courtney reached for the check.

"Wait," I said. "Let me get it. I can write it off as a business expense."

"You could, but that would be silly. I dragged you here against your very strong will."

I pointed at her. "That is true."

We paid and walked to the square, where we would part ways. "I hope that wasn't too painful," Courtney said.

"Surprisingly, I survived."

She chuckled. "Have a good day, Margaret. Thank you for having lunch with me." I nodded. "Let me know when you have more listings to show me."

"Will do."

I stood in front of the restaurant and watched Courtney walk away, bound for work or the B&B or who knows where, and felt the tiny pieces of my heart stand up to be counted, a reminder that she'd once broken it. Friends? Sure. But my guard was up. I was on high alert.

"Still as beautiful as ever," Rene said, stepping out of the restaurant to smoke a cigarette. "I wasn't sure we'd ever see that girl again."

"Yeah," I said quietly. "Me neither."

CHAPTER EIGHTEEN

Saturday night at Cricket's Lesbian Bar and Dance Club (a name I found a little indulgent in length) was packed. Women of all shapes, sizes, styles, and ages danced their asses off to Lady Gaga on remix.

Melanie Newcastle was one of them.

"Did you see that blonde with the ponytail whip me around the dance floor like a rag doll?" she asked me with the excitement of a gay man at a Barbra Streisand concert.

I bobbed my head to the music and spoke directly into her ear so she could hear me. "I did. She has me a little frightened."

"Is it weird that I'm also frightened, and into it?"

I smiled at Melanie, who I'd watched blossom from self-hating lesbian to Sapphic social butterfly in the span of just a few years. She wasn't a perfect human, but I'd come to appreciate her, flaws and all. "You do you, Mel."

"How's your night going?" she asked, dancing in place.

I took a pull from the longneck in my hand. "I've had worse." In the last hour, I'd met several highly attractive women, danced with two of them and managed to not embarrass myself, and allowed a third to buy the beer in my hand. Still, no one had really pulled me in. Was I losing my touch? I used to be good at this, and I needed to be good if I wanted to spice things up.

Melanie leaned in. "There's a redhead staring at you at three o'clock. Why don't you go talk to her and work a little Beringer magic?"

I touched my beer to Melanie's glass in appreciation. A second chance. "In fact, I think I will." In that moment, the clock struck midnight and the bar went nuts as the opening line from the song

"Thriller" played. I approached the redhead, feeling confident and light. I'd like to think I'd perfected my skills when it came to meeting women, and I rarely struck out. She turned to me expectantly. "I don't want to bother you, but I've been waiting for the right moment to say hello. I'm Maggie." I offered her my hand.

"I'm Lacey. Nice to meet you." She leaned in. "You know, I haven't seen you in here before."

I nodded and passed her my best smile. "I'm from Tanner Peak. I only make it into the city once in a while." The out-of-town angle always worked well.

"Then I consider myself lucky."

"Oh, you don't have to say that."

"I certainly don't. It happens to be true."

It was off to a good start, and Lacey was incredibly attractive with an air of sophistication. In fact, I might have been aiming outside my league, but the little touches, the laughs, and the sustained eye contact told me that she was interested. One drink later and the distance between us progressed to nonexistent.

"Are you in town *tonight*?" she asked, her breath tickling my neck.

I most definitely could be. Unfortunately for me, those were not the words that left my mouth. "I'm not exactly sure. I probably need to go back with my friend." Whoa. Major failure. System down. Mayday.

"I see. A shame."

I smiled apologetically. "I wholeheartedly agree. Maybe a rain check?"

She kissed my cheek. "I'm counting on it, Maggie from Tanner Peak." As she left me standing there, I took stock of all the ways I wanted to murder myself. What in the hell had just happened? But I knew exactly what had gone wrong. While my body was willing and ready for what would have been a memorable tryst with Lacey, my mind had been royally fucked with this week and wasn't bouncing back nearly as well as I'd thought.

"You guys looked cozy," Melanie said. "Well done."

I turned to her, dejected. "I think I'm broken."

"What do you mean?"

"That woman wanted to take me home, and I couldn't do it."

"Uh-oh. Let me guess who broke you." She stared hard. "Blond hair, blue eyes, yay high."

"I didn't know you knew alternate meanings of the word 'yay.'"

She glared at me. "Let's get out of here and you can tell me all about it."

"No frightening blonde for you tonight?"

"I'm looking for permanent, so frightening might be a deal breaker, no matter how hot she is. Besides, now I need you to tell me why you're broken."

And I did on the nearly two-hour drive home. To her credit, Melanie listened to me recount the insecurities, the dredged-up memories, the pain that never really went away. Really listened. When I finished, we were more than halfway into our drive.

She turned to me. "That's a lot."

"Right? And now we're friends apparently, which is only going to prolong the broken."

She shook her head as she exited the highway. "This is why you needed a plan. You can't let her affect you like that. Just don't. Make up your mind."

I laughed. "Like you did in high school when you decided you were better than all of us?"

She smiled over at me sweetly. "Yes, exactly like that." I enjoyed that I was able to tease her about it now. "And I was really good at it. See? Sometimes if you believe your own bullshit, you make it true."

"Or you're just delusional."

"Or you make it *true*," she said more forcefully. "Besides, I came around. Here I am, the class golden girl hanging out with the class outcast."

"Wow, we're really bonding now," I deadpanned.

She ignored me. "You know what I mean! Anyway, you just tell yourself that Courtney no longer has any power over you. Either that, or steer into the skid and have wild monkey sex with her. Now that I'm thinking about it, that doesn't sound like such a bad solution."

I sent her a look that said *really?* "I'm thinking the monkey sex is the wrong way to go."

Melanie shrugged. "Suit yourself. But I need my wingman back, so one way or another, you're gonna have to deal with this Courtney thing."

Yes, one way or another, I would. And that was the problem. "If I ever go and fall in love with someone, and I mean anyone, I want you to smack me with a crowbar, because it won't be half as uncomfortable as this whole thing is turning out to be."

"Deal. You're getting the crowbar." She held up her hand and I smacked it.

❖

A couple days later, I geared up for another round of Find My Rental starring Courtney and me. This time we'd agreed to meet late in the afternoon, as Courtney had a full day scheduled at the store. As I made the drive to Carrington's to pick her up, I had a very candid and necessary conversation with myself.

"You're going to be friendly, and professional, and maybe even joke around a little to make the day easier. You will not think about the past, or lust after your client, or fall into old patterns. Do you understand me?" I glanced at myself in the rearview mirror. "And just because you're talking to yourself does not mean that you are not in control of the situation. No, no, no. Many people in control converse with themselves. I bet Ulysses S. Grant had daily convos with himself. He did all right. Be like Ulysses S. Grant." I nodded at myself just as Courtney opened the car door.

"Hi. Thanks for driving this time." She wore a black suit today, with a royal blue shirt underneath and heels.

"No problem at all." As I pulled away, I decided to use the time to tell her about some of the listings, get her prepped in advance. By the time I got to the summary of the fourth house, it was clear she wasn't really listening, her gaze focused on the horizon. "So the final house is owned by a velociraptor who may or may not agree to take you on as a roommate." No reaction. "He bakes a lot of chocolate chip cookies, though, so you might enjoy him. Not sure how he does it with those claws. I doubt they make oven mitts to fit those things." I looked over at her for a reaction.

She blinked. "Okay, yeah, that sounds good."

"Interesting."

"What is?" she asked.

"I just tried to house you with a cookie-baking dinosaur and you agreed without question."

She laughed. "That actually doesn't sound so bad."

"You'll need to figure what you're going to bring to the table. He can't provide all the snacks."

Another laugh. "Sorry. It's just…have you ever had one of those days where it seems like the day is having you? Like you're not fully in control of the events and how they play out?"

I considered the question and knew immediately that I had. The other night at the club came to mind, as did our recent lunch together. "I can safely say yes to that question. Rough day?"

"I guess frustrating is the word." She looked over at me, seeming to see me for the first time today. "Oh. You look nice."

The comment caught me off guard. I ran my fingers through my hair. *Be Ulysses S. Grant.* "No, I don't. Just an old work outfit."

"Uh-huh. Still working on that compliment thing, I see."

"I'll try again." I bowed my head in acceptance. "Thank you for the compliment."

"You're welcome. I appreciate the dinosaur roommate."

"*You're* welcome."

We rode in silence. "Your hair is straighter than it used to be," Courtney said, surveying me.

I glanced at her and then back at the road. "I discovered this magical tool called a straightener, and now I bring all the girls to the yard." I was making jokes because I didn't know how else to handle myself. I'd wager Ulysses probably didn't have to employ that tactic.

She laughed at the quip, and I smiled automatically, the way Courtney's laugh always made me smile. Operation Humor came with side effects, I was finding.

"So are you seeing one of those girls from the yard now? I can't believe I just said that phrase." She shook her head at herself.

"I'm rubbing off on you in the best ways. Next up: twerking and why it ruins lives."

"I'd like to hear you give that speech to the junior history class."

"Don't think I won't."

She laughed and we fell into silence once again. "I hope it's not weird that I asked about the dating thing. I'm honestly just curious about your life. I promise I'm not hitting on you."

I stole a glance. "Good, because we both know where that leads."

"We do," Courtney said quietly and watched the scenery fly by.

Silence again, this time the weird kind. I shifted in my seat.

"I do date on occasion." Okay, so I stretched the meaning of the word. "Melanie and I were at a club in Santa Barbara just a couple of days ago, actually."

"A club? Aha. So maybe you're a little more like your brother these days than you're letting on."

I smiled at the comparison to Clay, and wondered what he'd think about that. "I take that as a total compliment."

"I meant it that way." She looked over at me, her expression softening. "I think about him a lot. Still."

I nodded. "Me too. I talk to him sometimes." I covered my mouth and slowly shook my head. I'd never told anyone that, yet somehow there it was, announced in my car.

"What is it?" Courtney asked.

"Just not generally something I share."

"For what it's worth, I'm glad that you did. I worried about you after we lost Clay. For years, I wondered how you were. Thought about calling you."

"But you didn't," I said flatly.

She blew out a breath. "I had a feeling you didn't want to hear from me."

I'd give her that. "Your instincts would have been on point." I opened the door and exited the car, making my way up the walk of the first house on our afternoon.

Her voice stopped me. "Regardless, I'm happy to hear that you still talk to him. Clay. I have a feeling he's with you every day."

"I know he is." I turned and met her eyes briefly. "There's not a doubt in my mind."

We spent the late afternoon touring the four properties that I'd set up for us and avoiding the hard topics, both of us still a little tender from the earlier conversation. While she seemed to really like the last house of our day, she still wasn't ready to pull the trigger, which was a little head scratching for a short-term lease.

"What's holding you back?" I asked her, as she walked through the space one last time. "You really like this house. It has plenty of room, an open floor plan, and you're hardcore in love with the garden tub."

She wrapped her arms around herself. "The tub is a nice touch.

I could do some serious soaking time in that thing." The image of Courtney, her hair up and her body surrounded by bubbles flashed, and I felt it all over. In places I shouldn't be feeling things. She studied me knowingly and suppressed her smile. "You okay?"

"Yeah, I just…think you should take the house."

"Of course you do, you're my Realtor. It's your job."

"It's my job to find you the *right* house. I just happen to think I have. Multiple times."

"Let me sleep on it."

I sighed loudly.

She grinned and waltzed past me, leaving a trail of mesmerizing vanilla. "I love it when you're dramatic."

I dropped Courtney at her car back at Carrington's and watched as she climbed inside and put the top down. That car was made for her. I pulled out of the parking lot and shrugged off the captivating image. I'd had a decent afternoon with Courtney, even if it had ended with little progress made toward the actual goal. This version of Courtney, I took note, seemed a lot more confident when it came to knowing what she wanted, which could be expected after years in the corporate trenches.

I stared at myself in the rearview. "You survived another battle. Ulysses would be proud."

❖

Thirty minutes later, my bleary-eyed cousin, whose hair fell in clumps from a loose ponytail and who sported a chemical spill on her once-white shirt, arrived at our table at Lonesome's Bar. "The white shirt might have been lofty," she said in greeting.

I grinned "You think?"

"I left two moody kids at day care this morning after feeding and clothing them, administered six cuts, three highlights, and one perm, ran payroll so employees can eat, picked up, fed, and bathed said children, now highly energetic children I might add, and now stand before you a woman in need of a glass of wine."

"It's good to see you, too, Berta," I said. "You take a seat and relax. I'll get that wine. I know where it lives."

She nodded numbly. "Bless you."

I made my way to the wooden bar across the room and rested my forearms against the wood. Dave, the part-time bartender, part-time house painter, made his way over. "What can I get for you, Maggie?"

"A glass of your finest cabernet for a woman on the verge."

He stared back apologetically. "We just have the one kind, so—"

"Sold."

"Red wine, coming right up." I watched as Dave poured the wine, something cheap from one of those huge bottles. "Saw you on Facebook earlier today. Didn't look on the verge at all. In fact, you looked downright cozy. You got people cheering for you two."

"No, the wine is for—what are you talking about, cheering for who?"

He took out his phone, scrolled a second, and slid it my way.

Right there in the middle of the screen was a photo of Courtney and me chatting at the café a few days back. She leaned in a little, and a soft smile played on her lips. My eyes drifted down to the caption: *Will love burn bright again for former Tanner Peak sweethearts?* My mouth fell open and I pointed to the screen. "This was a harmless business lunch! We're friends, and barely that!"

Dave's eyes widened. "I'm sorry."

I continued to motion to the phone, as patrons turned their heads one by one in my direction. "The misuse of social media in this town is rampant! This kind of insinuation is silly, and people have too much time on their hands."

He raised a worried eyebrow. "I'm not exactly sure what to do here."

"You know what? Not your fault, Dave!" I handed back the phone, dropped a ten, and grabbed the wine.

"You really shouldn't take it out on Dave, you know," Berta said, when I returned to our table.

"You knew about this?"

She nodded. "Everyone's seen it."

"Everyone's seen what?" Melanie asked, sliding onto a stool.

Berta turned to her. "The cozy café photo of Courtney and our own Margaret Beringer."

"Ah, yes."

I glared at her. "As one of the keepers of that site, you're part of the problem."

"Pshhh. No harm was done, and it's all in good fun." She glanced around the table. "What are we drinking? Red wine for Berta and the blood of social media vixens for Maggie? Perfect. I'll secure myself a little drinky-drink. Be right back, girls."

I watched her go. "Sometimes I feel like she hasn't changed a whole hell of a lot since high school."

"You're forgetting how awful she was." She shuddered.

"Good point." I turned back to my beer, and Berta squeezed my forearm.

"Incoming at two o'clock."

"Ow!" I grimaced at her. "Your mommy grip is on point."

"Just giving you a heads-up."

Curious, I glanced over my shoulder to see Courtney grace the doorway of the bar. Courtney in faded blue jeans and a white T-shirt. She made that outfit take on new meaning. Berta and I watched as she headed in the direction of the bar, nodding hello to the folks she knew as she went. Well, wasn't that just par for the course? I turned back to Berta, over it. "She wants a drink. Free country."

"She's talking to Melanie," Berta said, narrating. "Melanie's glancing at us. Now Courtney is. Now Courtney is waving." She raised her hand, and her lips barely moving. "I'm waving back."

"You should be a sportscaster," I told her and took another sip of my beer. "A ventriloquist one."

"Okay, Melanie has a drink. Now Courtney has a drink. They're chatting some more, and Courtney is laughing. Oh." She paused and an idea seemed to hit her. "You don't think Melanie likes Courtney, do you?"

"While I feel like that question takes me back to seventh grade, no, that would be crazy."

"Mel keeps touching her briefly and then pulling her hand away."

I narrowed my gaze, beer frozen midway to my mouth. "Short little touches?"

Berta pointed at me. "Exactly like that."

This was serious.

I sat up straighter and turned around—intrigued or annoyed, the jury was still out on which. Well, call me Betsy Ross. Berta was right. Melanie was on Courtney like wool on a sheep, and whether it should have or not, it dug at me. "Well, that's new."

"Are you annoyed?" Berta asked, lowering her voice. "I would be. Isn't that breaking some sort of code?"

I swallowed it back. "Nope. All is well."

"Good, because I hate to break it to you, but they're coming over." Berta broke into a radiant smile and straightened.

I too sat taller. "My lucky day."

"Would you look who I found lurking all alone at the bar?" Melanie cooed.

I smiled. "The star of Facebook herself." Courtney shot me a questioning look, but I waved it off. "Trust me, you don't want to know."

"We hear you've been hunting for a rental," Berta said.

"True," Courtney said. "Unfortunately, we've come up short so far."

Melanie placed a hand on my shoulder. "Don't worry. The star Realtor of Tanner Peak won't let you down."

Courtney met my gaze. "I have every confidence in her."

I nodded my thanks and glanced around. Was it warm in here? Because it felt a little warm in here. We drank and talked and drank a little bit more. I bought the second round. Berta regaled us with stories from the Travis trenches including how hot he looked in nothing but a towel, but how she wanted to murder him with it once he left it on the bathroom floor for the fiftieth time. "Such is marriage," she said. "You take the good with the bad."

"I wouldn't know." Melanie shook her head. "Haven't met the one who will make me forgive the towel on the floor. I still want to murder them."

I felt Courtney's eyes on me. I turned just in time to see her glance away and down. She stared into her glass, seemingly lost in thought.

"What about you, Courtney?" Berta asked. With two glasses of wine to bolster her courage, she went for it. "You gave the whole marriage train a whirl."

"And survived," she said, raising her glass.

"Any towel throwing?" Berta asked.

"Strangely, no. Nate was neat. Tidy. Almost too tidy."

"Boring?" Melanie asked, as if it were the cardinal sin of life.

Courtney considered the question. "Not boring. Just nice. Nate was extra nice."

"To Nate the nice guy!" Melanie said. And we drank. Courtney's eyes shifted to me again, and when I met them, there was that spark, and the hint of a shiver. No one had made me shiver like that but Courtney.

Melanie stood. "Next round is on me."

"Oh, no," Berta said. "Two is my limit. Kiddos are at home zonked and I don't want to keep Travis up late waiting on me. He can't sleep until he knows I'm safe somewhere."

I smiled at the sentiment. "You've got yourself a good one."

She nodded. "I'm lucky. I'll sit with you guys for a little bit, though."

"I'm good on drinks, too," I told them. "But you guys go ahead."

And they did. After their third drink and with a fourth in hand, Melanie and Courtney were bonding over just about everything in a past-the-point-of-tipsy laugh fest. "Do you think Dave would look good in suspenders? Like one of those little garden gnomes my neighbors had growing up?" Courtney asked.

"Yes!" Melanie pointed at her. "He so needs a little pointy hat."

"Pointy little hat," Courtney whispered.

"And knickers!" Melanie shouted. I placed a hand over hers to quiet her, as even the regular drinkers were shooting us looks.

"On that very amusing note," Berta said, and pushed herself up from the table, "I'm gonna head home, and take this one with me." She placed an arm around Melanie's shoulders.

"Me?" Melanie asked, overly flattered.

"You. Come on. You're on my way. I can drop you. You guys leaving, too?" Berta looked from Courtney to me.

"Soon," Courtney said. I offered Berta an I've-got-this wave and a nod.

"You sure?" she mouthed.

I nodded and watched as Berta followed behind Melanie, stopping her when she tried to readjust Russ Fielding's baseball cap. "Maybe don't touch people," I heard Berta say.

"All right, McDrunkerson," I said, turning back to Courtney.

"Finish that drink so we can get you home. Or, you know, don't finish it. That might be smarter for your day tomorrow. Cut back on the hangover quotient."

"Can I ask you a question?" She set her cocktail down.

"Sure."

"Why are you still so sexy after all this time?" She shook her head. "I needed you not to be Maggie when I got back to town."

"Um. I don't know how to respond to that. I'm still me."

She sat back and closed her eyes "Trust me. I know. It sucks, because you are the one person I cannot get caught up with."

"I hear ya." I stole a sip from her glass because I needed it.

She sighed in that overexaggerated way drunk people do. "Do you hate me?"

I shook my head. "I don't hate you. And I've tried to, believe me."

"I tried to hate you, too, to run as far away from you as I possibly could."

"Yet here you sit." I couldn't help but smile at the irony.

"I better head home. That stupid dimple is about to do me in." She stood and took a moment to get her balance, clearly righting herself. That decided it.

"I'm going to drive you."

"We've been drinking. We should walk."

"You've been drinking. I quit a while ago."

"Fine. We'll take your Maggie car. Good night, Mr. Garden Gnome."

Dave raised an unsure hand as we passed.

"Good night, Dave. Sorry for yelling at you earlier."

"No apologies needed, Maggie."

Courtney waved it off. "Gnomes are friendly. He's fine."

I turned back to the bar and addressed the five remaining individuals. "No one put this on Facebook, you hear me?"

I was met with tipsy little answers like, "Better get that girl home, Maggie," and "You two enjoy yourselves." I rolled my eyes and followed a very intoxicated version of Courtney into the parking lot.

"They think we're going to sleep together?"

"Yeah, something like that."

"Listen, there are worse things that could happen to me." She laughed and put her arm around me. Even flat drunk, she was still over-the-top attractive, and when she looked at me, the smile dimmed from her face. "You ripped my heart out once."

"Yeah, well, right back at you." I opened the passenger door to my car and waited as she climbed inside, and then made my way to the driver's seat.

"What does that mean, I ripped your heart out?" she asked. I could see her working to understand.

Oh, hell, why not go there? Wasn't like she'd remember much of this tomorrow anyway. I leaned back against the seat and turned my head to her. "I was packing for Chicago when I saw the newspaper and your wedding photo."

She blinked several times. "No, you weren't. You weren't packing for Chicago."

"You know what? It doesn't matter now."

We drove to the bed-and-breakfast in silence and I walked her up the quaint brick path to the pale blue door. "You going to be okay?" I asked. She nodded and pulled me into a hug. Because it was clearly motivated by alcohol, I didn't fight her.

"You may hate me, but it's really good to see you," she whispered.

I held her, my face pressed into her hair with the cool night air wrapping around us. I wanted to hate her, and though I still carried a lot of hurt with me from all those years back, hating Courtney was near impossible. As I held her, something squeezed in my chest as I inhaled the vanilla that would only ever remind me of one person.

She released me wordlessly, met my eyes for a long moment, and went inside the house.

CHAPTER NINETEEN

Mr. Noriander wore extra-short golfing shorts and a purple argyle sweater vest as he waited outside my office for me the next morning, tapping his toe.

"Maggie, you're here. Thank God."

"Where else would I be?"

"Sometimes you're off gallivanting on that berry farm."

"That's true. Though gallivanting might be a strong word." I flipped through my keys in search of the one to my office. "Something wrong, Mr. Noriander?"

"Well, I have an important appointment to get to but wanted to stop off first to tell you about what I decided."

"And what have you decided?"

He followed me inside, hot on my heels. "I'd like a three-bedroom now, because if I'm gonna have a girlfriend, I'll need extra space for my stuff. A man cave."

I turned to him in amusement. "I didn't know you had a girlfriend."

"Well, not yet. But I've decided to get one. A sweet one, who doesn't nag. And not one of those trashy sixty-somethings either, but someone my own age. Seventy or over."

"Got it. A three-bedroom house with a red door suitable for two people in their seventies."

"Do you know anyone?" he asked.

I smiled and placed a hand on my hip. "You want me to find you a house *and* a girlfriend?"

"If it's not too much trouble."

I laughed. "You have a lot of faith in me."

"Everyone says you're good at your job," he said, raising his palms.

"Well, no one comes to mind at the moment, but I'll give it some thought."

"Have you met Netta Carrington?" Courtney said, as she entered the office. Our heads swiveled in her direction.

Mr. Noriander walked to her eagerly. "Oh, she's a looker. Kind, too."

"She is both of those things," Courtney told him.

"Actually, that's not a bad idea at all," I told Mr. Noriander. "You should call her up. See if she wants to have coffee with you."

"No, no." He waved off the idea. "I'm bad on the phone. I stammer when I can't see a person. I need the eye contact."

Courtney considered this. "She plays senior bunco at the recreation center on Thursdays. You could talk with her there. Get in some eye contact."

"Thursdays." He grabbed a pen and a sticky note from my desk and scrawled the word. "Your Facebook buddy has been very helpful," he said to me, and hooked a thumb at Courtney, who shrugged and looked skyward in feigned modesty. "Keep looking for that red door!" he called out as he left.

Once we were alone, I took a seat behind my desk and looked up at Courtney in amusement. "So how are you feeling today?"

She widened her eyes and shook her head. "I've been better."

My smile grew. "I thought that might be the case. No buttery pancakes and heavy metal, then?"

"Please. No more talk of food. I beg you."

I folded my hands on my desk. "I can't make any promises."

"You seem to be enjoying my pain."

"Not at all," I said, shrugging. "But the bar sure enjoyed you last night."

She covered her face with her hand. "I didn't sing, did I?"

"You did not, sadly."

"Oh, not sadly at all. Trust me on that one."

"You did, however, harass poor Dave. If he has a garden gnome complex because of you, it's only right to chip in for therapy."

"Duly noted." She leaned against the doorjamb. "I'll start penning my apology letter later this morning, which brings me to the first reason I'm here."

"To apologize to Dave?"

"No." She smiled and took a moment. "To you first. You had to take me home last night because I was an idiot, and that was thoughtless of me. So this is my official 'I'm sorry and thank you' all rolled into one."

"No apology necessary. It's what anyone would have done. What's part two?"

Courtney took a seat. "Getting a little antsy at the B-and-B and wondered if you'd perhaps heard back on that pocket listing."

"In fact, I have. I got a voice mail from the listing agent in Helford." I glanced at her. "That's one town over. He says we're welcome to take a look."

"Great. When can we do that?"

I flipped through my planner. "How about next week? Friday afternoon?"

She grinned. "I'll clear my schedule."

A few days later, with my highlighted book in hand, I hopped into Melanie's Jeep Cherokee and we drove to Stoneyton, a half hour from Tanner Peak. More specifically, we set off for Micki Manning's house and our monthly book club gathering. Micki Manning was our dedicated leader, who Mel and I had secretly dubbed "Micki Mantle" because of her obsession with baseball and everything related to it. To her credit, Micki Mantle often volunteered her rather large and baseball-themed home as our group's regular gathering spot. She was good people.

Tonight's meeting began as all of our book club meetings seemed to, with Debbie, Monica, the two Jennifers, Donna, Melanie, me, and of course, Micki Mantle, who wore a Padres jersey and sneakers, all gathered in the living room (under the scoreboard), snacking and sipping wine.

"So there's a well," Melanie said dramatically to kick off our book club discussion. I smiled because I was pretty confident that, in typical Melanie form, she hadn't come close to reading the book. It was one of her standard tactics of deflection. If she offered up the first comment of the discussion (that generally said nothing about the book in any real depth), no one would notice when she failed to contribute further and instead nodded and smiled in all the right places. Her technique had to be commended. Flawless execution.

"Wonderful metaphor, wouldn't you say?" Micki Mantle asked. She'd pulled her dark ponytail through a ball cap, which she adjusted each time she spoke. It was endearing in an odd way.

Melanie nodded vehemently.

The two Jennifers looked at each other and nodded as well. "Definitely a strong metaphor," Jennifer Number One said.

I jumped in. "I found parts of the book frustrating."

"In what way?" Melanie asked, looking the part of a Rhodes Scholar. I had to give it to her. The doorbell rang just as I opened my mouth, and Micki dashed off to answer it.

"Well, for one, there was so much description. Too much. Usually that's a positive in my opinion, but Hall was beyond verbose. It cluttered the narrative."

"Yes, but you can't ignore the fact that she was trying to paint a very vivid picture of a specific time in history." We all turned to the voice, and I squinted to find Courtney standing behind the couch. How in the world? It was like seeing your fifth-grade teacher at the mall. Worlds were colliding.

"You made it!" Melanie crowed, moving to Courtney and putting her arm around her. "Everyone, meet my friend Courtney, who is in town from Chicago. I hope it's okay that I invited her to join us. She even read the book!"

Monica beamed at Courtney and fluffed her hair from her spot on the couch. The Jennifers sat a little taller. Debbie subtly applied lip gloss, and Micki looked like she'd just won the lesbian lottery. If Courtney had arrived with the words "fresh meat" scrawled across her forehead, the response wouldn't have been any less overt. These women were primed for new blood, and *this* new blood happened to be crazy attractive. I resisted an eye roll.

"We're happy you could join us, Courtney," Micki said. "Can I get you a glass of wine?"

"Anything red would be great." She looked around and beamed. "This place looks more like a party than a book club meeting."

"We like to have fun while we chat," Donna told her and then laughed way too loud.

"How about a snack? I baked blueberry muffins," Jennifer Number Two said. "From scratch. Let me grab you one. Warm butter?"

Courtney smiled at her as she passed. "Absolutely. Thank you. You're so sweet."

The sweetest. That was Jennifer Number Two.

Donna leaned forward, her chin in her hand, staring intently at Courtney like a lion gazing upon its next meal. "Tell us, Courtney, what were you saying about the book when you came in?"

Courtney flashed her killer smile and I felt the room collectively swoon. My emotion was dialed to Over It. "I think the point I was trying to make to Maggie, who I have nothing but the utmost respect for, was that the description of the book, which I believe she characterized as—"

"Excessive," I supplied. "I characterized it as excessive."

She turned to me. "Right. Was actually a tool for creating that early twentieth-century world so vividly for the reader. We needed those details as the world, to us, is foreign. Am I right?"

Six heads nodded in perfect synchronicity.

"Yes," I said, adjusting in my spot on the floor, "but at the same time it made the book clunky and needlessly long."

"I really enjoyed the description," Jennifer Number One said.

"I did also," said Two. "A lot."

"Okay, I like this discussion. This is all very good," Micki said, addressing the group. "Very good indeed. Let me ask you this. What do we think about the message of the book?"

"It has such a *strong* message," Melanie announced. She then took a delicate sip of her wine. She was going on the traitor list.

Courtney fielded the question. "I think it's clear that the author wants us to understand that it's important for gay people to be treated just like everyone else, which, for the time period, was lofty. She was a pioneer."

Given the events of the evening, the universe demanded I take the opposing viewpoint. "Right, but the message I walked away with was that if you're gay, be prepared to be lonely and miserable for the rest of your life, which is horrible. For me, that message just about overtook everything else. It ruined the book for me."

Courtney turned to me. I hated how beautiful she was. "I guess I'm trying to see the positive side."

I closed my eyes momentarily, frustrated that Courtney could drive me insane on one hand and still make me want her desperately on the other. How was that possible? How was it even fair? I wanted to draft a sternly worded letter to the fates to get their shit together and leave me out of it. "I think I need more wine," I proclaimed loudly.

I headed to Micki Mantle's kitchen and scooped up the already opened merlot, pouring a generous amount into my glass. Okay, and maybe even a little more for good measure. "Easy there. I don't want you overly fortified for our debate." Courtney. Damn. Would my luck never end?

"What are you doing here?" I asked, spinning around. Good God, she looked good. Jeans and a red T-shirt that came with a fantastic dip in its V-neck. I decided I hated all V-necks. I'd burn all I owned when I got home, because that view was criminal and nudged every erogenous zone I had.

She lifted a shoulder. "I wanted to participate in book club. Melanie invited me. Why else would I be here?"

"Apparently, to act as eye candy to those women out there."

She seemed taken aback by that, and a little amused. "Are you jealous? Is that what this is?"

No, she did not. "That's ridiculous. I just think we could use a little space given the whole…"

"Chemistry thing," she supplied.

"That. Yes. I can admit it. And you, here, at my book club meeting, is not offering me that space. You can mess with my head another time, I promise. But *something* has to be sacred, you know?"

She nodded and took a step in. I felt it. God, did I feel it. "So you don't want me at your meeting?"

I swallowed, wanting her and fighting it. "No."

She inclined her head, her blue eyes dancing. "I'm picking up on a few hostile vibes."

"Yeah, well, you're very intuitive."

"So I've been thinking about something. The chemistry."

Big gulp of wine. Huge. "Oh yeah?"

She leaned against the counter next to me, all casual and delectable, which wreaked havoc on my concentration ability. "It makes total sense, given our history. I'm not sure we should beat ourselves up about it."

"I completely agree."

"In fact, it's not a big deal at all."

"Great." Big bite of cookie. Chocolate would save me.

Courtney looked at me and smiled. "I don't want to violate anything sacred, but you have a tiny bit of chocolate…" She reached out and swiped her finger across the corner of my mouth. I looked on, dumbstruck, as she pushed off the counter and headed toward the living room. "See you out there for round two." She licked the chocolate off her finger and was gone.

Holy hell. What was I supposed to do with that? The chocolate was a turncoat.

"We're about to move on to characters," Micki said, peeking her head into the kitchen. "Everything okay?"

"Fine. Everything is just fine. On my way."

"Great," she said. "We need our resident smarty-pants."

I laughed because my actions of late could be described as anything but smart. Somehow Reckless Pants and Stupid Pants didn't have quite the same ring.

The best part about torrential downpours in higher elevations is that they can be merciless. And when I say the best, I mean the *worst*. The next afternoon, I squinted through my windshield attempting to see the thin, winding road in front of me. The journey to the pocket listing could be described as obscure and treacherous at best. I white-knuckled it out to the house, doing an impressive fourteen miles an hour for most of the trip, not at all surprised to find that Courtney had beat me there. She stood on the covered porch of a rustic little cabin surrounded by tall, lush trees and offered a wave.

Not anticipating this level of precipitation, I'd neglected to bring my umbrella and hated myself for it. There was only one way into that house. I was going to have to make a run for it. After a deep breath, I threw open the door and raced up the walk like a lunatic, bounded up the three stairs, and landed safely under the protection of the covered porch.

"I've never seen you move that fast in your life," Courtney said, laughing. "That was great! Do it again. More arm flailing, though. That was the highlight."

I took a bow. "It turns out I'm a fast runner when I need to be."

Courtney's gaze moved down my body and up again. "Not fast enough, I'm afraid. You're soaked."

I ran a hand through my wet hair, realizing she was right. I lifted my shoulders in an attempt to unplaster my shirt from my body, but it clung to me ruthlessly. I was a walking burlesque show. "It seems I am."

Her lips parted as she took me in. "Don't worry. It's not a bad look." We stared at each other for a moment to the sounds of the rain falling, thick and heavy as the tension blanketed us. *Danger, Will Robinson.*

"I should show you the house," I said quickly, rallying.

"Yes. We should probably get to that."

I typed the provided code into the lock box, which granted us entry into a highly intriguing space. "Oh, wow," I breathed, moving inside. The cabin had been staged with crisp, angular, and rather expensive-looking furniture in grays and blues. As for the design of the house, the architect had not spared on creativity. The place was a compact little playground of cool. A largely charcoal living room comprised the main floor, with the solitary bedroom located directly above, open and overlooking the rest of the house in dramatic fashion. A circular staircase wound languidly up. A gray kitchen to the left of the living room could be seen through a large, square, artistic-looking window on the wall that separated the two rooms.

"Would you look at this?" Courtney said, walking immediately to the back of the house. While the front was rustic and quaint, the rear was modern and fabulous, situated on top of a lake. The entire back wall was made of glass that extended to the floor, beneath which ran water from the lake. "We're standing on the lake. How is that possible?"

"This is fortified glass," I told her, reading from the detailed email on my phone. "Reinforced several times over, apparently a signature of the architect."

"Good to know because that lake is rising as we speak."

I frowned. "Let's hope that rain lets up soon." A clap of thunder punctuated that sentence. "Uh-oh."

"Yeah." Courtney pulled up an app on her phone and showed me the red angry mass moving over our location on the radar. "We're right in the center of it, and it doesn't look like it's moving too quickly, which means there's more on the way."

I shook my head. "I should pay more attention to the news. We probably shouldn't have come out here. The roads were horrible."

"It's not a problem. We can wait it out. Better to be safe than sorry." The thunder struck again and the walls of the house seemed to shudder. "You're sure about this glass? How fortified is fortified?"

"Oh, yeah. I mean, pretty sure." Honestly I wasn't sure at all. "To be safe, why don't we move to the front of the house? You know, the part with a floor we can't see through."

"Good call."

Courtney followed me on a tour of the rest of the home as the storm of the century marched on. When we finished in the kitchen, I turned to her. "Pretty awesome finishes, huh? I could see you living out your remaining glorious weeks here in style."

"They're beautiful." She trailed her finger along the sparkly Silestone countertop. "I've never seen a place quite like this."

"Think about it. It may not be a forever space, but I would say it's a pretty cool spot for a temporary stay. Tons of sketching opportunities. Let's sign the lease!"

She balked, apparently maintaining a level head. "If it weren't for the fact that we literally can't leave right now without fearing for our safety, I might agree with you."

"Stop focusing on the details."

"Says one of the most detail-oriented people I know." It felt good, the back and forth, and I let myself enjoy it for a moment. She pushed herself onto the countertop. It reminded me of the teenage version of her, playful and adventurous.

"Pshhh. What's a little monsoon when you have a winding staircase thing in your living room?"

"Very persuasive." She gestured at me, which had me noticing her hands. "I see why you're wildly successful at this whole real estate thing. 'Winding staircase thing' is some pretty technical jargon."

"I'm no department store heiress, but I do okay." Because we weren't able to leave, I pushed myself up on the counter across from her. It took me an extra try. Okay, and then a third attempt. The fact that I would never be as cool as Courtney was once again reinforced.

"You okay?" she asked, amusement sparking behind her eyes.

I waved her off. "Totally fine."

"Just checking." A pause as she studied the kitchen. "I'm a little jealous of you, if we're being honest."

"You are not."

"I am. Getting to go into all these different houses and close deals."

"Well, *yeah*." A beat. "But you always found the big city more your speed."

"I don't know," she said wistfully. "There's something pretty charming about this little town. I forget until I'm here." For whatever reason, it made me happy that she appreciated Tanner Peak. It *should* be appreciated, and she saw that.

"Speaking of here, you still haven't said how long you're staying."

She raised a shoulder and took a deep breath. "It's hard to say. Could be a month. Could be three."

"Or Two? Or six."

"Possibly."

I eyed her. "You're very Mary Poppins about the whole thing. Just gonna wait for the wind to change?"

She chuckled and tucked a strand of hair behind her ear. "I'm here for as long as it takes to get the store where it needs to be, or when I'm needed elsewhere."

"Vague."

"Like you haven't been."

I made a show of smiling at her. "Courtney, I'm an open book."

"Really? Then why didn't you tell me that you were coming to Chicago five years ago?" She said it as if it were the most casual thing in the world. While the reference sobered me considerably, I followed her lead and kept my tone light.

"I told you the other night."

"I'm talking about back then."

We stared at each other. "Because it wouldn't have mattered."

She shook her head. "You don't know that."

"I do. That ship had sailed. You were young and in love. With a senator's son, no less."

She seemed uncomfortable but held my gaze. "I was young and heartbroken. There's a difference."

"Yeah, well, apparently not *too* heartbroken."

"Don't."

"What?" I asked and meant it.

"Maggie, you have to remember—"

"Margaret," I corrected gently, doing everything I could to keep her at arm's length, but also feeling myself losing that battle. The memories overwhelmed me, and this was Courtney I was talking to, *my* Courtney, who knew me inside and out, who knew parts of me no one else did. "We all made the best decisions we could at the time," I said quietly.

She nodded. "Right. We did."

The room fell into silence, and not the comfortable kind. I slid off the counter and headed to the living room, suddenly feeling trapped in this small house with Courtney, who was making me feel things that I didn't want to feel ever again.

But she wasn't done.

"Maggie, wait." I heard the footsteps behind me and closed my eyes. "I didn't mean to make you feel uncomfortable."

"You didn't. I just…needed a moment." I felt her hand gently touch my shoulder, and she turned me to her. Her eyes widened, and she quickly ran both hands down my arms and up again in alarm.

"You're freezing. Look at you." She glanced around for a solution. "It's because you're soaked."

"I'm fine."

"You're not. Look. You have goose bumps." I didn't point out to her that they weren't from the cold. "I wonder if there are clothes in these closets." She headed to the nearest one and threw it open.

I cringed. "I'm not wearing some stranger's clothes! That's weird and unprofessional."

"We're caught in a storm. They would totally understand, and you don't have to be professional with me."

"No, I'll be in Realtor jail in no time."

"That's not a real thing."

"Still."

She passed me a look. "Stop being stubborn. We at least need to get you out of that shirt." The thought took me somewhere other than what she'd intended. She must have heard the sentence out loud and regrouped. "Hey, I'm just trying to be helpful. You know what? Here. You can wear my jacket." She shrugged out of her navy suit jacket and held it out to me. I reluctantly accepted the jacket because I was freezing and hated the impracticality of being stubborn just because it was Courtney doing the offering. I pulled my cold and wet shirt over my head and slipped into the jacket, which at the very least was dry... and oh, smelled a lot like her.

"Here, you've got the lapel flipped." She moved to me and I held up a hand.

"It's okay. Don't worry about it."

"No, I'll just—"

"Fine. Whatever you want." I huffed out a breath and dropped my hands to my sides in frustration as Courtney adjusted the jacket, turning the lapel right side in. And there she was. Right there in front of me. Everything seemed to get softer with her proximity. The world slowed. She must have felt it, too, as her movement stilled and her hands slowly dropped.

"There," she said quietly.

I watched her mouth as she said the word. It just wasn't fair. She had such a good mouth. She was now using it to form words, but I had no idea what they were because I was focused on the way the tip of her tongue slid across her lower lip. I don't know how or why, or whether it was the rain or the vanilla or my irritation, but I was moving to it, her mouth, drawn in by some sort of invisible force. We shared a breath for a moment as I hovered just shy of her lips, long enough for me to understand what was about to happen and feel the anticipation wash over me in a flood of delicious tingles. My gaze flicked to hers before it drifted down again to her full lips.

I needed this badly. I wanted it.

I kissed her.

Hungrily. Wantonly. And she kissed me back. Her lips moved over mine urgently. The force of the kiss propelled me backward a step, but her arms were there to catch me, to steady me, to hold me there. I reveled in the feel of her lips pressed to mine, the taste I'd dreamt about for years. Overwhelmed by the sensation of wanting someone that much and of being wanted in return, things got a little hazy. My hands combed her body as I pulled in a breath, moving up her back and then down again. Hers were inside my jacket, my tongue inside her mouth.

Alarm bells sounded. I ignored them. It was like I'd never been kissed before. Everything was new and wonderfully familiar at the same time. She kissed my neck, and I exposed it more. It was the one spot on my body that made my toes instantly curl. She knew that. Alarm bells, louder this time. Damn the bells. Damn them.

I pulled her mouth back up to mine and sucked lightly on that lower lip.

Sirens blared. The alarm bells were now sirens, obnoxious ones. For the love of all things holy.

"Courtney. Wait. Wait. What are we doing?"

"I think we're winging it," she said against my mouth and pulled me back in by the lapels of my jacket.

I could get behind that.

Sparks, sparks, and more sparks as she crushed her lips to mine for another searing kiss. The jacket fell to the floor moments later and I stood there in my bra. Courtney's fingertips traced the skin from my shoulders down my body to my wrist, pulling a delicious shiver. Our mouths danced, and I was reminded how perfectly they fit together. I'd never been able to match that perfection, and I'd tried over the years.

Thunder crashed and we jumped, separating, remembering ourselves. I stared at her, panting, searching for air. She put her hands on top of her head and took a couple steps back, relying heavily on the distance. Without it, there was no fighting what this was. None. The distance was a necessary evil.

"Momentary lapse?" I offered weakly, feeling the need to justify my very reckless behavior.

She nodded. "Totally. A lapse."

"We can't do this," I said, as much to myself as to her. "You know we shouldn't do this."

She shook her head. "God, no. We've tried before. It didn't work."

"And it won't work now. I mean, it shouldn't still be there. I shouldn't still…"

Ache for you like this.

"Yeah, well, some things never change. I should probably go."

She gestured to the door behind her with her thumb. "I think I'll brave the rain after all. Safer."

I understood her sentiment entirely. "Right. You go. I'll be right behind you. Just gonna make sure I close up properly." I glanced around the room, seeing it for the first time in several minutes. "Oh, Courtney!" She turned back. "Your jacket." I scooped it up along with my shirt, which I held to my chest, feeling exposed now and foolish.

"Keep it."

The door clicked shut behind her and I drew in an unsteady breath and let it out slowly, struggling to regain what I could of my equilibrium. When it came to Courtney, it seemed my mind and body were at war, and it was one for the record books.

I didn't know how I was going to survive it.

CHAPTER TWENTY

There was something wet and warm accosting my face, and I found it hard to breathe. I blinked, coming to on Saturday morning to find myself staring up at sixty pounds of gray. Ernie was apparently ready to get his weekend started early and thought the best way to do that was to rouse me with his tongue across my cheek and two big paws on my chest.

"Well, good morning to you, too," I managed to say, despite the collapsed lungs. Another swipe of the tongue. "You, large, excited fella, have to work on your morning etiquette," I told him, and pushed him off me gently.

He followed me around the cottage as I turned the coffee machine on, checked the morning headlines, and to his delight, set down his breakfast.

While Ernie rode the train to chow town, I showered quickly and put on cutoffs and a T-shirt. I added a plaid button-up that I left untucked and open, just to cut the morning chill. "Wanna walk?" I asked Ernie, sending the big lug into a jumping frenzy. When Ernie went vertical I loved it, and when he threw his head back and howled, I couldn't resist joining him. I'd trained him to walk with me off leash, which was how he spent his entire life, with free rein of the property. However, there was nothing Ernie enjoyed more than walking by my side, and the sentiment was mutual. We set out to roam the farm, him bounding ahead and then running back to me, the process on repeat. When we finally circled around to the big house, I found my mom sitting on the front steps.

"Well, hello, little granddog," she said to Ernie, who promptly bounded the steps and placed two paws unceremoniously in her lap. "Is your mama taking you for a stroll today?" A lick. She recoiled in laughter.

"Sorry," I told her. "His manners are a work in progress."

"I don't mind Ernie." She looked up at me. "Time for coffee?"

"I would love some. Thanks."

My mother disappeared inside and returned with two steaming mugs and a dog biscuit for Ernie. I took a deep inhale from my mug, the way I sometimes did when I pretended to star in a coffee commercial. I felt like Ernie and I would make an excellent casting choice.

It hadn't escaped my notice that my mother had a faraway look in her eye, so I decided to check in. "You doing okay?"

She smiled, but it faltered. "Just thinking about things."

"Oh, yeah? Like what?" But I knew the look.

"Clay would be thirty later this year. I can't help but wonder what he'd be up to these days." I smiled, imagining all the trouble he'd have gotten into, only to be completely forgiven because he was Clay. But the concept that he'd never be thirty still sliced deep. I'd done a ton of healing over the past few years, as had the rest of my family, but the loss of someone that special never really goes away. The pain changes and shifts, but it's always there.

I gestured with my chin out at the farmland. "He'd be really proud of all the work Travis and Dad have done on this place."

"That he would." She took a sip of her coffee. "What about you?" she asked.

I scratched Ernie behind his ears. "What about me?"

"What do you want to be doing by the time you're thirty? It's not so far off anymore."

"If I could visit all the major Beatles monuments, I'd be thrilled." I was deflecting, but that felt a whole lot more comfortable than asking myself those daunting long-term questions.

She rubbed the back of my neck affectionately. "In addition to that."

I sucked in some air. "I think I'm just trying to play it all by ear."

She met my eyes. "See, I wonder about that philosophy. I wonder a lot."

"And what do you wonder, Mom?" I felt some sort of lecture coming on and wondered if maybe I had forgotten an important get-together I could conveniently dash off to.

"I can't help but worry if 'I'll play it by ear' is just a cop-out for 'I'll let life pass me by.'"

"Gasp. Are you implying I have no life? That I'm boring and pathetic?"

She moved her head from side to side. "Not exactly."

"So a *little bit* you're implying that I have no life and am boring and pathetic? It's okay. You can say it. There's no pretense necessary."

"Maybe a tad."

My jaw dropped. "When your own mother tells you you're boring, it really strikes a chord." And it did. Ouch. This was unfortunate.

"I saw your photo on Facebook last week, however." A smile crept onto her lips. "It made me happy. That's all I'm going to say."

I sent her a look. "Mom, you know that villainous Facebook page lies. It's the TMZ of Tanner Peak and needs to be shut down for good. Melanie's involved somehow. Rene, too. It's a whole racket."

She ignored my theory entirely. "Maybe the page lies and maybe it doesn't. She's divorced, you know."

I covered my eyes. "Not you, too. Mom." I groaned. "You need to know that that ship has sailed. Many years ago."

She pulled me into a hug. "I'm just saying that sometimes those sailed ships come home for a reason."

My phone buzzed. She released me and I checked the readout, shaking my head at what I saw. Courtney. "It's like you conjured her up."

"Well, well. Looks like your ship's come in."

"Stop that," I said, though I couldn't stop myself from laughing at her utter persistence. Standing, I pointed to Ernie, who lay on the porch, all four feet in the air. "Can this circus dog stay with you? I think I'm about to close a deal on a house at long last. Courtney's finally ready to sign."

"For a real estate deal, we will certainly entertain our granddog. And, Margaret, I want you to think about what I said."

"Don't be boring at thirty. Got it."

"You don't want to be my age and still on your own."

"Mom!" The jabs kept coming. My mother thought I was an old, boring spinster.

"Come on, Ernie," she said. "Let's see what Granddad is doing in the barn. At this rate, you might be the only grandchild we get."

I placed my hand over my heart to brace against the twisting of the knife.

As I drove to Carrington's in response to Courtney's message, I heard that horrible sentence from the conversation with my mother invade my thoughts over and over again.

Don't be boring at thirty. Don't be boring at thirty. Don't be boring at thirty.

Gah!

"Yeah, well, boring isn't so bad," I argued to myself in the rearview mirror, only half believing it. "I have a perfectly wonderful dog. And a job I like. And once a month I go to book club." Hearing it out loud was only confirmation of my lonely, old lady existence. I should probably take up quilting and humming and cat collecting. Though I did like cats. That part wouldn't be so horrible.

Feeling utterly boring, I marched through Carrington's, passing stylish mannequins (probably with torrid mannequin sex lives), upscale-looking sales people (probably with exciting Saturday-night plans), and said with purpose to the administrative assistant (who was way more put together than I was), "I'm here to see Courtney Carrington. I'm her real estate agent."

"One moment, please. I'll let Ms. Carrington know you're here."

I took a seat on the expensive-looking leather love seat. After just a few moments, a large oak door opened and Courtney smiled at me. "You're incredibly fast."

"You've said that to me twice in one week." I owned it as I walked past her into her office with purpose. I was feeling a mixture of insecurity over my boring status and celebration over finishing up my real estate duties to Courtney. "When a client says they're ready to sign, you don't give them time to overthink."

"One of the secrets of the trade, I take it."

I winced. "I probably shouldn't have revealed that. So which house are we offering on? Oh." I paused to look around. "Your office is large and intimidating."

"I can agree with both assessments. It used to be my father's before he headed back east. I'm trying to put some softer touches in place, but it's slow going." The spacious room came with dark walls and heavy maroon draperies. In the center stood a large oak desk that I imagined weighed hundreds of pounds.

"You have a desk like Mr. Blankenship's!" I said, pointing.

She laughed. "I never really looked at it that way, but you're kind of right."

"Well, why would you put too much effort into changing much when you're only here until the wind changes?"

"Right. There is that." Silence.

"So, the rental?"

"Yes," she said, springing into action and moving farther into the room. "Let's go with the first house."

I balked. "The first house?"

"Right. The first. I loved it. Six-month lease if we have to, but three months is better. If they try to force a year, we walk."

"Got it. A girl who knows what she wants," I said, jotting a note.

She laughed sardonically at the comment and lost herself in something on her screen.

Okay, then. "Give me a few minutes to talk with the agent and we'll see if we can't get the paperwork signed today."

"I guess you're ready to be done with me," she said, eyes still never leaving the screen.

I looked back at her from my spot at the door. The truth fell from my lips. "Not at all. That's the problem." Her lips parted and her gaze flew to mine. Damn it. I left her there, fleeing the scene to place the call, my heart beating fast and furious. But she was ready for me when I returned.

"Why did you say that? Before you left just now. That you weren't done with me."

I sighed and realized that we were going to go there. It was probably for the best, because the situation needed to be addressed and handled in an adult fashion. Courtney and I weren't teenagers anymore. "Because spending time with you since you've been back...has been tricky. That's all I meant."

"Define tricky."

"Courtney."

"Humor me. Please." She came around and sat on the corner of her desk, and my stomach clenched. I'd give this a shot.

"Okay. You and I never had any shortages in the electricity department. I think we can both agree to that."

"I think that's more than fair." She bit her bottom lip, and I closed my eyes briefly because really?

I pointed at her in frustration. "Okay, stop with the lip biting when I'm trying to have a serious conversation and not make out with you. That one mannerism is a perfect representation of the whole problem."

She stood and held up her hands palms up, frustrated now. "What, that you're attracted to me?"

"Yes, that I'm attracted to you!"

"Well, I'm attracted to you, too!"

"Fine!"

"Great!"

Don't be boring at thirty. Don't be boring at thirty. "Come to my place for dinner tonight. You can sign the lease, and I'll get out of your hair."

She took a moment, perhaps sensing the danger of that invitation. "Seven thirty?"

"Done."

❖

The sun hung low in the California sky that warm July evening. I watched the brilliance of the pinks and oranges intermingling from my kitchen table as music played softly from a local Americana station on the radio. I asked myself what the hell I was doing.

I had no answers.

Restless, I pushed open the screen door of the cottage and sat on the steps in front. I spotted Ernie snoozing on his side about thirty yards from where I sat. His favorite things in life included chasing dragonflies, dinnertime, and sleeping outside. Inside, the dinner I'd made was set to warm. I'd sautéed a couple of chicken breasts, made a salad, and put some white wine on ice. Courtney and I could talk, and sign the lease, and—

I heard the tires on the gravel before I saw the Mercedes, and then there it was, winding slowly up the drive. When Courtney exited the car, her eyes found mine, and I understood exactly what would happen. I knew that look and it had me undone.

The chicken would have to wait.

I stood from my spot on the porch and watched expectantly as she walked up the stairs, all confident and beautiful. Her gaze was on me, moving over my body. I literally felt it. That was all it took to send me into action. I reached for her hand and tugged softly, pulling her in. My eyes never left those charged blue ones.

Neither one of us said anything. We didn't have to.

The sun slanted across our faces as she kissed me, deep and thorough. I lost track of everything when Courtney kissed me. Every. Time.

I realized then that I'd never wanted someone so much in my entire life. It was everywhere, the wanting. In the air all around us. In the way that she kissed me. It beat in rhythm with my pounding heart.

Her mouth moved to my jaw, then my neck, her hands equally busy, molding to my body beneath my T-shirt, across my cutoffs.

"Inside," I whispered.

"Yes," she said softly and pulled me inside.

We kissed our way in the direction of the bedroom but got hung up in the hallway, needing more of each other, and now. My hands slid into her hair and gripped as I kissed, licked, and sucked on her neck. She moaned, and my response was visceral. I was wet and throbbing and more turned on than I imagined possible, but I wanted her first. I needed her like I needed air. I pulled her earlobe into my mouth and unbuttoned her jeans. The zipper was next. I skimmed a hand between her legs on the outside of her jeans and she strained against it.

"Bedroom," she said breathlessly. "Unless you're planning to take me right here."

I considered it briefly before leading the way.

She'd not been in the room in years, and in that time, much of it had changed. Gone was the drawing she'd done of us once upon a time, as well as the framed posters and bargain-basement bedspread. I'd upgraded to more mature paintings, metal art, matching curtains, and a white down comforter. I'd even painted the walls a dusty sage. Her eyes scanned the space and she nodded in approval before turning back into my arms.

"You're all grown up now."

I nodded and watched as she pulled my shirt up and over my head and took a moment to just look at me in my black bra. She touched the tops of my breasts with her fingertips, and I closed my eyes. Delicious shivers, right on time. She dipped her head and kissed through the lace of my bra, first one breast and then the other. As she straightened, she slid a thigh between mine and pressed it upward, pulling a gasp from me, my mind ceasing all thought. She tugged the straps of my bra to my elbows, trapping my arms at my sides and revealing my breasts.

"Look at you," she whispered.

She dipped her head, sucked a nipple into her mouth, and bit down softly. I heard myself cry out as little shock waves of pleasure hit. I began to rock helplessly against her thigh.

I'd lost control and I needed it back.

I pulled her mouth back to mine and walked her to the bed. With my hand behind her back, I lowered her. As she looked up at me, I lost the bra entirely and watched her eyes darken. I didn't have time for her jeans and pulled them down her legs. I ran my hands along the smooth expanse of her skin from her ankles, to her calves, to her thighs. When my thumbs met at her apex, she hissed in a breath and arched her back. I looked down at her, watching her expression shift as I moved a finger across the fabric between her legs. Once, twice, three times. Her underwear was damp, and I had to close my eyes to steady myself.

They had to go, too.

With my thumbs I slid them down and tossed them over my shoulder. I pushed her legs apart and placed an open-mouth kiss between them. Courtney hissed in a breath and squirmed beneath my mouth.

But I hadn't even gotten started.

I slowly licked my way around her perimeter, nearing where she wanted me to touch most and then moving away, keeping her on the verge. The give and take had her hips straining for purchase, but I held her in place with my arms wrapped around her legs.

I kissed my way up her body, caressing her stomach, pushing her shirt up to reveal a white and pink bra. "You're killing me," I murmured at the display and dove in, kissing the tops of the breasts that no other woman's had compared to.

Good God, Courtney had fantastic breasts, and I needed to see them.

I pushed up the cups of her bra and greeted each one with my mouth. Her hands were in my hair, holding me in place as I took my time. All the while, her hips moved in little circles. I ran my teeth across her nipple before pulling it into my mouth firmly, sucking hard, biting down. She cried out, but I remembered how much she liked that move.

"You remember me," she murmured.

"In detail," I said, and did it again.

She gripped my hair harder when I bit down, pushing herself against my thigh, desperate now. I slipped a hand between her legs and played, pulling a succession of helpless little sounds. "Maggie," she breathed. The sound of my name inspired an intense flutter low in my body that rocked me, and I realized I might come before she did. Unable to wait any longer, I slid inside her, and she gripped the bedspread. "More," she said, opening for me, and I was happy to oblige. As I moved within her, the slow build inside me climbed and spread out. I buried my face against her neck and, with my palm, pressed into her fully. The sound of her cry as the orgasm hit was all it took to send me with her into blissful oblivion. Spent and satisfied, we lay there side by side, staring up at the ceiling.

"I missed this," she murmured finally and looked over at me. "Missed *you*."

I propped myself up on my elbow and rested my head in my hand. "What if we just made everything harder?" I asked.

She thought on the question and traced the outline of my breast. "How can anything be harder than trying to resist you all these weeks?"

I shook my head at the truthfulness of that statement. "You make a valid point. The book club." I covered my eyes. "The stupid book club where you were all scholastic and hot and leading those poor women on."

She gasped. "I most certainly wasn't leading them on. I was being friendly, which is what you do when you don't know people well."

"Doesn't matter. To them you were walking lesbian catnip."

She laughed. "All I know is that I couldn't take my eyes off you that night. It was like Abraham Lincoln all over again, when you start making points and getting all worked up about them. That's when I knew there was no going around this, around you."

I kissed her because I had to and luxuriated in it, memorizing the taste as if I could ever, in a million years, forget. "I wanted you that night," I confessed. "Badly."

"If I'd known the badly part, we might have been here sooner."

The reality of our situation began to creep in. "What do we do now?"

Her smile waned and she sat up. We weren't touching anymore, which was a startling reminder that this wasn't Courtney and me young and in love. We were now the adult versions of ourselves, and this had been a transaction. "I'm only here for a little while," she said simply.

Right. We both knew what this was and what it was not. But if anything, the temporary quality felt like a much-needed safety net. Courtney's impending departure date would act as an ever-present reminder that what we were doing came with an expiration date. Neat. Tidy. We had shelter against any sort of terrifying entanglement. I wasn't stupid. There were feelings for Courtney buried deep, and it was best to keep them right were they were.

Done. Decided.

"Until the wind changes," I said, and met her gaze.

"Until then."

It seemed we'd reached an informal agreement, and I felt lighter somehow, as if a burden had been lifted. My heart was safe. I looked on as she dressed, still mesmerized by her body. "Why the first house?" I asked. "After all that time, all that energy, and it was the first one all along?"

She sighed and turned back to me after pulling the T-shirt over her head. "It's possible I loved the house right off. And it's possible I knew it all along."

I narrowed my gaze. "No way. You're a big fat liar?"

"Way." She laughed. "I am. It's embarrassing but true. You didn't want anything to do with me, so I had to get creative."

"You hoodwinked me?"

She came back and sat on the bed. "Only a little. I just dragged out the process a bit. And trust me when I say that I didn't expect us to fall into bed. It was just nice talking to you again. Spending time with you."

I softened at the kind remark. "Way to ruin my angry face."

"You should also know that your angry face is really, really attractive."

I shifted my lips to the side. "I'll need to work on it, then."

"Impossible." Then her eyes widened. "Oh no! You were going to make dinner, and then I…sidetracked us."

"Is that what we're calling it?" She laughed. "I did make dinner, a nice chicken. And we're both guilty of the sidetracking."

She covered her mouth. "I am so sorry, Maggie."

"Don't be." I ran my fingers through what had to be my sex hair. "Best consolation prize ever."

Her concern melted into a lazy smile, and she leaned down and kissed me. "That's very true."

"I can pop it in the oven." I slipped a hand up the back of her shirt. "Are you hungry?"

She looked down at me and nodded, her eyes dancing. "But not for anything to eat."

"What are you hungry for?" I asked. She slid down the bed and showed me.

More than once.

I fell asleep somewhere before two that morning, exhausted, sated, and happy.

When my eyes fluttered open at three, she was gone.

CHAPTER TWENTY-ONE

W hy are you so bleary eyed and slow this morning?" Berta asked over her giant latte. "You're like a happy little sloth sitting on a couch." I stared at the red mug enviously. I never had mastered the whole hot coffee in the summer thing. Best laid plans and all.

"Not a ton of sleep last night," I told her and attempted to suppress a smile. She was too good for that and zeroed in on it immediately.

"Why?" She rested her chin in her hand, bursting with curiosity. "Why would you say that you didn't get a ton of sleep?" She pointed at me. "I heard about book club, so don't try deflecting. I'll see your deflection coming a mile away. I'm raising a seven-year-old."

Someone had definitely had her caffeine today. Berta was like a dog with a bone, and I knew better than to try to keep something like last night from her. It would be impossible. "I had company."

She sucked in air audibly and her mouth fell open. "You had *Courtney* company. I knew it. It was only a matter of time, really." Then she sobered. "Are you sure you know what you're doing?"

"No, not at all, which is why we're keeping it very light. She's in town for a handful of months max."

"And then?"

"And then nothing. I go about my life. Not getting involved in any drama. Been there. Done that. This is nice and neat and casual, and then it's over." Berta looked at me strangely. Her cup shielded the bottom part of her face. "What? What is that look?"

She shook her head. "Oh, nothing. I'm just wondering if you two have met yourselves."

I went on the defensive. "I'm not the girl I used to be. Courtney and I don't work in the grander scheme of life. We're a math problem that will never add up."

Berta passed me a dubious look. "If you say so."

"We're both on the same page."

"Because you're afraid of more." She set her mug down like a judge leveling a gavel after a decision.

"I'm sorry?"

"You blame a lot of your initial trouble with Courtney on geography. But we both know that's not the basis of the problem." I opened my mouth to argue and she held up a hand. "Don't get mad. Just hear me out."

"Fine. I'm listening." I gestured for her to go on.

"You love Tanner Peak, but it's always been a security blanket for you. When you lost Clay, you clung to it even tighter, fearful of the rest of the world, and that meant Courtney. Because of that fear, you wound up hurt in the end, which only made you *more* fearful. It's a vicious cycle of fear with you, Maggie."

"Thank you, Dr. Phil," I said, laughing, trying to make light of the whole thing. It was certainly easier that way, because something about Berta's theory had me uncomfortable.

She shrugged. "Laugh if you want, but I just spelled out your whole life for you."

"I'm not sure about that."

She leaned in, energized now. "Think about it, Maggie. If you somehow found a way to take a risk, do something scary that puts you outside of your comfort zone, trust me when I say that you could conquer the world. I've always believed that."

I nodded, trying to wade through her theory and remain objective. Okay, so Berta had a valid point. I could admit that, as even now, I felt that ripple of fear at her very hypothesis of fear.

It *was* a vicious cycle!

I forced myself to move past it. "You now what, Berta? You don't have to worry about the cycle because there's nothing to be afraid of."

She shook her head, not accepting that answer. "Okay, then tell me this. Did she sleep over?"

"Absolutely not. Trust me. I have this under control."

She stared at me knowingly, skepticism in her eyes. "If you say so."

"I'm late!" Melanie announced and collapsed onto the sofa. "My eight a.m. appointment ran long. I have thirty minutes before I have to be back for my ten a.m., who, bless her heart, has dyed her hair pale blue in an attempt to cover the white." Melanie seemed to enjoy this, which reminded me of her high school self.

"Don't make fun of her," I said. "That sounds like a hair emergency."

"Well, bingo is tomorrow, so in her world, it is." She glanced around. "Did I miss anything important?"

I turned to her. "Tim got in trouble at day camp for painting the other children again."

"Good for him," Melanie said.

I nodded. "Right? Painting people sounds fun. I don't see the problem."

Berta leaned in. "And Maggie slept with Courtney."

"Oh yeah? Finally." Melanie punctuated the word with a widening of her eyes.

"Finally?" I balked. "*Finally?*" Melanie shuffled through her bag and begrudgingly handed Berta a ten-dollar bill. "Whoa. What is *that* about?" I asked, pointing at the traitorous transaction. "You were betting on me? On if I would sleep with Courtney?"

Two pairs of innocent eyes turned my way. "No. Of course not," Berta said. "We wouldn't do that."

"We were betting on *when*," Melanie supplied.

"Well, that's just perfect," I grumbled and threw my hands up. Then a thought occurred to me. "Wait. I thought you were into her," I said accusingly to Melanie. "All touchy feely."

"She is movie-star beautiful," Melanie said, "but she only notices you in any given room, so that was pretty much a dead end from the start. I was just trying to speed along the process. Jealousy works wonders, and there was ten dollars at stake."

I let the meaning of that sentence wash over me in mystification. "Unbelievable."

"Oh, don't get too bent out of shape," Melanie said. "You had sex last night."

"Why, yes." I grinned into my coffee cup. "Yes, I did."

❖

"We're four days out, just to remind everyone," I said to the ten Beringer employees gathered around the conference room table.

One of the joys of my hybrid career path was that I could chart my own course when planning my schedule. While I generally spent most of my workweek wearing my real estate hat, with Beringer's hosting our annual open house in just a few days, I'd switched into event planning mode and was surprisingly good at it.

"Okay, after the Pick-Your-Own demonstration, each group of visitors will then move to the cooling room where Shelley will offer an explanation. Next, they take the hayride trip to the northern fields for a talk given by Byron on seasonal adjustments. Finally, they'll stop and feed the goats. We're switching the order from last year. Sammy, can you make sure you rotate the goats so we don't make any sick from overfeeding?"

Sammy nodded. "Way ahead of you. Already have a schedule in place."

I nodded. "Perfect."

"What about the face painting?" asked one of the teenagers standing at the back of the room.

"Right. Great question. There'll be two different stations set up for kids to get strawberries painted on their cheeks in front of the big house. Stephanie and Todd, I have you two scheduled to help facilitate."

"What about adults?" Travis asked with hope in his eyes. "Can the adults get their faces painted?"

"You're in luck. They can."

"And there's still free ice cream at the end?" he asked.

I relaxed into a smile, indulging him. "Yes, Travis. There will still be free ice cream with all the fixings at the end of the tour."

"Yes!"

The room collectively chuckled at Travis. While very much the comedian, he had honestly shocked us all with his rise to leadership over the past few years. Everyone on the farm liked and respected him, which said a ton about his ability to manage others. He was knowledgeable, personable, and dedicated. It was clear to me who would take the reins and run the day-to-day operations on the farm once my father retired, and I was more than okay with that. We made a good team.

The weekend arrived before I knew it, and the rain that had been forecast missed Tanner Peak entirely. The Open House was framed with blue skies all around, and you couldn't have wiped the smile of relief off my face. By midafternoon, the farm was bustling with families from near and far who'd come to check out the inner workings of Beringer's.

I'd just completed my third tour and swung back by the big house to pick up my fourth—two families with kids, a young couple, and Courtney Carrington wearing white shorts and a yellow sleeveless top.

"What in the world?" I asked, pulling her aside.

She smiled. "I want the official rundown. Is that allowed?"

"There's not a rule, but," I stared at her in amusement, "you know the rundown."

"Well, I want to hear it again. I also heard a rumor that there are goats being fed somewhere, which I didn't even know was a thing here."

I laughed. "We added the goats three years ago. They're a big hit."

"And you didn't send word? I'd have been on a plane like that," she said, snapping her fingers.

"Well, now I know the trick. Follow me for goats," I said, leading her back to the group.

The tours each lasted thirty minutes, and for my part, I did my best to keep the information interesting and accurate without being overly technical.

"So *people* still pick the strawberries?" one woman asked midway.

"Yes. In the midst of all the technological advances, human hands are still best for the fruit. That's not to say we don't use machines to make their job a little less strenuous physically. We do."

I saw a hand go up on my left and turned to Courtney. "Yes, ma'am?"

"Is it true that when I purchase a carton of strawberries at the grocery store, the last pair of hands to touch a strawberry were the hands of the person who picked it?"

I suppressed a grin because I'd taught her that very fact when we were kids. She was the perfect audience plant for the tour. "Yes, that is true. You're very smart."

She placed a hand over her heart. "Thank you."

I turned to the group. "Because of this fact, there is a lot of attention paid to properly educating farm workers on hygiene and food safety. Their job is incredibly important on our farm."

The rest of my tour nodded in surprise at this little-known fact as we headed to the goat pens.

As we walked, she leaned in. "I don't think you understand my level of excitement."

Courtney, when excited, reminded me very much of her as a kid. "I'm picking up on it."

"Do you have a favorite?" she asked, her eyes dancing. "I mean, is there one goat in particular you would recommend I meet? I want to use my time wisely."

I laughed but understood that to Courtney this was a very serious question. She didn't get to hang out with goats in the big city. "If Cotton is out, you definitely want to meet her. She's an attention whore and very sweet."

"Got it. Cotton." She headed off to the goat pen like a doctor into emergency surgery. I stood along the fence as Sammy distributed a handful of grain to each of my charges. I watched as Courtney checked in with him only to be shown to the solid white goat we affectionately named Cotton. Courtney held her hand out flat, just as she'd been instructed, and smiled as Cotton eagerly ate from her hand. Slowly, she stroked the goat along the neck and shook her head in wonder. That's when it came over me: pure, unencumbered happiness. The moment playing out in front of me was so simple that it shouldn't have carried that much weight, but it did. The happiness, I understood finally, came from Courtney's happiness, seeing her so carefree, taking such enjoyment in her time with the little goat. The whole thing had me smiling like an idiot.

Which meant that I might be in trouble.

Refusing to examine this new revelation any further, I waited for the group to finish up before hopping back on the hay bale–filled trailer that would take us all back to the barn. Courtney sat next to me as the tractor pulled us slowly across the property. Once it was clear that the other members of the tour were lost in their own conversations, she leaned in very close to my ear.

"That was fun."

I nodded, aware of my thigh up against hers. "It was."

She dropped her voice to a whisper. "I love watching you speak in front of a group. It makes me want to do delicious things to you."

I quirked an eyebrow.

"I'm behaving myself right now only because I have respect for this farm and your family."

"What things would those be?" I whispered back with a smile, my mind already running with the possibilities.

"Oh, I'm making a list."

I met her darkened eyes and ordered my libido to settle. "You're killing me. You know that, right?"

"I'm not thinking the list will *kill* you, but it definitely might wear you out."

I glanced at my watch. "I have a break after this."

Her interest was piqued. "It seems the stars are lining up for us."

"And I just live a quarter mile up that road there."

"What are we waiting for?"

While it would be rude to report that I unceremoniously dumped the rest of my tour and hightailed it with Courtney back to my cottage, that's exactly what happened. "I've never had an afternoon tryst before," I mused, exhausted and happy in the luxurious afterglow.

"Oh, I'm pretty sure we've had afternoon sex before," Courtney said as she walked naked around my bedroom, gathering her clothes. "In fact, I know we have."

"Doesn't count. We were young. This was an adult tryst."

"I'd say, given what we just did." Once she'd compiled them, she set them in a neat little stack on the bedside table and climbed back in bed. "How much time do you have?"

I glanced at the clock next to the bed. "Nine minutes until I have to be back."

"I'm a fan of the way you taste," she said, and nibbled on my neck. I wrapped my arms around her waist and pulled her in, loving the feel of her weight on me, loving the feel of her. She lifted her head. "So three minutes to walk back to the big house."

I thought on this. "That's about right, if I'm expeditious." She palmed my breast, and my eyes fluttered at the overt sensations it released.

Another overly thoughtful expression crossed her face. "Two minutes to get dressed and tame that gorgeous hair."

I nodded. "More or less."

"Which gives me four whole minutes with you." She slipped a hand between my legs, and holy Mary Todd. My lips parted and my body melted to Jell-O at her slow strokes. That very familiar spark took hold and was already building.

"We can't. Courtney, I have to…" But she shifted to circles, and all meaningful words failed me. "Oh, wow. Okay."

"I thought I could persuade you." She wrapped her other arm around my waist to anchor me and continued to use the other hand to take me to ever-growing heights. "I have three minutes," she whispered as I found the rhythm of her hand.

"Mm-hmm."

"Maggie."

"Yes?" Torturous circles.

"I want you to look at me while I touch you."

I opened my eyes and locked my gaze to hers. What I saw looking back at me had me struck. It wasn't the desire in her eyes that had me struck, though that was decidedly there, but the unabashed tenderness. "Maggie," she said again simply, as she entered me. In that moment, I was hers and came in a wash of intense gratification amplified by emotional reward that left me limp, sated, and mystified.

She kissed me softly. "You are so beautiful." She smiled down at me and shook her head in reverence. Recognition flared and she seemed to remember herself. "Ninety seconds to spare," she said, much lighter now. She stood, picked up her clothes, and headed in the direction of my bathroom to dress.

"Courtney, wait a sec." But the door clicked quietly closed, ending the connection that had rocked me so potently. The history between us was vast. That part was no secret. But was what I was feeling now a mirage of what had once been or something rooted more terrifyingly in the here and now?

I dressed and waited for Courtney, no longer concerned with the ticking clock. When she reemerged, gone was the sincerity, and in its

STRAWBERRY SUMMER

place, the kind of levity she excelled at. "I was thinking about the face painting. I could do that, ya know. Make a few extra bucks on the side of the whole retail thing." She stared at me curiously. "What? What's that look?"

I opened my mouth to explain, to articulate the blaring questions that now stood at attention in my mind, ramrod straight and unbending. There was a part of me that couldn't help but wonder *what if.* "I think you'd make a fantastic face painter," I said instead.

Her smile faltered, but only for a moment. "Me too."

• 237 •

CHAPTER TWENTY-TWO

When we weren't together, I thought about Courtney a lot, wondered what she was doing, how her day was going. The more time we spent together, the more I felt an unexpected warmth and affection for the Courtney she was today. I lusted after her blatantly. True. That part hadn't changed, but I'd also developed a new appreciation for how her mind worked. She was intelligent, driven, and thoughtful when it came to business, plus she had this artistic streak when it came to sketching and fashion that was like sprinkles on an already impressive sundae.

Courtney had moved into the small rental shortly after signing the lease and seemed to really enjoy it, adding a few personal touches of her own to make it feel more like home. We'd fallen back into the pattern of seeing each other at the end of every day, texting here and there throughout. In bed, we were more combustible than ever, and our talks were always full of easy shorthand. Maybe that's because we stayed away from the heavy topics. And true to our arrangement, she never slept over. Yet there was an ever-approaching day on the calendar that I didn't let myself think too much about.

Others did that for me.

"Have you let go of all that anger yet?" my father asked as I packed up at the end of our meeting. We'd spent the afternoon going over the calendar for the fall, cementing in the important events and their dates.

I blinked at him as I swung my attaché on my shoulder. "What anger are we talking about? I'm still not okay with Yoko, if that's what you're referencing. I don't even like her children."

He inclined his head to the door. "You're running around this town with Courtney Carrington joined at your hip, and I want to know if you laid down the anger you've been carrying with you ever since the day she got married."

Married. The word itself caused me to bristle, which I guess was evidence that I hadn't. "Not really something I choose to dwell on." Total lie.

"Maybe it should be. Anger sucks," he said, and left the office whistling.

Later that night, as Ernie snoozed at the front door—guard dog that he aspired to be—Courtney and I stayed up late eating post-sex ice cream in my kitchen.

"So I don't understand why the right side of the store is getting all this new design effort," I said, taking a seat next to her at the table. "Why the right?"

Courtney licked the back of her spoon. "It's the most important The average person will usually start their shopping on the right side of a given retail space, as their gaze travels there from the left. The Tanner Peak store is missing that pop on the right, so we're redoing it. The goal is to add eye-catching colors to grab the customer's attention instantly."

"I don't start shopping on the right."

"Yes, you do. You probably just don't realize it."

"No."

She laughed at my obstinateness. "I'm guessing you read right to left, too?"

I pointed at her with my spoon emphatically. "Hey, you don't know."

Her smile waned. "I know that there's no one like you, Maggie."

I felt that one like a burst of warmth right in the center of my chest. Alarm bells flared, because we both knew what this was between us and also what this wasn't. I attempted to move us out of it, finding my smile again. "You're trying to distract me with kindness while I'm attempting to learn something here."

"I'm sorry," she said, following suit. "What else would you like to know?"

"I want to know more about the psychology aspect as it applies to shoppers that aren't me."

"Of course. The not-yous of the world. Well, let's see. As a retailer, we're always going to do better if we provide breaks in the display of merchandise. The average shopper, present company excluded of course, will generally skip over twenty percent of the products available for sale if everything is strung together. Breaks in their perusal are shown to increase sales."

I'd missed all this the past five years.

The interesting conversation. The kidding back and forth. The explosive chemistry. I found Courtney utterly sexy when she talked shop. "I get the feeling you're good at your job."

"I'm glad I've left you with that impression, at least. Come here and I'll tell you all about window displays," she said, holding out her hand. Unable to resist that sexy smile, I made my way around the table, catching sight of myself in the mirror. Lips: swollen. Hair: wild. Skin: glowing. Nipples: hard.

Sigh.

"I don't know what you've done to me," I said, covering them through my T-shirt.

Courtney grinned. "I haven't done anything. They just like me, is all."

"That part is true." I straddled her lap, lacing my arms around her neck. She wore the short silk robe that Berta had given me for Christmas the year prior. Seeing Courtney in it gave the robe brand-new meaning.

"Window displays," she said, as she slipped her hands under the fabric of my T-shirt and rested them on the small of my back, "should tell a story. They're the eyes into the store."

"I like that. The eyes into the store."

"I do, too."

We shared a smile for a long moment, and the world seemed to slow down. "Tell me something you're thinking," I said quietly, wanting to know what was going on behind those heartbreakingly beautiful eyes.

She looked skyward. "How well I feel ice cream and bedroom activities pair together."

"I can agree to the stellar pairing." I nibbled on her neck. "What else?"

"I was thinking that I love your giant teddy bear of a dog."

"Me too. He's a keeper." More nibbling. "Anything else?"

"Sometimes I wonder about us."

Silence. I went still but wanted to hear more. "In what way?"

She looked up at me, and I disentangled my arms from around her neck. "I sometimes wonder what it would take to get you to fight for me."

I didn't react right off because the stab of pain I felt in my chest stole my next breath. The expression on her face read vulnerable. I swallowed. "I did fight for you once upon a time. It didn't go so well."

She eased me off her and walked to the sink. I could no longer see her eyes and that had me feeling powerless. "If you had, I'd imagine I'd know about it."

Whoa. "Courtney, you got married. *Married*," I said, emphasizing the word. "If that isn't the universal sign for I've moved on, I don't know what it is. You found someone else. Maybe he made you happy in a way I never did."

"You know that's not true." Her voice was low and shaky.

"Actually, I don't."

She turned back to me, her eyes brimming. "He *wanted* me, Maggie. And you didn't."

I swallowed the lump that had formed, but the anger from all those years ago wasn't so easily dissolved. "And that was enough for you? That's all it takes? For someone to want you?"

She looked at me, incredulous. "You have no idea, do you, Maggie, what it was like to be someone like me. Are you really that oblivious?"

"I don't know what you're talking about."

"You had this wonderful family overflowing with love. Two parents who would have walked to the moon and back for you. A community of people who adored you, and a best friend who had your back at every turn. I had *you*." The tears fell from her eyes. "Do you understand that? And when I lost you, I had to find a way to be okay again."

I didn't know what to say. For the first time, I looked at the breakup from Courtney's point of view, a luxury my anger hadn't allowed in the past. It was like turning on a light in a darkened room. "I'm sorry you felt alone," were the words I heard leave my lips. They came straight from my heart. "I was mad at you for so many years. But I can say now that I'm sorry. For hurting you. For pulling so much of myself away."

She nodded. "Thank you." Silence hovered between us, and she slowly took a seat at the table in contemplation. Finally, she looked up at me. "For a long time, I didn't let myself imagine how you'd feel when you heard about Nate and me. I didn't let myself think about you or my life back here at all. I'm good at that when I need to be."

"Why'd you come back?" I had to ask. "The truth this time."

She stared at the ceiling for a few moments before leveling her gaze on me. "Because when I walked out of this cottage five years ago, I lost the best part of myself. Maybe subconsciously, I thought I could get it back. Silly, right?" She chuckled sardonically and shook her head.

"Yeah," I said, not really believing it was because I'd lost the best part of myself that night, too.

"Well," Courtney said loudly, pushing herself up from the table. "Things have gotten entirely too serious in here, and that's my fault. I apologize. I'll go. I shouldn't have—"

She didn't get to finish that sentence because my lips were on hers in a kiss I hoped would communicate all the things that I could not. The heartache, the confusion, the passion, the lust, but most important of all, the love. Because of course it was still there, and always would be. I'd loved Courtney with all of my heart back then and I still loved her now. I'd just found a way to live without her, if you could call it living at all. I wasn't sure I wanted to do that anymore. I also wasn't sure I was capable of doing anything about it.

"Maggie," Courtney whispered. I nodded against her lips, because I knew. She loved me, too. I took her to bed wordlessly where we made love. Before we fell asleep, I made a point to kiss her like I was drowning and she was my only hope.

In so many ways, it was true.

We fell asleep tangled in one another beneath the covers as the blue moonlight slanted through the room. I held her close and woke every hour or so to make sure that she was still there. When the glowing numbers on my alarm clock read 7:14, I was sad to find the spot next to me empty. I turned over and ran my hand across the sheet where Courtney had been, feeling the loss.

When the sound of the shower hit, my heart squeezed. *Stop that.* I was in automatic self-preservation mode, a habit I'd developed from years of practice. But I did something a little crazy then and let myself enjoy the squeeze.

Just for a few minutes.

I sighed happily, reveling in the little upshot in energy I got thinking about our sleepover. How wonderful it was to have Courtney sleeping in my arms or the inverse, holding me. Both were equal parts heaven. The languid daydream was interrupted by the bathroom door opening. "What time is it?" Courtney asked in a panicked voice.

I glanced at the clock. "Seven sixteen."

"Damn it." She moved quickly into the room, completely naked. I sat back and enjoyed the show. "I'm late."

"You're in charge. You can't be late."

She held up a finger. "*Because* I'm in charge, I shouldn't be. Have you seen my bra?"

"Next to the dresser?" I rested my head in my propped-up palm and watched her look.

"Nope." She turned back to me and smiled. "You're enjoying this way too much."

"Probably next to my jeans. They came off around the same time."

Her eyes lit up. "That they did." I watched as she shook out my jeans, located her wayward bra, and put it on.

"Aww, now that's a shame."

She passed me a glance as she gathered the rest of her clothing. "Stop tempting me."

I shrugged. "I would do no such thing. You're going to have to go home and change anyway. I'm just thinking you could spare five minutes."

"It takes me at least ten."

I raised an eyebrow. "Didn't last night. Come here."

"No way," she said, and swatted my hand away. "If I do that, you're going to kiss me."

I grinned. "I definitely am. And do other things."

"Must be strong," she said more to herself than to me. With her clothes in a jumble, she retreated to the bathroom. Next to me on the bedside table, a phone buzzed. Courtney's. "Hey, Court, your phone is talking to me!" No answer. Moments later it buzzed again. I didn't want to be nosy, but I couldn't help myself. I picked up the phone and glanced at the readout. It was from someone named Jonathan. Wasn't he the CEO?

I know you're enjoying yourself in that little town, but I need to pull you back to Chicago ASAP. CALL ME.

The bathroom door clicked open and I dropped the phone like a hot potato. I was flooded with guilt for having looked at the text, and dread at what it told me. Courtney emerged and stared at me questioningly. "You look like you forgot to study for a test."

I shook myself out of it. "No. Just got lost in my own thoughts."

She came and sat on the bed next to me. She'd pulled her hair up, and it looked so pretty. "Thank you for last night." I nodded and accepted the gentle kiss she placed on my lips. At the same time, my stomach churned. The wind had changed, and the little fantasy world I'd created for myself over the past few weeks would soon vanish. I'd be left with nothing, a familiar story. She retrieved her phone and slipped it into her bag, heading for the door.

"Have a good day at work," I said softly.

She smiled at me over her shoulder, and my chest ached because she was looking at me differently now. Heart-stoppingly different. Her guard was down and she was letting me in. "It's certainly off to a good start. I'll call you later."

"Great."

Alone in my bedroom, I went about getting ready for the day, my heart exposed. I felt vulnerable, sad, and terrified. It took everything I had to put one foot in front of the other to get myself to the office.

Once there, I kept busy as best I could, walled myself up in a stack of annoying paperwork I'd put off. Today, it was a solace. All the while, my thoughts zigzagged and tugged. I hadn't meant for things to go this far with Courtney. I knew Courtney hadn't either. Regardless, our comingled best intentions had flown right out the window with the night we'd just shared. It had been telling, each moment.

The way we'd touched each other with such tenderness.

The way Courtney had looked at me, deep in the throes.

The way my heart yearned.

Berta had been right all along. She'd known exactly where this was heading and had tried to warn me. I loved Courtney. But it didn't matter. She would leave, I would let her, and life would resume as it had been. It wasn't going to happen for us.

I would have to settle for what time we had left, for right now. It felt sickeningly familiar.

❖

The porch light glowed in front of the rental even though it wasn't yet dark out. I'd waited until I knew Courtney would be finished with work for the day before stopping by. She'd been noticeably silent today. I knew why. She was leaving, and the little bubble we'd created for ourselves was no more.

I made my way to her front door, but she opened it before I could knock.

"Maggie." She was still dressed for work and seemed out of breath, as if she were in a hurry. Her mouth was tight, and her eyes carried sorrow. But then her gaze softened and she took my hand. "Hey, come in. I didn't know you were coming over."

"Sorry I didn't call." Her bedroom door was open and I caught the open suitcase on the bed. My heart twisted at the confirmation. "I didn't mean to interrupt."

She followed my gaze to the suitcase. "I was going to call you."

"Now you don't have to."

She nodded solemnly.

Our eyes connected, but she felt a million miles away. She was already gone, and the pain slashed through my chest, razor sharp. "How soon do you have to go?"

"I'm on the eight o'clock flight."

I closed my eyes briefly against the news. "Must be a department store emergency."

She lifted a hand in explanation. "There's some shuffling on the board. I need to be there."

We spoke at the same time.

"Maggie, I just—"

"I suppose we should—"

We smiled at each other the way people do when they're being extra polite. Our easy give and take was gone. This wasn't us and I hated it. "You first," I said, gesturing to her.

Courtney seemed to make a decision. "It was really nice to see you again, Maggie," she said finally. "You don't know how nice. I needed this."

"I think I did, too." I searched for the words I needed, the ones that would tell her I loved her, that I didn't want her to go, that if there was even a sliver of a chance for us, I wanted to take it.

But the words wouldn't come.

I stood there too terrified to take the leap.

"Tell me you don't hate me anymore," she said.

"I could never hate you, Courtney. You're Courtney. My first love. You'll always be that."

Her eyes filled. "I will be, won't I?" I nodded. She gestured to her bedroom. "I suppose I should probably—"

"Yeah." We were talking over each other again, when all I wanted to do was pull her to me and never let go. My chest ached and the lump in my throat grew. "I'll let you get back to it."

"Don't be a stranger, okay?" she said. The tears were contagious, it seemed. I felt them pool in my own eyes. "If you're ever in Chicago, you call me. I'm serious."

"Of course." A long silence ensued and we stared at each other. Finally, I opened my arms and she fell into them. We'd been through so much together. Love, hurt, fear, tragedy. The memories swarmed, and it was all too much. As soon as she let me go, I turned. I had to get out of there. I had to find air.

"Maggie."

At the sound of her voice, I turned back.

"I hope you find whatever it is that will make you happy."

What she didn't realize was that I already had, only I was powerless to hold on to it.

I walked to my car, and once safely inside, the tears came fast and hard. I pulled over two streets away because they no longer allowed me to see the road. The choking sobs shook my body and I gripped the steering wheel with everything I had.

The emotion I'd held back for years assaulted me with staggering intensity. Everything. All of it. I cried for Clay, for the lost years with Courtney, but most of all for myself and the cowardly person I'd become.

They were right. I was a shell of who I used to be and lived a lonely little life.

I'd been certain that protecting my heart had been the right way to go. That Courtney and I didn't mix in the long term. That love was not for me.

I'd been wrong on all counts.

CHAPTER TWENTY-THREE

For the entire next week, I avoided the rest of the world. I closed down my office and locked myself away in the cottage, telling friends and family that I'd caught an awful bug and that they would do best to keep their distance. I'd retreated once again, spending my time in front of a television I wasn't actually watching or staring out at the vast farmland around the cottage for some sort of answer. By the eighth day, I was pulled in a very specific direction.

Tanner Peak had one cemetery, and I spent a lot of my time avoiding it.

In fact, the thought of visiting my brother's grave left me petrified. I'd only been there once, the day of his burial. Because the grounds were impeccably kept, many in town strolled through in way of a shortcut from the library to the center of town. I never did. I couldn't bring myself to enter its gates.

Today was different.

Today I needed to be closer to Clay, to talk to him, to find a way to get my head straight. So I decided to go visit him, as hard as that might be. After having retreated from the world for over a week, it was time to start conquering some of my fears.

I entered the grounds on foot, my heart thudding rapidly and my breathing shallow. Fear trickled through me one inch at a time. I rolled my shoulders to stave off the clammy perspiration that crisscrossed my skin.

One step at a time. Just keep walking.

And there it was.

I blinked my surprise when the terror drifted away the moment I found his grave, almost as if a magic wand had taken the fear from me. I looked down at his name carved into stone and smiled the first smile in days. He was with me. I could feel it.

"What's up, big bro?" I asked, taking a seat on the freshly cut grass. I ran my fingertips across the etching and let my hand linger there for a moment, closing my eyes and lifting my face to the sun. Its warm embrace comforted me. It was peaceful here. I'd never realized just how peaceful. "Bet you're surprised to see me here? Yeah, well, me too."

I sat in silence for a bit, basking in the serenity of the space. The blue sky went on for miles that morning, and I could hear birds chirping from the Douglas fir trees nearby. The cemetery stood empty, except for me.

"I don't know why I'm here." I studied the sky as I spoke. It helped me gather my thoughts. "I need help. I guess maybe that's the reason. Courtney's gone, and it's pretty much my fault." The stupid tears came again, and I was beyond sick of them. Something about hearing the words out loud helped, though. I ran my fingers through the grass and tore off a couple of blades. "I love her, Clay. But you already know that. You always have. My heart is telling me to go with her to Chicago, to fight for her once and for all, the way I should have all those years ago. But it's like my feet are stuck in this town. It's who I am and means everything to me, even more since we lost you."

I thought on it as an understanding hit.

"But it's not the same here without Courtney. It would be easy and tame, my life, but it would never be great, ya know? Just good enough." I felt a burst of frustration. "So maybe I do this thing." I smiled. A modicum of courage gathered behind my words. Courtney had always been the secret ingredient that made my life great. Without her, everything was gray and passable.

I couldn't lose her again.

"I don't remember the first time you called me Scrapper. Mom says it was when I was eight and you were twelve and I carried just as much firewood to the log pile as you did." I took a moment to think on it. My nickname and its meaning. "I haven't felt much like a scrapper since you left. I know what I want, but I need the strength to put myself out there, to take the risk. Can you help me through this?"

Clay didn't answer me with words, but this was one of those times when I didn't have to guess what he was telling me. I could feel his guidance and I shook my head, marveling at the difference I already felt in myself. Bolstered. Upright. Strong. I could do this.

"Chicago is nice this time of year, right?" I nodded a few times as the excitement glimmered briefly. I ran my hand across his name one last time. "Thank you for being my brother, Clay. You've always been there for me and you still are. I love you." I stood and lingered in silent gratitude a moment longer, staring down at his grave before turning to go.

Traversing the same path I'd taken into the cemetery, I didn't feel any of the same fear that had crippled me on the way in. In fact, I felt about ten feet tall and ready to take on the world. In the back of my mind was an image of Courtney smiling at me from behind her sketch pad, and my chest felt about to burst. I knew what I wanted and it was her, for always.

I could only hope that she'd give me that chance.

❖

I surveyed myself in the full-length mirror on the back of the hotel room door. I'd rented a suite, a small living room that adjoined a bedroom. This was, after all, a special occasion.

Chicago was different than I'd imagined it. Fast paced, but also friendly. I'd taken a walk earlier and stopped into a popcorn shop to purchase their famous mix and browsed a farmer's market right there in the middle of the city hubbub. I liked the fast-paced feel of it all, so different from what I was used to.

Staring at myself in the mirror, I adjusted the red and charcoal belted dress I'd selected and paired with black pumps. That dress always got me compliments, and I wanted to look my best. My hair was pulled back on top, with the sides falling loose around my shoulders. It was my best shot at a more sophisticated big-city look, perhaps the first of many to come. I glanced at my watch, taking note of the fact that it was approaching four o'clock. I'd chosen my hotel for its across-the-street proximity to Carrington's Corporate.

It was now or never.

I pulled in some air and adjusted my hair for the fifteenth time before heading out.

Carrington's operated multiple floors in the thirty-two-story monstrous building with the towering atrium. I consulted the directory and headed up.

"Ms. Carrington's office is two floors up," the friendly administrative assistant informed me. She was right. "Courtney Carrington, Vice President of Operations" was mounted on the wooden wall outside the office in gold block letters. My heart sped up and skipped. Suddenly, this whole thing felt a little crazy. Who was I to walk in there unannounced and declare myself?

"Can I help you?" a handsome older gentleman asked. His suit looked like it cost several hundred dollars.

"I was hoping to see Courtney Carrington."

"Follow me," he said, and led me into the office. A woman sat at a sleek and simple wooden desk in the small yet welcoming lobby. The space felt vastly different from the office in Tanner Peak, made up of soft green chairs, but then Courtney would have designed this one herself. The man gestured to her. "This is Crystal, Ms. Carrington's assistant. She can help you."

"Good afternoon," Crystal said warmly. She was close to my age, and somehow that relaxed me.

I smiled. "Hi. I was hoping she was in," I said and gestured to the large oak door behind her. "We're old friends and I'm visiting from out of town."

Crystal nodded. "Unfortunately, Ms. Carrington is gone for the day. I would be happy to tell her you stopped by."

"Oh. Well, thank you anyway. Will she be back tomorrow?"

"No, ma'am."

I turned to go. My heart sank. I would have to call her.

"It's Maggie, isn't it?" Crystal asked as I pushed open the glass doors to the hall.

I paused. "Yes, how did you know?"

She dropped the professional tone and leaned in. "Courtney and I are also friends. I've seen your photo."

"It's nice to meet you."

"You, too. Tell you what…" She glanced at the office door next to Courtney's. The one the handsome man had disappeared into. "I'm going to do something that could get me fired. But because I know Courtney so well, I tend to think that won't be the case." She scribbled something on the back of a business card and handed it to me. "Her address. Five blocks east."

"Thank you." I smiled. "You didn't have to do that."

"Yes, I did."

I held the business card up and nodded. "Five blocks east."

The sun had dipped behind the buildings when I emerged, and there were more people on the street as rush hour crept closer. I followed Crystal's directions, dodging pedestrians as I went. I located the building easily enough and was able to slip in the door just behind a resident. Her apartment on the fourteenth floor was easy to locate, and I stood in front of the red door for only a moment before knocking.

"On my way, Albert. Just hang on a sec and I'll—" The door flew open and Courtney, in an off-the-shoulder sweatshirt and yoga pants, paused midsentence. "Whoa."

"Hi." I eased a strand of hair behind my ear. "Sorry I'm not Albert."

"Maggie?" Her glance moved behind me in the hall as if trying to piece together the puzzle that had me on her doorstep. That's when the soft smile hit. "I don't understand. What are you doing here?"

"Right. I imagine you're wondering that. I'm here in Chicago because I love you."

She stared at me. "You do?"

"I didn't mean to just blurt that out, but it's true." I nodded, feeling the energy flow through me, ready to put it all out there. "You asked me, not too long ago, what it would take for me to fight for you. I guess it would be the thought of losing you. I never stopped loving you. Not for one second."

"Maggie, I—"

I held up a hand. "Let me just say this and then you can shoot me down or tell me to go home and never call you again. Your choice." She nodded. I had absolutely no idea what she was thinking. Her face was carefully blank, and my heart was hammering so loudly I could barely hear myself speak. I pressed on, taking another step out on that limb. "Courtney, I was drawn to you from the first moment I saw you. When I'm with you, I feel like the world is full of possibilities. Without you, it dims. When you left five years ago, I constructed a wall around my heart, and you decimated it once again. I'll move to Chicago. I'll do whatever I have to, but I want you back. I want us back."

"Wow. I never thought you would…" She stood there a moment, grappling. She ran her hands through her hair and her gaze brushed the ground. "You know what? I can't think out here. Come in. I just need to wrap my head around this for a minute."

I followed her into the apartment, through a well-put-together beige and turquoise living room that was littered with half-packed boxes. I looked to the kitchen. The boxes continued in a never-ending parade. Tape, paper, and packing supplies were stacked on a stylish-looking kitchen counter. "Are you moving in or out?" I asked, trying to understand. My stomach clenched. This was bad.

"Out," she said quietly. "I'm leaving. Maggie, I didn't expect any of this, so I—"

"Oh. I'm sorry. I didn't mean to—" I paused so my racing thoughts could catch up. "Can I ask where you're going?"

She nodded. "Tanner Peak."

I replayed the words. "What?"

Her eyes met mine. "I'm moving back to Tanner Peak. I love Chicago, but when I really think about it, Margaret Beringer, the happiest times in my life were all in that little town. Were all with you." She shook her head. "I've been chasing that kind of happiness ever since, when all along, I knew right where to find it."

My entire being went warm. I felt the smile take root. She wanted me back. What was a hope moments before was now a reality. "What about Carrington's?"

She smiled back at me and slowly took my hand in hers. "I told them I either work remote, or not at all."

"And?"

She slid her other arm around my waist. "I can home-base at the Tanner Peak store, but I'll have to be flexible about travel. There might be a decent amount."

"I'll come with you."

She laughed. "I would love that." A pause. "Maggie."

"Yes."

"You came to Chicago for me. For *me*. You don't know how much that means, that you—" Her voice broke, too thick with emotion to finish the sentence. But I understood the gravity. She took our entwined fingers and brought them to her chest. I could feel her heart beat against the back of my hand, and it was everything.

"I had to come. There was no way around it," I said. "You were here, so I had to be."

Her eyes sparkled as she wiped away the errant tears. "And you love me?"

"And I love you," I said very seriously. "Desperately. More than the Beatles. Way more."

Her smile only grew. "I love you, too."

I closed my eyes and let the words wash over me. "Does that mean there's an us? What do I have to do for there to be an us?"

She inclined her head to the side in thought. "Well, I need somewhere permanent to live."

"I know the best place. All the strawberries you can eat. What else?"

"There should be a dog. I prefer large, goofy ones."

I grinned. "Your lucky streak continues. Anything else?"

"I'm partial to kissing, given it's with the right person."

I took a deep breath. "Let the audition commence."

I pulled her in and kissed her, threading my fingers through her hair. I felt her smiling against my mouth and fully endorsed that sentiment. When we came up for air, she cupped my face and looked at me quite seriously. "This is all that matters, okay? We have to remember that. Everything else is just details to be sorted through. Promise me we'll remember."

"We will. For always. I promise."

EPILOGUE

I waited patiently as my thorough clients took another lap through the three-bedroom bungalow they'd already proclaimed to love passionately three times and counting. He was a meticulous accountant. She was an elementary school teacher. They were very sweet, but I'd pay them eight times my commission to wrap up this outpouring of real estate love.

While I wanted the couple to be happy, I was also aware of the fact that I had a dinner date with a beautiful woman who'd just gotten in from a business trip the day before. Courtney and I were scheduled to leave in just over an hour, and I so wanted to freshen up for the night out. She'd taken the day off, and it had been excruciatingly hard to come into work this morning with her still in bed and stealing my heart. The idea of spending the evening with her (and the later-evening beyond that) had me already a little checked out of the last part of my day. I would make it up to this nice couple later, I decided. Maybe a congratulatory fruit basket when the deal went through. Toss in some extra strawberries for good measure.

"So it sounds like we have ourselves a winner!" I said excitedly to the wife, who was now walking around the house with her hands clasped to her heart as if in the midst of the most touching moment of her life. Okay, so my own heart was warmed at the sight whether I wanted it to be or not.

"Thank you, Maggie," she said, beaming. "I never knew a house could feel so much like family."

"Can I use that quote on my website?" I laughed and accepted the hug she offered me. She really did sound like a commercial.

"We'd like to put in a full ask offer," the husband said. "Unless you think we should go over-ask."

I raised a finger. "Let's not get crazy. I'll submit a full ask tomorrow, only because it's new to the market and the brokers are swarming. If there's a competing offer, we can adjust. Tanner Peak is suddenly very popular. Small-town life is on the rise." And there it was, right on time, that jolt of excitement that came with every potential deal. I really did love my job.

"Babe, let's take one more walk through."

Sometimes.

Sometimes I loved my job.

When I arrived home forty-five minutes later with sore feet and low coping skills, I was met at the cottage door by a gorgeous woman who handed me a glass of red wine. "Hi, baby," Courtney said. "How was your day?"

"Better now," I said, grinning at her and accepting the kiss she placed on my lips. "Do I have time to drink this?" I held up the glass.

"Take your time. Dinner can wait. I made a cheese board for us."

"An appetizer! I could kiss you!"

"I will take you up on that." She stole another kiss and placed the elegant little platter on the table in front of me. She'd seemed so much lighter lately. Happy, that was the word, and I was right there with her. Life was infinitely better since Courtney had moved in six months prior.

"Any deals today?" she asked from the bedroom as she slid into a pair of heels. She had on the navy dress she knew I loved, the one that brought out the blue in her eyes.

"I have an offer I'm submitting first thing in the morning. Time will tell." Ernie bounded into the room and I offered him a few head rubs before he leapt up onto the couch and stretched out. "What about your day?" I asked. She'd been taking a lot more days off now. I loved it.

"I read a book on the porch and did some sketches of the northern field. This lug made an appearance in one of them." She scratched Ernie behind the ears and he sighed loudly. She looked so relaxed, so rested. It was contagious, and I found myself joining her there as the day slid off me little by little.

"Maybe," I said, catching her hand as she passed, "we skip dinner and stay in."

"I see what you're up to," she said, taking my face in her hands. "But it will have to wait until I'm properly fed. You'll want my stamina up. Trust me." She winked at me for effect, and boy, did it work.

"You make a valid point. In that case, let's get this show on the road." I dashed into the bedroom and shimmied into my newish yellow cocktail dress and straightened my hair, very much liking the tamer look. Courtney appeared behind me in the mirror and wrapped her arms around my middle.

"You are stunning. Do you know that?"

I smiled at her in the mirror because she really made me feel that way. "Thank you."

"Ready to get out of here?"

I nodded. "I am."

She released me and led the way to the car. As we drove from the property, she tossed me a glance. "Do you remember when we used to make out on the recesses of the farm?"

I laughed fondly at the memory. "Like I could forget. Day would turn to night and we didn't even notice."

Courtney made a right when she should have made a left and I smiled. "You're heading over there, aren't you? To our spot?"

She raised a shoulder. "I just thought we could reminisce for a moment."

"Okay, but I'm not getting my dress dirty before dinner. Unless of course you want to take my advice and skip the meal altogether. I think you already know my opinion on the..." My voice trailed off because as we rounded the corner to what had been "our spot" as teenagers, I saw the most unexpected gathering. Standing there along the edge of the field were Berta, Travis, and the kids. Melanie had her hands on little Tim's shoulders. Next to them stood my parents, who held hands and grinned at me with tears in their eyes.

"What's going on?" I asked Courtney, but I already knew. Emotion welled within me and tears sprang to my eyes. "What are you doing right now? Courtney?"

She calmly got out of the car, walked around to my side, opened my door, and offered me her hand.

"Courtney, talk to me." The butterflies in my stomach were on speed. Luckily, they were happy butterflies. Friendly ones. Courtney didn't say a word.

I followed her to where our friends and family had gathered. Everyone was smiling and exchanging anticipatory glances with one another. These were all of the people I loved, and this felt like the most wonderful dream. Courtney paused and turned to me in the same stretch of grass where we'd once talked and kissed and dreamed out loud until her curfew or mine.

She smiled at me and took my hand. I reminded myself to breathe as the excitement bubbled. "Eight and half years ago, you gave a speech in history class and my life was never the same. Six and a half years ago, in this very spot, I asked you to marry me. You laughed and I told you that one day I would ask again. I had no idea then the obstacles that lay ahead for us. I had no idea that the great love I had for you would grow exponentially once we'd weathered them. But I know so much now, Maggie. Most importantly, I know that I want to spend the rest of my life with you." She sank down on one knee, and I covered my mouth in shock that this moment had finally arrived. "Margaret Beringer, I love you and I want everyone to know it. I promise to always be there for you through the good moments and through the tough. Will you marry me?"

"Say yes!" Travis yelled to laughter from my family and a slug from Berta.

"Sorry," she whispered and covered his mouth.

But I was focused on Courtney and the way the setting sun haloed her blond hair and her blue eyes shone bright. She had always been the most beautiful woman in the world, but tonight she simply radiated. "Of course the answer is yes," I said simply. "It's always been yes."

The spectators cheered, and Courtney stood and kissed me thoroughly, lovingly. My father attempted to take a photo with his phone and my mother stepped in to help him. The baby fussed and Courtney dried my eyes as I laughed at my own sentimentality. Shortly after, we all headed off to dinner together, where we toasted with champagne and playfully talked wedding details.

"While I can't wait to plan a wedding," my mother said, "I'm counting the days until grandchildren."

"I'll drink to that," my father said.

"So who will carry the baby?" Travis asked in genuine curiosity. This time Berta didn't slug him.

Courtney and I exchanged a look. She lifted a shoulder. "I've always wanted to be pregnant one day."

I couldn't stop smiling if I'd tried because we had so many "one days" ahead of us and I couldn't wait to get to each and every one of them. The table erupted in conversation and I turned to Courtney. "Boy or girl?" I asked her quietly.

"Both," she said decidedly. "I already have a boy name picked out."

"Tell me."

She leaned in close to my ear. "Clayton Carrington Beringer."

I kissed her softly. "I love you."

She grinned at me. "Never stop saying that."

I looked down the table at the faces of the people I loved and reflected on the journey that had brought me to this very moment. The world wasn't an easy place. In fact, it came with pain, sorrow, and strife. But interwoven were moments of unencumbered joy when I reminded myself how wonderful it was to be alive, to love, and to be loved in return.

I knew beyond a shadow of a doubt that Courtney and I would have the most wonderful life together full of laughter, adventure, and warmth.

For that, I'd be thankful until my dying day.

Life was good.

About the Author

Melissa Brayden (melissabrayden.com) is a multi-award-winning author of eight novels published with Bold Strokes Books. She is hard at work on her ninth and loving the writer's life in San Antonio, Texas.

Melissa is married and working really hard at remembering to do the dishes. For personal enjoyment, she spends time with her Jack Russell terriers and checks out the NYC theater scene several times a year. She considers herself a reluctant patron of spin class, but enjoys hitting a tennis ball around in nice weather. Coffee is her very best friend.

Books Available From Bold Strokes Books

Escape in Time by Robyn Nyx. Working in the past is hell on your future. (978-1-62639-855-9)

Forget-Me-Not by Kris Bryant. Is love worth walking away from the only life you've ever dreamed of? (978-1-62639-865-8)

Highland Fling by Anna Larner. On vacation in the Scottish Highlands, Eve Eddison falls for the enigmatic forestry officer Moira Burns despite Eve's best friend's campaign to convince her that Moira will break her heart. (978-1-62639-853-5)

Phoenix Rising by Rebecca Harwell. As Storm's Quarry faces invasion from a powerful neighbor, a mysterious newcomer with powers equal to Nadya's challenges everything she believes about herself and her future. (978-1-62639-913-6)

Soul Survivor by I. Beacham. Sam and Joey have given up on hope, but when fate brings them together it gives them a chance to change each other's life and make dreams come true. (978-1-62639-882-5)

Strawberry Summer by Melissa Brayden. When Margaret Beringer's first love Courtney Carrington returns to their small town, she must grapple with their troubled past and fight the temptation for a very delicious future. (978-1-62639-867-2)

The Girl on the Edge of Summer by J.M. Redmann. Micky Knight accepts two cases, but neither is the easy investigation it appears. The past is never past—and young girls lead complicated, even dangerous lives. (978-1-62639-687-6)

Unknown Horizons by CJ Birch. The moment Lieutenant Alison Ash steps aboard the *Persephone*, she knows her life will never be the same. (978-1-62639-938-9)

The Sniper's Kiss by Justine Saracen. The power of a kiss: it can swell your heart with splendor, declare abject submission, and sometimes blow your brains out. (978-1-62639-839-9)

Divided Nation, United Hearts by Yolanda Wallace. In a nation torn in two by a most uncivil war, can love conquer the divide? (978-1-62639-847-4)

Fury's Bridge by Brey Willows. What if your life depended on someone who didn't believe in your existence? (978-1-62639-841-2)

Lightning Strikes by Cass Sellars. When Parker Duncan and Sydney Hyatt's one-night stand turns to more, both women must fight demons past and present to cling to the relationship neither of them thought she wanted. (978-1-62639-956-3)

Love in Disaster by Charlotte Greene. A professor and a celebrity chef are drawn together by chance, but can their attraction survive a natural disaster? (978-1-62639-885-6)

Secret Hearts by Radclyffe. Can two women from different worlds find common ground while fighting their secret desires? (978-1-62639-932-7)

Sins of Our Fathers by A. Rose Mathieu. Solving gruesome murder cases is only one of Elizabeth Campbell's challenges; another is her growing attraction to the female detective who is hell-bent on keeping her client in prison. (978-1-62639-873-3)

Troop 18 by Jessica L. Webb. Charged with uncovering the destructive secret that a troop of RCMP cadets has been hiding, Andy must put aside her worries about Kate and uncover the conspiracy before it's too late. (978-1-62639-934-1)

Worthy of Trust and Confidence by Kara A. McLeod. FBI Special Agent Ryan O'Connor is about to discover the hard way that when you can only handle one type of answer to a question, it really is better not to ask. (978-1-62639-889-4)

Amounting to Nothing by Karis Walsh. When mounted police officer Billie Mitchell steps in to save beautiful murder witness Merissa Karr, worlds collide on the rough city streets of Tacoma, Washington. (978-1-62639-728-6)